Dear Reader,

Growing up, I led a double life. During the day I was an all-American girl going to an all-American school doing all-American things. But the moment I got home…I spoke fluent Polish, knew the latest Polish movies/songs, all without ever touching Polish soil until I was fourteen. You see, my parents were born and raised in Poland. Unlike me. It was difficult being raised with cultural expectations that differed from the ones surrounding me. I totally related to *My Big Fat Greek Wedding*.

Back then, I rolled my eyes whenever I had to attend Polish rallies with my father. Hordes of people throughout the Chicago metropolitan area would gather to wave Polish flags before the Polish consulate. At the time, I considered them to be patriotic freaks. Until I studied history. Those Poles had gathered to support the Solidarity movement that was happening in their country on the other side of the world. It was a movement that led to Poland's historic freedom in 1989 after being oppressed by the Russians for a total of 173 years. My heritage and Poland's incredible history inspired me to write *The Perfect Scandal*. I always wanted to read a historical romance featuring a Polish heroine. It is my hope you will love this story about as much as I loved writing it.

Cheers and much love,

Delilah Marvelle

**Don't miss the rest of the Scandal series,
available now!**

Prelude to a Scandal
Once Upon a Scandal

DELILAH MARVELLE

the *Perfect* *Scandal*

HQN™

Recycling programs
for this product may
not exist in your area.

ISBN-13: 978-0-373-77554-5

THE PERFECT SCANDAL

Copyright © 2011 by Delilah Marvelle

This edition published by arrangement with Harlequin Books S.A.

For questions and comments about the quality of this book please contact us at Customer_eCare@Harlequin.ca.

® and TM are trademarks of the publisher. Trademarks indicated with ® are registered in the United States Patent and Trademark Office, the Canadian Trade Marks Office and in other countries.

www.HQNBooks.com

Printed in U.S.A.

ACKNOWLEDGMENTS

I know I'll only find myself thanking Harlequin Books and HQN and its amazing editors and its entire staff over and over. But I have to say it again. THANK YOU for all those unseen hours each and every one of you at Harlequin put in. Thank you for giving me an opportunity to share my stories with the world. In particular, I wanted to thank my new editor, the ever-wondrous Tracy Martin. Thank you, Tracy, for your enthusiasm, your guidance and your wisdom in the process of ensuring that my words, my characters and my stories live up to their full potential. Ours is the beginning of a beautiful relationship.

I wanted to thank my agent, Donald Maass, who is a freakin' genius in all matters of writing (and agenting, too!). You'll never be rid of me, Don. Ever. Bwahahaha.

Thanks my incredible husband, Marc, who always shoulders everything so that I can make my deadlines. If we weren't already married, darling, I'd marry you all over again. A huge thank-you to my two wonderful little inspirations, Clark and Zoe, for cheering me on instead of grumbling about the hours I spend writing. Disneyland or Paris? It's on Dad. Smirk.

And last but not least, thank you to my chapter of almost fourteen years, Rose City Romance Writers, and all its incredible members. I really don't know how the hell I would ever have survived the chaos of writing without all of you. Muah!

To my dear Poland and each and every Pole
who dedicated their breaths, their lives
and their souls to its freedom.

the Perfect
Scandal

A PRELUDE TO A SCANDAL

A lady should only ever trust her family. There are simply far too many ~~assholes~~ souls aspiring to take advantage of a woman who trusts too easily.

—How To Avoid A Scandal,
Moreland's Original Manuscript

28th November 1828

To the King's Most Excellent Majesty,

May it please Your Majesty to know how endlessly grateful we are that the long-standing private agreement between my uncle and the great former Sovereign of England is being considered. As Your Majesty is well aware, the Countess must be cared for in an environment that will oversee her well-being. That environment is no longer here in Warszawa. The upcoming formal coronation of the Emperor as our King is bringing more political unrest than anticipated. The whispers over the lack of civil liberties governing the constitutional monarchy of our Kingdom are likely to result in an uprising. I fear there is too much unrest amongst the people to hope otherwise. As per Your Majesty's inquiry, my cousin is indeed of notable beauty and is most accomplished, being fluent in English, Italian, German, Latin and French. Whilst I hope for a respectable match, one that will prevent her from becoming a political pawn, her inability to walk may hinder that result. If my thoughts in this prove to be true, arrangements will be made to relocate her to France by summer's end so as not to impose upon Your Majesty's generosity for too long. Out of respect for her mother, who has long since passed, I ask that no one from the Russian Court be allowed to call upon her. My family and I are humbled and grateful for your intervention in this delicate matter and hope you will grace her with the opportunity to know peace.

Ever your humble servant,
Karol Józef Maurycy Poniatowski

SHORTLY AFTER it was received, this letter was destroyed for the protection of those involved.

SCANDAL ONE

*Be wary of the flirtations you engage in. No
matter how respectable a man may appear,
he cannot and should not ever be trusted. ~~For
even the most honorable of men still only want
the same thing from a lady that a seasoned
rake wants from a Drury Lane whore. The only
difference is that a Drury Lane whore gets paid
for her disgrace, whilst a lady only gets paid in
ruin. Being ostracized by all of society is not
nearly as exciting or as profitable as receiving
a guinea for one's amorous efforts.~~*

—*How To Avoid A Scandal,*
Moreland's Original Manuscript

*Late evening, 11:31 p.m.
16th of April 1829
Grosvenor Square— London, England*

AFTER THE CARRIAGE had clattered off into the silence
of the night, back toward the coach house, Tristan
Adam Hargrove, the fourth Marquis of Moreland,

continued to linger on the shadowed doorstep of his townhome. He eyed the entrance door before him, knowing full well that when he opened it and stepped inside, there would be no Quincy scampering over to greet him. There would be nothing but a large, empty foyer and eerie silence he wasn't in the mood to embrace.

Readjusting his horsehair top hat with the tips of his gloved fingers, Tristan turned and descended the paved stairs he had just climbed. With a few strides, he crossed the cobblestone street and veered beneath the canopy of trees dimly lit by several gas lampposts.

Though the hour suggested he retire, with the recent death of his revered hound Quincy, it had become far too quiet in the house. The silence punctuated the reality of his own life: that he was still a goddamn bachelor, and now he didn't even have his dog for company. Fortunately, he occupied himself well enough from day to day and did not dwell too much on his lack of prospects or the fact that his dog was dead.

On Mondays, after a long ride through Hyde Park, he met with his secretary for the day. On Tuesdays, he visited his grandmother. On Wednesdays, he tarried at Brooks's, almost always evading discussions with fellow peers about the debates plaguing Parliament. No one ever pestered him about it because they all knew his political views weren't held by the majority anyway.

On Thursdays, he spent the entire day at Angelo's Fencing Academy, relentlessly scheduling match after match against the best opponents in an effort to remain fit. On Fridays, he roamed the British Museum, the National Gallery or the Egyptian Hall, never tiring of the same exhibits, although he did pester the curators more than any decent man should.

On Saturdays, he answered correspondences, including any letters forwarded by his publisher, and though he designated most evenings to balls, soirées and dinners in the hopes of meeting marriageable women, the invitations were usually sent by individuals he either detested or didn't care to know. He was desperate for a companion, but not that desperate. On Sundays, he became a moral citizen and went to church. There, he prayed for what all men pray for: a better life.

Tristan scanned the grouped homes around him, the endless rows of darkened windows reminding him that he ought to retire himself. Just as he was about to turn and do exactly that, his gaze paused on a brightly lit window high above, belonging to the newly let townhome opposite his own. His brows rose as he came to an abrupt halt, the soles of his boots scuffing the pavement.

There, lounging in a chair at the base of a window whose curtains had been pulled open, was a young woman brushing unbound, ebony hair. She brushed with slow, steady strokes, the oversized sleeve of her white nightdress shifting and rippling against the movement of her slim arm. The elegant curve of her ivory throat appeared and disappeared with each movement, displaying an exceedingly low neckline. All the while, her gaze was dreamily fixed up toward the cloudy night sky above.

In that single breath of a moment, Tristan's intuition insisted that this stunning vision before him was the divine intervention he'd been waiting for since he was old enough to understand a woman's worth. Hell, golden light was spilling forth from above with enough glorious intent to make the blind notice. All that was missing were the soft notes of a flute and the yearning strings of a violin. It really couldn't be any more obvious what God was telling him to consider.

Love thy neighbor.

Though the realist corrupting his soul demanded he retire and ignore his moronic intuition, the romantic that occasionally peered out from time to time whispered for him to stay. Wandering closer, he moved beyond the shadows of the trees and focused on the features of that oval face as it came into better view. The light in her bedchamber illuminated her entirely, tinting one side of her smooth, porcelain face and the edges of her dark hair with a soft, golden hue that was mesmerizing.

Who was she? And what sort of woman left her curtains open at night for the world to see her in a state of undress?

Weeks earlier, he'd noted that the house, which had been standing empty for months, had finally been let. Various footmen, attired in royal livery, had been carrying in furniture and trunks for days. Prior to tonight, however, he'd never once seen this woman.

Reaching the pavement leading to the entrance of her home, he lingered, sensing he would remember this night for years to come.

The woman paused. She lowered her hairbrush, shifting toward the window. Sections of her face faded into the soft shadows cast by the streetlamps, making him keenly aware that she was now privy to his presence.

He didn't know why he continued to stand there like some perverted dolt, but he did. He supposed limiting his association with women throughout the years had led him to do very strange things even he did not understand.

She hesitated, only to then wave, as if there was nothing wrong with waving to an unknown man lurking outside her bedchamber window at this time of night.

His pulse thundered as he stared up at her. Was she mistaking him for someone else? She had to be. Did he care that she was mistaking him for someone else? Hell, no.

Unable to resist, he touched his gloved hand to the curved rim of his hat in a gentlemanly salute, and hoped there wasn't a husband there in the room with her. A husband who could already be loading lead balls into a pistol whilst enlisting his wife's assistance in setting up the target.

The woman snapped up a forefinger, wordlessly requesting his patience, then unlatched the window and, to his astonishment, pushed it wide open. She leaned out, her wavy black hair cascading past the window in a single sweep, and casually propped herself against the sill as if she were Rapunzel in the flesh. The ruffled décolletage of her billowy, white nightdress shifted and spilled forward, exposing the golden glint of a locket swaying on a chain as well as the most stunning pair of breasts he'd ever had the pleasure of encountering.

Tristan fisted his gloved hands, forcing his mind *and* his body to remain calm.

She smiled flirtatiously down at him and spoke in a sensuous, foreign accent he couldn't quite place. "'Tis a pleasure to finally meet you, my lord. You live in the house directly across from mine, do you not?"

He couldn't help but be flattered, knowing she

had been waving to him, after all. Trying not to stare up at those lovely breasts that taunted him beneath the low hanging scoop of her nightdress, he offered, "Yes. I do."

Awkward silence hung between them.

Should he ask for her name? No. That would be crass and overly familiar. So what should he say? Stupid though it was, he couldn't think of anything.

She half nodded and glanced up toward the cloudy night sky above, tapping the brush against the bare palm of her other hand. "A rather pleasant evening despite all the clouds. Is it not?"

Weather as a topic was death to any conversation. Why couldn't he be more dashing? Why couldn't he be more…debonair? Why couldn't he—"Yes. Yes, it is."

"And is it always this cloudy in London?"

"Unfortunately." Christ, he was pathetic.

Awkward silence hung between them again.

A playful, melodious laugh rippled through the night air. "Is that all I am worth? Two or three words at a time and nothing more?" She wagged her silver hairbrush down at him. "You British are so annoyingly coy. Why is that?"

He cleared his throat and glanced about the quiet darkness of the square, hoping that no one was watching him make an oaf of himself. "Coy? No. Not coy. Curt. Curt best defines us."

She laughed again. "Yes. Curt. That certainly explains everyone's apparent lack of conversational skills. Might I venture to ask how a woman, such as myself, is ever to befriend a man, such as yourself, when all forms of conversation here in London appear to be so…stilted?"

Though the last thing he wanted was to expose this sultry foreigner to any gossip by continuing their conversation, ass that he was he couldn't resist. There was a playful intelligence in her demeanor that was as bold as it was fortifying. Even more intriguing was that delectable, soft twang of an accent. Unlike most foreigners whose English was irregular, coarse and difficult to understand whilst they struggled to find words, hers was clipped, perfect and beyond well versed.

Moving closer, Tristan grabbed hold of the iron railing lining her home. Propping his leather boot on the ledge between the railings, he hoisted himself up, wishing there weren't three whole floors separating them.

He observed her heatedly, admiring the way her long, dark hair framed her pale face and how it swayed past the window against the soft breeze. A sharp nose and wide, full lips, made her exotic-looking in a subtle way, though he couldn't quite make out the color of her eyes against the shadows and the light filtering out from behind her.

Damn, but she was alluring. A bit too alluring. "I am afraid, madam, that even if my conversational skills were to exceed all of your expectations, we still couldn't be friends."

Her lips parted. "Why ever not?"

Because friendship is not what I have in mind for us, he wanted to say. Instead, he smiled tauntingly and tilted his head, the weight of his top hat shifting. He wished he could reach up and glide his fingertips across her exposed throat. "I think it best I not comment on any of my thoughts."

She arched a brow. "Are you flirting with me?"

"Attempting to." And failing miserably....

"Shall I assist you in your attempt?"

"No. Please don't." Unlike most men, who eagerly chased after beautiful women, he avoided such stupidity at every turn because he knew what it would lead to: disaster. He had to be sensible when it came to women and do things properly to ensure nothing fell outside of his control. And this was not proper. Nor did he feel as if he were in control. He needed to retire and consider how to go about pursuing this in a civil manner.

He leaned against the railing he was balancing himself on. "Before I say good-night, madam—which I am afraid I must—being the gentleman that I am, I feel compelled to say something that I hope will not offend."

She smiled. "I rarely find myself offended."

"Good." He lowered his voice. "Despite my pathetic attempt to capitalize on your naiveté, for which I can only apologize, you really shouldn't be flaunting yourself like this. 'Tis indecent. Come morning, regardless of whatever did or did not happen between us, everyone in this square will assume we are lovers and you will be ruined. Is that what you want for yourself?"

She shrugged. "What others have to say about my character does not concern me. After all, I am a foreigner *and* a Roman Catholic, and as such, everyone will seek to condemn me in whatever it is I do. Though I suppose if a man of your size quakes at the thought of what others will think, perhaps we should end this conversation. I most certainly do not wish to place *your* reputation at risk."

He tightened his hold on the railing, squelching his urge to scale the wall, grab her and drag her over to his house for the night. "I suggest you cease being so flippant. London is extremely vicious when it comes to the reputation of a woman."

She rolled her eyes. "If you are so worried about my reputation, why ever did you initiate this conversation?"

"Me?" He laughed. "I beg your pardon, but I didn't initiate this conversation. You did."

"In theory, yes, I did. But in fact, no, I did not. You did."

"What?" he echoed, his brows coming together.

"*You* wandered over to *my* window, not I to yours. Whether my curtains were open or not, ultimately it was *your* decision to stay and watch me in a state of undress. Upon discovering you had no intention of departing, even after you had noticed that I had noticed you, I was therein compelled to open my window and offer you conversation, because I did not want any of our neighbors to think the worst of *you*. Regrettably, that makes *you* accountable for tarnishing *both* of our reputations. Would you not say?"

Damn. That actually made sense.

He dug the palm of his hand harder against the rail, the sting relieving his tension. "I assure you, I don't usually wander the streets at night seeking to—"

"There is no need to apologize." She grinned, her cheeks rounding. "I am well aware of your respectability, my lord. Do you think I would have opened my window if I had any doubts as to who you are or did not know of your sterling reputation? Although this may be our very first formal meeting, I know everything about you and your renowned gentlemanly ways."

He smirked at her adorable naiveté and leaned back, allowing a gloved hand to fall away from the iron railing he remained perched on. "I recommend you not place too much faith in the rumors you hear. I play the role of a gentleman for a reason, and I assure you, it has *nothing* to do with respectability."

She tilted her head to one side, observing him intently. "You are utterly fascinating."

"Am I?"

"Yes. I ardently hope that you and I will be able to pursue this to its fullest extent."

Tristan's grip almost slipped. He grabbed hold of the railing with his other hand to quickly balance himself and glanced up at her. Was she…? "The fullest extent? The fullest extent of what?"

She playfully rocked back and forth against the window sill, swaying her hair along with it. "Must I say it? Our neighbors might be listening."

This was officially getting out of hand. And he was entirely to blame for it. "No. Do not say it. Do not even think it."

She shifted her weight against the sill, swaying the locket around her throat, and met his gaze. "You obviously think the worst of me." She sighed. "Though I cannot blame you. Allow me to confess what it is I hope for us."

"Please do."

"I am in need of a husband by summer's end and you, my lord, fit all of the qualifications I seek."

"Oh, do I?" He let out an exasperated laugh,

released the iron railing and jumped back down onto the pavement with a solid thud. It was time to leave. Or by God, he would end up married to a foreigner and a Catholic by the end of the night. His staunchly Protestant grandmother would have a fit.

Stepping further back, he met her shadowed gaze and confided in a low, raw tone, "Here in London, there are rules as to how things are conducted between men and women, and I confess that as of right now, you and I are breaking every single one of those rules."

She sighed. "You British have rules for everything. How did this country ever populate itself?" She winced, shifting against the sill, and then set her chin. "Advise me as to how we should go about progressing this and I promise to adhere to whatever rules there may or may not be."

There had to be something wrong with her. Beautiful, intelligent women didn't miraculously appear in a gentleman's neighborhood and enthusiastically offer relationships through a window in the middle of the night. Not respectable relationships, anyway.

He'd best pretend to be indifferent until he knew more about her. "I regret to inform you, madam, that I am not interested in pursuing this." *Not yet.*

"I disagree." She gestured toward him with the tip of her brush. "You appear to be very interested. Otherwise you would have never stayed this long."

He snorted, realizing she'd called his bluff. "Allow me to take my leave before you drown in all that vanity. Good night." He gave her a curt nod, turned and strode away, telling himself to keep walking. He needed to go home before he did something ludicrous. Like turning around, striding back and asking her if he could come up for the night.

"I am *not* vain!" she called out. "I was simply making an observation based on your mannerisms!"

He quickened his pace before she figured out anything else based on his mannerisms.

"Might we at least part amiably?" Her voice echoed across the entire square. "We *are* neighbors, Lord Moreland. Or might I call you Tristan? Or Adam? Or do you prefer Hargrove?"

He jerked to a halt. How the devil did the woman know his entire list of names? Who had she been talking to?

He turned and stalked back toward her, determined to instill a flick of sense and respectability into that head. "Keep your voice down. And for the sake of whatever reputation you may or may not have, do not *ever* call me or any other man by their birth name. It insinuates far too much. Now, I suggest you retire and that we avoid each other until I say otherwise."

She looped a shorter section of her hair behind her ear. "Avoid each other? Why?"

"We don't want others to think we are involved."

She lowered her voice. "But I want us to be involved."

He stared up at her, wishing he could dig into that mind and understand what it was she really wanted. His money? His title? What? Because he wasn't *that* attractive. "You, my dear, appear to be on a path of self-destruction."

She tartly stared him down. "You know nothing about me or the path I am on."

"Oh, I know more than enough. You are overly determined, a bit too fond of yourself and, sadly, possess far more beauty than you know what to do with."

She eyed him. "You are very odd."

He pulled in his chin and pointed to his chest. "You find *me* odd?"

"Most men usually do not see beauty as a vice."

"Yes, well, I am not like most men."

"So I have noticed. Would you care to elaborate as to why that is?"

He pointed at her. "Do not make me climb that wall and nail your window permanently shut. This conversation is over. We avoid each other until I decide otherwise. Good night." He heaved out a breath and swung away.

She tapped her brush against the sill of her window

like a judge demanding order from him with a gavel. "I have one last thought to convey. Might I?"

He swung back, agitated with himself for wanting to stay and hear it. "Of course. What is it?"

She hesitated, lowering her gaze to her slim fingers, which were skimming across the bristles of her brush. "Do you believe in intuition and fate?"

He drew his brows together, surprised to find her taking on a much softer tone and a more serious demeanor. It lulled him into wanting to take on a softer tone himself. "Yes. Very much so. Why?"

Her fingers stilled against the brush. "Intuition tells me, despite your air of indifference, that at heart, you are anything but apathetic. I confess that I used to be very much like you until I learned to embrace what matters most. What you are witnessing is a woman seeking to bring change to the world through a plan that involves marrying into a perfect political platform. *You* are that perfect political platform. 'Tis fate that brought me into your neighborhood. 'Tis also fate that brought you here to my window tonight, as I have been seeking an introduction between us for weeks. Grace me with an opportunity to prove my worth, my lord, by getting to know me and my aspirations, and I vow you will not regret it."

He rumbled out a laugh. Parliament could make use of her. She was relentless. He pointed up at her. "I want a wife. Not a politician."

She paused. Glancing over her shoulder, she slid off the sill and leaned back into the room. "Our conversation must end," she whispered down at him, yanking up her hair and shoving it back over her shoulder. "Call on me tomorrow at four. I insist."

His chest tightened. "I am afraid my schedule will not allow for it and I would prefer—"

"*Shhhh!* Tomorrow at four. Be punctual." Flinging her brush over her shoulder, she yanked the window shut, latched it and leaned over to the side, fumbling with the curtains around her. She yanked at the nearest curtain in an effort to close it, but appeared unable to. A robed elderly woman breezed toward her side to assist.

He cringed and spun away, forging his way back home. Tomorrow at four? Not bloody likely. He hated rearranging his schedule for anyone or anything. It only led to chaos and lack of good judgment. Which is why, tomorrow at four, in his stead, he would have the footman deliver a copy of his etiquette book, *How To Avoid A Scandal*. Hopefully, it would be a polite enough message to convey that despite their conversation, he was still a very respectable man.

SCANDAL TWO

A lady may find herself tempted to become involved with less than savory individuals. Not because she is naive or unintelligent, but because the lives of these individuals appear to be far more fascinating than her own. She must resist this urge at every turn. Their glittery ways are but an invisible web meant to entangle prey. In truth, predators have no choice but to appeal to their prey by being dashing, witty and amiable. Otherwise, they would never be able to trap what it is they seek to cradle and devour. ~~I confess I often find myself fascinated by predators. Though certainly not enough to warrant my becoming one.~~

—*How To Avoid A Scandal*,
Moreland's Original Manuscript

28th of April, Late morning

FOR SOME REASON, the *London Gazette,* which Tristan always enjoyed reading every morning with his coffee, seemed to blur into a pyramid of letters he could not decipher. After vacantly staring at it for a prolonged period of time, he refolded the newspaper and slapped it onto the lacquered walnut table before him.

It appeared he was now illiterate, and he damn well knew his neighbor had everything to do with it. Though it had been twelve days since his footman had delivered his book, and though he'd heard nothing since, he still could not remove her from his head. Huffing out an exhausted breath, he tightened the belt of his embroidered oriental robe, leaned forward in his chair and grasped his ever-reliable cup of coffee.

Coffee always set him right each and every morning. Which he needed this late morning more than any other, because he most certainly hadn't been sleeping very well. If at all. Not since he'd realized *his* bedchamber window was aligned directly with *her* bedchamber window, just on the other side of the square.

Determined not to stray, for the past ten nights, the moment he retired into his room he had yanked those bedchamber curtains shut and had refused to look in that direction. Yet his thoughts lingered on that lush, accented voice, that alluring, pale face, the shifting of her nightdress against those soft, full breasts and that delectable mouth he wanted to get to know on a very, very personal level.

And then…last night…on the eleventh night before the eleventh hour, his well-molded, gentlemanly resolve finally fissured. He dug out his best riding crop, along with a spyglass, and toted them both into his bedchamber.

After extinguishing every candle in the room with the tips of his fingers, he leaned his shoulder against the frame of the window and extended the brass eyepiece, pointing it in her direction. Fortunately for her—though not so fortunate for him—she had learned to keep her curtains drawn. He'd only been able to make out a few passing shadows, even after diligently watching her window for over twenty minutes.

Unable to rest or think or sleep, he'd stripped, snatched up the riding crop from the windowsill and set his back against the nearest wall. After thwacking his thigh just enough to heighten his awareness of his body, he tossed the crop and pleasured himself into oblivion.

All the while, he had envisioned himself wearing only trousers, kneeling before her. She worshipped him, told him that he was everything she would ever want and need, while she seductively rounded him on bare feet, draped in that flowing nightdress that slid off her right shoulder. Her eyes would never leave his as her hand gripped the thick handle of a whip he'd given her to play with. She would then smile ever so softly, ever so charmingly, while delicately smacking the braided leather end against his thigh or back, causing him to suck in breaths of anticipation. She would further tease him by placing sections of the leather whip in her mouth and biting it between her teeth to show him how much she really enjoyed playing with him.

When every last inch of his body and mind pulsed in awareness and desperation, he'd envisioned rising, yanking up her nightdress above her waist and quietly instructing her to release the whip and set both hands against the pane of the window. He'd envisioned ramming into her, her pale hands sliding down the glass, unable to find stability, as he kept ramming into her from behind, again and again and again.

It was the best orgasm he'd had in a very, very long time. Which, yes, was pathetic. But then again, that was his life: pathetic. Hell, here he was, at the age of eight and twenty, and aside from several dozen tolerable nights throughout the years with women he shouldn't have even bothered with, he'd never experienced true passion or a meaningful relationship. He wanted that. He'd always wanted that. Sex for sex's sake made him feel so…vulgar. Especially the sort of sex he enjoyed.

Bringing the porcelain cup up to his lips, Tristan

swallowed a mouthful of hot, gritty coffee and paused, drawing his brows together. Smacking his lips against the acrid bitterness and granules coating his tongue, he refrained from spitting out his own saliva into the cup. Why was his coffee so mucky?

He set the cup on the porcelain saucer with a solid *chink* and sighed in exasperation. Instead of complaining to the servants, he rose and trudged back upstairs, toward his dressing chamber. He was already an hour late anyway.

After the valet assisted him in dressing, he surveyed his appearance in the full-length mirror one last time, only to pause, noting something wasn't quite right.

His boots.

Glancing down, he drew up his right foot, to better inspect the black leather, before setting it back down. For some reason, his boots were scuffed.

He blinked, realizing they were the same boots he'd worn the night he had met...*her.* He must have scuffed them against the railing he'd climbed. He hated scuffed boots. He hated it about as much as he hated being late. It was obvious his focus was waning.

Before leaving the house, Tristan rang for his valet one last time and had the man repolish his boots. Slamming the front door behind him, he stalked out toward his waiting carriage, annoyed with his inability to focus. Settling into the upholstered seat, he rapped on the ceiling to signal his driver onward and yanked out his pocket watch.

It was almost noon. Blast it. His entire schedule would have to be rearranged. Tristan glanced toward the house across the square and shifted his jaw. He was already an hour behind. He supposed it wouldn't matter if he casually drove by her house on the way out. Perhaps if he could glimpse her in passing, and in full daylight, he could convince himself that she wasn't as attractive or as interesting as he had allowed himself to believe. He could then move on with his life and not worry about it again. And though, yes, it was a very stupid approach toward rationalizing his own preoccupation with a woman whose name he didn't even know, he was well used to stupid approaches when it came to women.

Shoving his watch back into his vest pocket, he unlatched the window of the carriage, pushed it open and called out to the driver, "Round the entire square once before our departure." He hesitated. "Slowly." He hesitated again. "Though not too slow." He didn't want to be *too* obvious.

"Yes, my lord!" the driver called back.

Tristan slid closer to the window and waited as the neighboring townhomes alongside the stretch of the street dragged past. And dragged and dragged and dragged past.

He rolled his eyes and refrained from cursing. Though the carriage was going *far* too slow, so slow he could actually see into every single window that passed and see all of the furniture and servants belonging to every family in the neighborhood, he didn't bother to yell out to the driver again lest he bring even more attention to himself.

Eventually, the carriage rounded the end of the square. The sun, which had been partly hidden behind a large cloud, poured a bright patch of light across the vast whitewashed Georgian home.

Tristan leaned forward and casually glanced over to the long row of glinting windows, pretending he was merely admiring the architecture.

To his disappointment, each window that edged past held no movement or the face he was hoping to see. As the carriage clattered past the last four rows of windows, he froze, noticing a dark-haired woman tucked in a chair, sitting beside one of the windows. Her eyes were downcast as her bare hands appeared and disappeared above the sill, fastidiously occupied with intricate needlework.

It was her.

And unlike the last time he'd seen her, her thick, black hair was prettily swept up into a simple chignon. An alabaster cashmere shawl covered her slim shoulders, obscuring the curve of her breasts and sections of her azure morning gown.

She glanced up from her needlework and momentarily met his gaze through all the glass separating them. Her hands stilled at the exact moment his heart did.

Haunting gray-blue eyes, highlighted by the bright sun streaking her face, intently held his as the carriage edged on. He'd never realized a woman's eyes could force a man to reconsider his entire life.

She shifted against her wicker chair, her bold gaze following him as he rolled past. He leaned far forward in an effort to hold her gaze and offered a curt nod in her direction, wishing to inform her that despite the fact that he hadn't called, it did not mean he wasn't smitten.

Her full lips spread into a stunning smile that rounded her elegant cheeks. She waved him over, silently inviting him to call.

God save him, she needed to learn that respectable women did *not* wave men over. He shook his head, signaling that he wasn't quite ready to entertain the idea of calling on her. He needed more time.

Her smile faded. She shrugged, cast her eyes downward and occupied herself once again with her needlework.

As his carriage rounded the corner and headed out of the square, Tristan edged back against the seat and sighed. Sometimes he really wished he was capable of being more spontaneous. Sometimes.

On the outskirts of London

TRISTAN JOGGED UP the set of stairs leading to his grandmother's vast terrace home, reached out and twisted the iron bell on the side of the entrance. Moments passed, and with them the occasional clattering of coach wheels and clumping of horses' hooves from the cobblestone street behind. He waited and waited, yet for some reason, no one answered.

Leaning back, he eyed the vast windows, noting all of the curtains were open. His gut tightened as he twisted the iron bell again, praying that nothing was amiss. Eventually, eight solid clicks vibrated the large door and at long last, it swung open.

"Oh, thank the heavens!" Miss Henderson bustled out, grabbed him by the crook of his arm and yanked him inside.

Tristan stumbled to a halt, his top hat tipping forward as the chambermaid released him. Stunned, he blinked past the lowered brim of his hat at the hall decorated with potted ferns. "Miss Henderson." He pushed his top hat back into place. "Was that necessary? I could have easily walked in."

"Beggin' your pardon, milord." She scurried around him to shut the door. "Seein' how you always insist on knowin' the particulars, here it be plain— Lady Moreland's been in a foul mood all week. More foul than I've ever been privy to, to be sure. And with you bein' late, it appears to have agitated her into a state of panic."

"I see." Tristan eyed the silver tray laden with food that sat unattended on the bottom landing of the sweeping staircase. He pivoted toward Miss Henderson. "Is there a reason you've been tasked to answer doors? Assure me Lady Moreland hasn't dismissed yet another butler."

She sighed. "That she did. Turned the poor man out not even two days ago when he complimented her on her appearance. She doesn't give a rottin' fig for men, does she?"

That was an understatement. "No. I am afraid she has endured far too much hardship to warrant that."

In her debutante years, his grandmother had been hailed as an extraordinary beauty by all, including her own esteemed cousin, His Royal Majesty. Her beauty had seen her married to an extremely wealthy Marquis, which had pleased her father far more than herself. Sadly for her, the match had resulted in many years of vicious beatings at the hands of a libertine husband who flew into irrational, jealous rages brought on by cruel whispers that she and her cousin, His Majesty, whom she had always intimately associated with, were lovers. Which they were not. As a result, now it was Tristan's poor grandmother who was irrational.

Miss Henderson finished bolting each of the eight locks on the main entrance door. "The butler wasn't the only one to receive the shoe. Up and dismissed four others, she did." She clasped her hands together and grinned, her round cheeks dimpling. "Always lovely havin' you call, milord. Makes all the difference. Softens her quite a bit, I think."

"Does it?" He never knew his grandmother to be remotely soft. Or pliable, for that matter.

He blinked, noting Miss Henderson's white serving cap was tipped atop her blond, pinned hair, and that her embroidered white apron was propped almost entirely on the left side of her hip. It was obvious she was overworked.

He dug into his pocket and withdrew a ten-pound banknote from a small roll he always carried with him. He held it out for her. "Here. This will assist in keeping that lovely spirit of yours afloat. I appreciate everything you do for her."

Her eyes widened as she eyed the banknote. "Truly?"

He leaned toward her and waved it. "I never offer something I don't intend to part with, Miss Henderson. 'Tis a rule of mine."

She hesitated, then slipped the banknote from his gloved fingers and bobbed an awkward curtsy, stuffing the bill into her apron pocket. "You are too kind, milord."

He gave her a curt nod. "At least someone thinks so. Inform Lady Moreland of my arrival."

"That I will." Miss Henderson adjusted her apron into place. Smoothing it against her gray serving attire, she bobbed another curtsy. "Pardon my frayed appearance, but with the butler and the housekeeper and two others gone, I am well without a wit. Surely you understand."

"More than you realize," he drawled. There was a reason he'd moved into separate quarters at twenty, after only five years under his grandmother's care. The woman meant well, but she had been territorial, obsessive and overly demanding. Still was.

Miss Henderson gestured toward the grand parlor off to the side, patted her cap back into place and hurried past. She heaved up the large silver tray from the bottom step, then clumped up the staircase. At the top, she glanced down at him, smiled and disappeared around the corner.

The ticking of the French hall clock pierced the deafening silence. He turned and eyed the bolted door behind him, which consisted of more iron latches than the Bank of England would ever require.

God help him, why did he always put himself through this? Guilt, he supposed, and a deep affection he was forever cursed to feel. For despite all of his grandmother's faults and the fact that she was a recluse of the worst sort, she and she alone had compassionately seen him through the darkest hours of his youth.

Knowing no designated servant was going to fetch his hat, he stripped it from his head and tossed it toward the entrance door before heading into the parlor. He paused upon reaching the middle of the room and eyed the empty expanse of the gilded cream-and-yellow drawing room. His brows came together as he slowly turned left, then right. Where the devil had all the portraits and furniture gone to?

He turned, rounding the room. Except for a side table that had been set on the edge of a Persian rug, the rest of the furniture he'd only seen last week had been stripped and removed. The lone lacquered table that remained was stacked high with untouched correspondences. A quill and an ornate silver-and-onyx inkwell sat upon the marble mantel of the vast hearth just across from the table.

He shook his head. He never knew what to expect when he visited.

A loud crash from upstairs sent a tremor through the corridors and the walls. He jerked toward the doorway.

After a prolonged moment of silence, there was a rustling of skirts and the rushing of booted feet down the main stairs. Miss Henderson jerked to a halt in the entryway of the parlor and curtsied, tears streaking her flushed cheeks. "Her Ladyship insists you visit her private chamber, milord."

Tristan eyed her. "Are you unwell, Miss Henderson?"

She pressed her thin lips together but said nothing.

Poor thing. At least she was getting paid to deal with his grandmother. He most certainly wasn't. "I will do my best to rein her in."

She nodded and hurried out of sight.

Tristan strode out of the parlor, tackled the sweeping length of stairs, taking two steps at a time, and upon reaching the landing, veered right. He passed door after closed door, until he paused at the second to the last, leading into her bedchamber.

Drawing in a deep, calming breath, he knocked. "'Tis me," he called out. "Moreland."

Only silence pulsed. Grabbing the round brass handle, he turned it and edged the door open. The heavy scent of rose water clung to the stagnant air. His boots echoed as he made his way into the large bedchamber. He stepped over the upset silver tray, mashed food and shattered porcelain, his eyes drifting past the blue-gold pinstriped silk wallpaper and the oversized four-poster bed.

He paused, noting the curvaceous, tall figure, dressed in an embroidered cobalt gown, lingering before the lattice window. His grandmother stared out, angling herself just enough for him to glimpse the regal profile of her powdered face and her mass of snowy-white pin curls.

She didn't turn or acknowledge him. No doubt because she was displeased with him for being late.

He sighed and closed the remaining distance between them. "Is there a need to be so harsh with Miss Henderson? The poor woman was in tears."

"I was not harsh with her at all," she quibbled in an overly dry tone. "I was merely pointing out that I do not appreciate my heirloom china being smashed into countless shards I cannot use."

He rolled his eyes. "If that is the worst she will ever do as a servant, be grateful. I once had all of my silver swiped."

"Oh, that will come next, I am sure. I may have to dismiss her. She is far too emotional for my liking. I cannot even rationally point anything out to the woman without her blubbering at every turn."

"If you dismiss Miss Henderson, there will be no one left to serve you, let alone answer the door. I suggest you offer her a bit more compassion. She is being sorely overworked and, knowing you, probably underpaid."

"I advise you not to be foolish enough to actually defend one of my own servants to me. I pay her very well. In fact, I pay her more than I should."

He sighed. "I suggest we make better use of our time. I have to leave earlier than usual today."

She hesitated but still didn't turn. "Why? You always dedicate Tuesdays to me."

Yes, and even that was sometimes a bit too much dedication on his part. "The House of Lords will be swearing in the Duke of Norfolk, Lord Clifford and Lord Dormer today. I intend to show my support by making an appearance."

A brittle laugh escaped her lips. "Show your support to the Catholics, indeed. Low-hanging fruit is all they are. No good will ever come from giving such men seats."

"You sound like a damn bigot. Reducing religious discrimination reflects the moral progress of a nation."

"Ah, yes. You always were an idealist, Moreland. Much like your father." She set her chin and continued to gaze out the window. "So, why are you late? You never are."

He cleared his throat, not wanting to think about *why* he had overslept. "Forgive me. I was behind schedule."

She glanced at him from over her shoulder, her arched silver brows rising. "You never stray from your schedule. It would be like a bird displacing its wings." Her voice was patient, warm and steady, as it always was when addressing him. "Who is she?"

He dragged in a breath, knowing if he admitted having any interest in a woman, it would only rile his grandmother into investigating his neighbor's entire life, right down to the cosmetic creams she wore. "You are assuming far too much. I was merely slow to rise."

"You haven't been slow to rise in thirteen years, Moreland." She snickered suggestively. "I only hope whatever is responsible for your…*unease* will cease vexing you."

He would either have to move or marry his neighbor for her to stop vexing him.

His grandmother turned toward him, the long lace sleeves of her muslin gown shifting against her wrists. Dark, playful eyes met his. Raking the length of his body, she sighed. "Why do you never put any effort into your appearance, Moreland? You always wear far too much gray. And if it is not gray, it is black. Can you not invest in some…color?"

He set his gloved hands behind his back and strategically set his booted feet wide apart to better display all his gray. "I dress for comfort. Not entertainment purposes. If the good Lord had wanted me to be a peacock, he would have *made* me a peacock, don't you think?"

"Let us move on to a more notable matter of importance, shall we?"

He smirked. "By all means."

She folded her hands before her as if trying to settle on how she ought to begin lecturing him. "During my usual weekly inquiries into society, I was astounded to hear that my dear, respectable grandson had been secretly vying for a certain woman in a most unconventional manner. A woman who, by the by, has undergone several Seasons untouched for reasons relating to some ruined fop in Venice. Why did you not inform me of your interest in Lady Victoria? Is it because you knew I would disapprove?"

He tightened his jaw and tried to remind himself that she was the only relative he had left, and that she loved him. Or at least she tried to love him. "I will admit that Lady Victoria has always fascinated me, and when the opportunity to vie for her was presented, I was intrigued enough to pursue it. I was never meant to live alone. You know that. Unlike you, I prefer sharing conversations and meals with someone other than myself."

"Do not chastise me. This has nothing to do with my objecting to you taking a wife. I am objecting to your choices."

"Same thing."

"I don't want you associating with that family. You need a good, stable alliance."

He glared at her. "Lord Linford was my father's closest friend. He also offered support when everyone else chose to toss gossip. Be mindful of that. From what I understand, the poor man's life is at an end and he doesn't have much longer to live."

She lowered her chin but didn't break her unwavering gaze. "Are you privy as to why?"

He glanced away, sensing she already knew what he did. Lord Linford was dying of syphilis. "I have heard rumors."

"They are not rumors. He is wasting away. Do you truly mean to inform me, Moreland, that watching your own father-in-law die of the pox appeals to your sensible tastes?"

It really was astounding how much gossip the woman always managed to unearth about him and everyone else, considering she never left the house. Of course, thanks to the death of his grandfather, her wealth now well exceeded his own. And with her also being cousin to the King—*and a favorite cousin, at that*—her hold on London society was as firm as ever. With the toss of a word and a few banknotes to the right person, she was able to play God with everyone's life. Including his own. "I am endlessly astonished to hear that all of your inquiries failed to inform you that Lady Victoria was already wed by special license to that 'ruined fop' from Venice you were just yerking about. So you needn't worry about her and me."

Her stern features softened and a smile feathered her thin lips. "You are better off. The Linfords, though pleasant enough, would have only offered you hardship."

He dreaded knowing what his future wife would have to contend with. Between himself and his grandmother, she'd have to be indestructible. "I am beginning to think you are terrified that once I am married my priorities will no longer rest with you. But I can assure you, Grandmother dearest, that my priorities haven't rested with you since I was twenty."

Her smile faded. "You are being rather unpleasant today. Why? What is agitating you?"

He huffed out a breath. His new neighbor. These past twelve days and eleven nights, the woman had made him realize that despite all the barriers he kept putting up to maintain a sense of command over his life, all he really wanted was a meaningful relationship with a respectable but passionate woman who wasn't going to make him feel like the walking freak that he was.

He stared his grandmother down. "Perhaps I'm not in the least bit pleased with the way you continue to pry into my life. Your inquiries into the Linfords is but another pathetic example of what I have to contend with. I have enough difficulties relating to women without you digging into their affairs. I prefer learning about a woman through conventional means and allowing her the privilege of doing the same.

Civil society refers to it as courtship. You may have heard of it?"

She shook her head from side to side, not in the least bit amused. "Courtship only ever offers a stage strewn with actors. I courted your grandfather for seven whole months and it was the only time in our association that brute never raised a fist to me. You may not appreciate my efforts, Moreland, but after your disastrous involvement with Stockton's widow last year that resulted in you slicing your arm yet again, when you swore to me you were well done with it, 'tis my responsibility to ensure these women offer you the sort of stability you require. The sort of stability you obviously cannot offer yourself."

He seethed out an exhausted breath. Despite what his grandmother thought, Lady Elizabeth Stockton had been a beautiful blessing in helping him understand that even the most eccentric women of his class held no respect for him or his needs. His penchant for the whip and blade had amused her into thinking that was all he was and all he really wanted. "You needlessly worry."

"You needlessly make me worry."

He glared at her. "Do you realize that the number of invitations I receive each year is beginning to progressively dwindle?"

"And you blame me?" she echoed.

"'Tis obvious people are terrified of having their

daughters associate with a queer whose deranged grandmother aspires to maliciously expose every detail of their lives. Hell, at this rate, I'll never be married. And I have an income of almost nine thousand a year!"

"You are far too agitated for my liking. Off with you. I will see you next Tuesday." She swept up her pale hand and held it out toward him. "Rest assured, I will unearth everything and set it right for you. I always do."

The older he got, the more he realized he was not strong enough to shoulder her relentless need to protect him. He didn't want or need protection. All he wanted was to be an ordinary man with an ordinary life that included a beautiful wife, a houseful of children, a hunting dog and maybe even a cat. But how could he even *try* to strive for the ordinary when she kept on bloody reminding him he was anything but?

Tristan made his way toward her, keeping each and every step controlled and steady. He paused directly before her, but refused to take her outstretched hand. "My life became my own when I walked out that door. Remember that. It has taken me *years* to crawl toward a civil understanding of myself. I don't need you breathing on every decision I make. I am in complete command of everything I do." *Except for when it comes to my neighbor's breasts.*

"I worry about your definition of *command*." She lowered her hand to her side and observed him tartly. "Someone was kind enough to inform me of an evening rendezvous you had with a young woman in your square. She must have been quite the flavor if you were willing to entertain her in public for almost an hour whilst she was in a state of undress. What do you know about her? Aside from whatever attraction you may feel? Are you pursuing her? Or wanting to?"

Christ, she already knew about her. "Have you nothing else to obsess about?" he growled, trying and failing to retain a respectable tone. "I find it disturbing. You need something other than me to occupy your life. I suggest you remarry, or step outside of this house from time to time."

She stared at him. "I only ever do what I believe is best for you, Moreland. Despite your claim that you are well and done with the blade—"

"I am well and done with it."

"Are you?"

"Yes. I am."

She observed him for a long moment, her dark eyes flitting toward his coat pocket. "Are you still carrying your razor case? Be honest."

He glanced away and shifted his jaw, knowing his razor case was in fact in his coat pocket. Not because he used it—hell, he hadn't used it in almost a year—but because it gave him a sense of…comfort. It also challenged him to try to rise above his baser needs. "I don't use it."

She sighed. "You will always mar yourself. That is a sad fact I have had to accept. Who is to say it will not lead to more should you end up involving yourself with the wrong woman? I suggest you avoid this neighbor of yours until I find out more about her. Give me a week. My footman will deliver you a detailed letter pertaining to all of my inquiries. You can make a decision then."

The trouble with her meddling was that she had a tendency to not only expose all of the grisly details to him, but to all of London. Then neither him *or* London would want anything more to do with the poor woman.

He leaned in and pointed at her, barely missing her nose. "The devil you will. Leave it be. Leave *her* be. Your meddling will only expose her to gossip. I will call on her when I am ready."

She narrowed her gaze. "Remove your finger from my face, Moreland, and then remove yourself from my presence. I have had more than enough intimidation in my lifetime and I most certainly don't need it from you."

Dropping his hand to his side, Tristan swung away and stalked toward the open door, agitated with her for always choking him like this. "I'm leaving. Before I realize I don't like you."

He grabbed at the brass handle and slammed the door hard behind himself, the tension in his body progressively rising. Pushing himself down the length of the corridor, the sudden need to escape not only that corridor, but his entire life, swelled.

No matter how much distance he tried to set between himself and the past, no matter how quietly he went about leading a good, respectable life he could be proud of, his grandmother always managed to burrow herself in and point out how much further he had to go. He was well aware more needed to be done. For one, he needed to stop carrying his razor case.

He glanced toward the long row of paintings and jerked to a halt, noting a new painting was hanging on the corridor wall. He turned and stared at a green field set against a low, setting sun. He swallowed, unable to push away the unsettling clench of his stomach.

He hadn't seen that painting in almost thirteen years. Mahogany-paneled walls flashed within his thoughts, and despite not wanting to see it, he did. He always did. His father's lifeless body forever remained slumped over his writing desk, dark blood smearing the polished wood, tendrils of it spreading over estate ledgers. A bloodied shaving razor lay angled upon the floor beside his father's booted feet, having fallen from his large hand, whispering of the tragedy that had occurred. Tristan had never thought his own father capable of destroying himself. Especially after they had spent months battling to keep his mother from doing the very same thing.

Noting the painting was crooked, he edged toward it and nudged each end of the carved frame until it was even. He stepped back and pushed out a breath, wishing he had it in him to rip that painting off the wall and smash it through a window. Of course, it wouldn't change anything and would only make him feel like a petulant child.

"I found it in the attic," his grandmother offered cheerfully from down the corridor. "Rather lovely, isn't it? It was your father's."

Tristan turned toward the direction of her voice. "Yes. I know. It was also hanging four feet from the desk where he slit his throat. Might I request you remove it from the wall before my next visit? I don't care to see it."

She hesitated. "Forgive me, I didn't realize—"

"Don't apologize. Just do it."

"Yes, of course."

He pointed at her. "And no inquiries. Do you understand? *None*."

"I beg your forgiveness, but no amount of intimidation will keep me from ensuring you don't end up like your father. Whilst I cannot protect you from yourself, I can protect you from the vile nature of others. And protect you I will. I intend to fully investigate this woman and set not only your mind at ease, but my own."

He lowered his hand and stared her down, ensuring she felt the pulsing intensity of his displeasure. "If you expose her to any gossip—*any*—I will marry her without even bothering to know her name, merely to demonstrate who is really holding the reins here."

She set her chin, her taut, pale features now marked with cold dignity. "I dare you to defy me and what I deem best for you."

He stepped toward her and tapped on his chest. "I dare you to defy *me*. I define what is best for me. Not you. Whether I choose to get involved with her isn't for you to control or decide. I may be a queer in your eyes, and in the eyes of every goddamn woman I stupidly allow myself to get involved with, but lest you and those women forget, I am first and foremost a gentleman. *A gentleman!* And I will not be treated otherwise."

"Moreland." She hurried toward him, her features twisting in anguish. "You are no queer. I have never looked upon you as such. But you cannot expect me to—"

"Good day to you, Grandmother. I take my leave."

Before I start ripping paintings off the walls and swearing at you for always treating me like a child.

Without deigning to give her another glance, he turned and stalked off down the corridor, down the stairs and to the entrance door, wishing she would spare him from enduring any more of her stupid manipulation at the cost of his own sanity. It was as if she truly believed he was on the brink of suicide. If she of all people didn't believe in him, who the hell ever would?

Settling into the upholstered confines of the carriage, Tristan impatiently waited until the door was secured by the footman. The need to rip out almost a year's worth of pent-up frustration from his mind, body and soul rose with each uneven breath he took. He couldn't tolerate it anymore. He simply couldn't tolerate forever trying to avoid what he was and what he knew he would always be.

When the carriage clattered forward and away from his grandmother's house, he yanked the curtains shut over each window. What did it matter anymore? He was a queer and would always be a queer.

Shifting against the seat, he stripped his gloves from his shaky hands and dug into his coat pocket, sliding out his razor case. He set it on the seat beside him and rolled up the sleeve of his gray morning coat, as well as the linen shirt beneath, exposing a section of his forearm.

With a flick of his thumb, he unlatched the hinged brass lid of the slim casing, revealing a folded white handkerchief, an ivory-handled razor and that damned faded piece of parchment he could never bring himself to burn despite trying to do so many times.

Setting his exposed arm on his upper thigh, he plucked up the razor and unfolded the straight blade, strategically positioning its edge on a clear patch of skin between the raised scars marring his entire forearm. He paused, his jaw tightening.

He had promised himself he wouldn't do it anymore. He had promised. How was he to become a good husband to any respectable woman when he couldn't even control his demented need to—

He swallowed against the tightness of his throat and hastily refolded the blade. He was going to be making an appearance at the House of Lords, for God's sake. He couldn't show up bandaged and bleeding.

Reorganizing everything back into his razor case, he secured the hinged lid and shoved it back into his coat pocket. Covering his arm, he swiped a trembling hand over his face and prayed he made it to Parliament without giving in to his need for release.

SCANDAL THREE

Devious behavior never benefits anyone.
~~*Although sometimes...*~~
—*How To Avoid A Scandal,*
Moreland's Original Manuscript

The 12th of May
Evening

DARK, DARK TIMES had descended upon the Kingdom of Poland. Yet again. For upon this day, the Emperor and Autocrat of All the Russias had officially crowned himself the Tsar of Poland and all of its people. And here she was, countries away, banished to fester in some town house in London, unable to so much as spit upon the man's boot *or* leave the house.

But that would soon change.

Although Countess Zosia Urszula Kwiatkowska was being bullied into marrying an Englishman by the end of what the British called the Season, she wasn't about to marry just *any* Englishman, despite what His Majesty thought. It was all about playing the right pawn on the board at the right time, when one's opponents weren't looking. If there was anyone who could single-handedly win at any game, be it chess, piquet, loo, whist, pope or charades, it most certainly was her.

Despite His Majesty's growing agitation, she refused to marry any of the strange men he kept sending to her door. Aside from none of them having a personality or any real influence on London society, they all treated her like she was some feral animal in need of restraint.

There were only so many things she was willing to sacrifice in the name of avoiding the monastery, and dignity most certainly was not one of them. She needed to marry an intelligent, progressive and influential man willing to accept her for what she was. Not whatever he expected her to be.

Of course, finding such a man was an involved process that was making His Majesty think she was overly ambitious and completely daft. Though she wasn't really too worried what His Majesty thought. After all, she could always blame any lapse of judgment on her laudanum.

Locking her bedchamber door with a quick turn of the key so her nurse wouldn't interrupt, Zosia wheeled herself around the bed toward the window on the other side of the room. Maneuvering her wicker chair before the drawn curtains, she gathered them up and buried herself and the chair within the vast material, allowing them to fall down around her and onto the wooden floor.

She edged the large wheels closer to the window, until the tip of her slippered foot, which was set upon the padded footrest, was propped against the wall below the sill. Readjusting the embroidered curtains around her, she secured them more firmly together to ensure no candlelight filtered out into the night beyond, to better keep her hidden from the outside world.

Well satisfied, she snatched up her spyglass from the sill of the window and extended its brass length, determined to stay privy to all the goings-on with her oh-so-dashing British neighbor, the Marquis of Moreland. The one with the mysterious dark eyes and brooding features.

Although she'd planned to coordinate an introduction between them with the assistance of His Majesty, she was astounded to find him standing beneath her window late one night, observing *her* in the manner she'd been observing him through her spyglass all along. Lunging at the opportunity to meet him, she discovered he was far more impressive in full size than he was palm size.

Everything about him, from his appearance, to his prospects, to his respectability, to his political seat, to his wit, intellect, demeanor and even his dialect was perfect. Too perfect. It made him untouchable to a one-legged Polish Catholic such as herself. But no man could be *that* perfect. He had to be hiding something beneath that cultivated, regal facade. But what?

Annoyingly, instead of calling on her, as she had invited him to do, his footman had merely delivered a red leather-bound book about British etiquette. It made her wonder if the man was onto her ostentatious scheme. Though it was unlikely. A man only considered a woman to be a threat to his money or his heart. Neither of which she wanted or needed. Wealth she had, and her heart…her heart was already spoken for by something far more important than a man.

With the delivery of that etiquette book—which she'd tossed after briefly skimming—she was beginning to think he was simply too respectable to crack. Until he'd rounded his coach past her home one afternoon, peering in through all of her windows. *That* was when she knew he wasn't as civil minded as he was leading her and the rest of the world to believe.

A movement on the cobblestone street below made her pause and glance down toward it. Her fingers tightened on the spyglass, the cool brass pressing against her moistened palm, upon seeing a broad-shouldered figure saddled upon a snowy stallion, dressed from head to boot in dark military attire. Lingering beside the lamppost, he was strategically aligned beneath her window.

Her heart skipped, realizing he'd actually been watching her all along while she had been situating herself. A large military hat shaded his nose and eyes, only revealing the shadowed outline of a strong, shaven jaw. He hesitated, as if wanting to dismount.

Instead, he swept off his military hat, revealing dark, shoulder-length hair, and inclined his head, gallantly acknowledging her as he pressed his feathered hat to his chest with a large gloved hand.

She blinked, trying to make out that shadowed face against the dim light of the lamppost, but he had already reaffixed his hat and veered his horse away from her window. Glancing back up at her one last time, he nudged his riding boots into his stallion's sides and galloped down the cobblestone street, his black riding cloak flapping behind him in the wind. He galloped out of the square, down one of the streets and disappeared from sight.

Wide-eyed, she leaned forward, pressing the tips of her fingers against the cool pane. Who was he? And why did he acknowledge her with such reverence? It was very odd.

Instead of being concerned that she and the house were now under military surveillance ordered by the crown, she sensed there was something far more to him. It was as if he'd been lingering in the hopes of glimpsing her. Similar to what Lord Moreland had done.

She hesitated, then sat back against her wicker chair and rolled her eyes. Glimpse her, indeed. She'd be nothing short of vain to think every man in London ardently longed to linger beneath the window of a one-legged Catholic for a glimpse. Unless it was for amusement purposes.

She paused. Speaking of amusement purposes—

Zosia leaned back toward the window and propped up the spyglass to her right eye. She squinted, edging it toward the direction of Lord Moreland's window, until she could see straight into his candlelit bed-chamber. Fortunately, the curtains draping his window were not entirely drawn, allowing her to peer past into a small section of his room. A section displaying a four-poster bed.

It was a very nice bed, actually. Certainly much nicer than her own. It had a silvery, plush coverlet with an assortment of burgundy and dove-gray pil-lows piled high against the carved headboard. It made her want to marry the man merely for an opportunity to roll around in it.

She smirked at the thought. Her cousin Basia, who'd been married for almost a good dozen years, had enthusiastically informed her all about what *really* went on between a man and a woman. And if she was going to do *that* with a man, he had better well look as good as Lord Moreland.

A shadow passed across the lens, and though she tried to follow the movement, it was too quick. The side of the curtain obstructed the rest of the view. She pulled the spyglass away and eyed his window to decipher where she was supposed to point the lens.

Realigning it, she tried again. A bare, sculpted chest came into view. She fumbled, momentarily losing sight of said broad chest. Her heart thumped as she scrambled to set the telescope back against her eye. She leveled it again, trying to keep it steady.

Having glimpsed many bare-chested men working in the fields during harvest whilst she and her cousin rode out of Warszawa and into the country, she had learned to appreciate a good chest. And this man had a good chest.

He turned away, tossing a robe onto the bed, his broad, muscled shoulders shifting. With a few swift movements, he dropped his trousers and undergarments around muscled legs, leaving him gloriously naked.

Zosia gasped. Only the support of her own chair kept her from toppling over. Whilst she considered giving him his due privacy, ultimately, she decided against it. After all, if she planned on marrying him, she had every right to know what his body looked like.

The muscles in those long, lean legs and firm backside flexed and rippled like satin as he leaned over and grabbed up his nightshirt. To her disappointment, he never once turned around to present what she was *most* curious to see.

The length of his body disappeared in a single sweep beneath a long, white linen nightshirt. He grabbed up a robe that was also on the bed, slid it on and adjusted it into place around his solid frame.

She'd never thought British men could be as attractive as Polish men. Her cousins were always telling her how stoic and uninteresting the British were. Of course, none of her cousins had ever been to Britain.

Lowering the spyglass, Zosia slid the brass extension back into its casing and set it on the sill of the window, letting out a breathy sigh. She tugged out the braided chain buried beneath her nightdress and fingered her ruby-studded locket, wondering how she could get him to call on her. Without annoying him.

A movement made her release her locket as the partially closed curtains she'd been keenly watching were swept wide open. The bright glow of countless candles filtered out, fully displaying Lord Moreland as he casually braced the frame of the window and stared out toward...*her.*

Mother in heaven. He was going to think she was obsessed. Her heart pounded as she grabbed hold of the spoked wheels and pushed back. For some reason, her chair resisted movement. Her chest tightened as she glanced down toward each large wooden wheel and realized it wasn't the two side wheels that were caught, but the small wheel behind her chair. The rotating wheel had embedded itself atop the long ends of the curtains behind her, locking her in place against the window.

Jezus i Maria. Of all times.

She violently jerked forward and back, forward and back, trying to move the chair. The curtain rod above rattled. She gritted her teeth and jerked back again. This time the curtain rod jumped off the hooks in the wall and crashed with a huge clang and a thud behind her. Her hands jumped up to cover her head as the last of the curtains whooshed past, barely missing her and the chair.

She groaned, realizing she had not only completely destroyed the curtains, but was now on full, candlelit display for Lord Moreland. Her cheeks burned as she lowered her hands primly back onto her lap. Knowing there was no point in wheeling away from the situation, she eyed him across the distance of the square.

His hands slid down the length of the window frame he'd been bracing. Though she couldn't make out the expression on his shadowed face, it was obvious he was intrigued as to why she had ripped off the curtains and was flaunting herself before him.

She lifted an awkward hand and waved, hoping that by being friendly she would appear a little less devious.

He hesitated, then lifted his own hand and offered a single, curt wave with the flick of his wrist.

She drew in a shaky breath and let it out. Maybe *this* was the opportunity she'd been waiting for. Words were not always needed to spark interest. Zosia waved again, ensuring this time it was far more enthusiastic and visible.

He casually set his hands on his hips and shook his dark head from side to side, attempting to convey his complete disappointment in her lack of maturity.

But he stayed.

She giggled. Pushing her dark braid over her shoulder, she shifted forward in her chair, closer toward the sill. It was obvious by his stance and the way he lingered that he wanted to play.

Zosia leaned far forward and balanced herself on the ledge of the sill. Setting her lips against the pane, which sent her swinging locket to *chink* against the window, she playfully smothered kiss after kiss across the entire window, before leaning back and admiring the moist, smeared marks she'd left all over the glass.

He readjusted the belt of his robe, his broad shoulders shifting, and braced the frame of the window again. Only this time, he stared her down as if restraining himself from leaping across the square and collecting those kisses himself.

"So you do like me," she announced softly. How very curious. Why would a bachelor who was supposedly in the market for a wife avoid a woman he appeared to like? Did he already know about her amputation?

The door rattled, startling her into veering her whole chair toward the direction of the door.

"Countess?" There was a tapping and the rattling of the knob. "You should not be latching your door."

Zosia rolled her eyes and dropped her hand into her lap. Mrs. Wade. Forever tending to her needs as if she were two. "I am quite well, Mrs. Wade," she called over her shoulder. "There is no need for you to come in."

"I heard a terrible noise from within your room. Please assure me all is well."

"Yes, yes." She waved her hand about. "The curtains and the rod fell off the wall. As old as this house is, I dare say everything will fall off the wall in time.

But there is no need for concern, I assure you. All is well. You may retire."

"You cannot possibly expect me to retire without even knowing what—"

"Mrs. Wade," Zosia snapped, turning her chair and glaring at the door. She wished the woman would cease treating her like an invalid. A missing leg did not denote a missing brain. "I have a right to privacy. Do I not?"

"Yes, Countess, of course, but—"

"Good night. Or as we Poles say, *dobra noc."*

"And what of your laudanum?"

Zosia smoothed the lace and linen nightdress against the length of her sore thighs and winced. She needed to use her crutches more, lest she become too sore. She hated being dependent on a rancid liquid that made her feel like she was drowning in a hazy fog. She considered pain a much better option than missing out on reality. "I feel content to sleep as I am, thank you. Tomorrow, I intend to make use of my crutches and take a few turns about the square. That should relieve whatever discomfort I am in."

"You know full well you aren't permitted to leave the house without His Majesty's approval. If you seek a turn about the square, Countess, you must send him a missive."

She was surrounded by wardens, not servants. She'd already sent His Majesty countless missives asking for permission to leave the house, only to be told it wasn't advisable. "His Majesty seems to be under the delusion that I have no rights left to my name. I am tired of his games and refuse to be confined to both a chair *and* a house and will find my way to the door whether it pleases His Majesty or not. I suggest you send him a missive telling him *that*. Now I bid you a very good night, Mrs. Wade."

The door rattled again. "Please. Unlatch the door. What if you should require assistance during the night?"

Zosia sighed. "I do not mean to be ungrateful, Mrs. Wade, but I am increasingly agitated by everyone's misguided devotion to my well-being. Now, I demand you retire and will not ask again."

Mrs. Wade hesitated. "As you wish, Countess." Steps clicked down the corridor and faded.

Zosia veered her chair back toward the window, ready to resume her play, only to discover Moreland's curtains had already been drawn shut.

She huffed out a disappointed breath.

She could easily blame Mrs. Wade for interrupting her strategic flirtation, but she sensed she'd intimidated the poor man into retiring. Karol had warned her that the British, especially the aristocracy, were as reserved as nuns during prayer, and that she needed to be mindful of that. She supposed it was time to play God, whilst all of the nuns prayed.

TRISTAN PACED before the curtains he had dragged shut, wishing he had it in him to dash across the square and be a rake. When he'd earlier wandered over to the window in hopes of glimpsing her, he was astounded to find her enthusiastically waving and smearing kisses all over the glass of her window. Kisses he desperately wanted to feel against every inch of his skin. Kisses he had no doubt every neighbor in the square had seen, including whatever neighbor was spying for his grandmother.

For all he knew, his grandmother already had a very long list bearing each and every one of his neighbor's faults. Aside from being overly protective, his grandmother had always foolishly believed that those who broke the rules of genteel society were of no worth and deserved to be humiliated. Little did his grandmother realize that genteel society and its vicious hold on everyday life had ultimately created the terrible situation that she had been forced to accept as a woman.

Her struggle to retain her dignity despite having been completely stripped of her own mind by society, her parents and a man who was supposed to be her protector, had prompted him, at the age of three and twenty, to unleash his quill and write *How To Avoid a Scandal*.

He had wanted to offer women a weapon. The sort of weapon both his mother and his grandmother never had. One that would give women a true glimpse into the reality of society's ruthless expectations and its governing men. Due to a very sheltered upbringing and no life experience outside of dancing, singing and pianoforte lessons, his poor grandmother had never been mentally prepared to become the wife of one of the most powerful men in London.

Of course, it had been quite a nuisance trying to write anything of value or merit considering he had to censor most of his commentaries, lest the book be considered a scandal itself. Given its unprecedented popularity with the ton, he supposed he had created the balance of respectability and reality he had been looking for.

Tristan turned toward the window again. He hesitated, feeling like a youth of fifteen, and separated the curtains with his hand by an inch. He peered out to see if she was still there watching and waiting for him. To his disappointment, only a darkened window greeted him.

Would she have entertained him longer if he had allowed her to? He released the curtain, letting it fall back into place. Setting his hands behind his robed back, he slowly rounded the room and his bed.

He'd never been pursued by a woman before. Most women gave up on him very quickly, thinking him cool, arrogant and unapproachable. It was a superficial role he played into quite easily, for it provided a form of protection from those he knew would never accept him for what he truly was.

But this...this was different. He could sense *she* was different, though he had yet to understand how and why. He supposed it was time to cease procrastinating and see if it were at all possible for this fascinating little flirtation between them to lead to something more.

SCANDAL FOUR

*Gossip is but a weapon that enables many
in society to sustain power over those that
threaten their way of thinking and their way
of life. Retain your power by not giving them
anything to gossip about. Life will be boring,
yes, but it is far better than dealing with a ~~fuck=
ing~~ mess.*

—*How To Avoid A Scandal,*
Moreland's Original Manuscript

*The following day
11:45 a.m.*

So much for taking a turn about the square.

Or ever leaving the house again.

For some reason, an endless parade of calling
cards had been delivered to Zosia's door over the
span of one short hour. Even more astounding than
that was the incredibly long line of gentlemen, as
well as servants and footmen in livery sent by their
masters, all patiently waiting to deliver *more* cards to

her door. The never-ending line of gentlemen actually rounded about the entire square!

Even long after the butler had politely stepped outside and announced to the crowd that no more cards were being accepted for the day, they all continued to incessantly linger as if expecting the butler to change his mind. Surely, such outrageous behavior, and on such a vast scale, wasn't normal. Not even for the Brits.

Seeing as none of the footmen were able to answer any of her questions pertaining to this most bizarre situation, she knew it was time to step outside and ask some of these men a few questions of her own.

Zosia swung a slippered foot forward, propelling herself and her crutches across the foyer in the direction of the stout butler and the lanky footman. Both men strategically set themselves between her and the door like the annoying wardens they had all been tasked to be.

She sighed, pausing in the middle of the foyer. "I have a right to know why half of London is standing outside my doorstep. Do I not?"

The butler, Mr. Lawrence, offered an apologetic nod, his tonic-slathered gray hair glinting. "That you do, Countess, but there is no need for concern. We were expecting them."

She blinked. "We were? *All* of them?"

"Yes. They came to deliver their cards." He

gestured toward the velvet-lined silver box filled with stacks and stacks of cards, set on the French side table beside the door. "I was instructed to cease accepting any more once the box was full. And as you can see, Countess, the box is quite full."

Zosia eyed the box and then squinted at the man. "And why are we acquiring such a disturbing number of calling cards?"

"His Majesty intends to personally wade through them."

"Ah. And I imagine there is a reason for it?"

"Yes, Countess. There is."

She hesitated, waiting expectantly for said reason. When he did not provide it, despite an insinuated prompt of silence, she sighed. "And what is the reasoning, Mr. Lawrence?"

"His Majesty will decide which of these men are to be granted interviews."

"Interviews?" she prodded.

"Yes."

Why did the British never fully convey their thoughts? It was so annoying. She sighed again. "Interviews for what, Mr. Lawrence?"

He cleared his throat. "For your matrimonial consideration. I was notified of it last night by royal courier and thought it best not to alarm you."

She didn't know whether to be flattered or upset. Shifting against her crutches, she eyed her servants, trying to understand why they seemed to know far more about her own life than she did. After all, she was the one expected to take a husband. Not them. "Why would His Majesty call for my matters to be conducted so publicly? It is neither respectable or acceptable to have this many men loitering outside my home."

Bringing his white-gloved hands together, Mr. Lawrence respectfully replied, "We are all but loyal subjects. We never question His Majesty's intent."

"Someone ought to." The naughty old sovereign, though kind, was proving to be more of a nuisance than a salvation. Not even a week after her arrival in England from Warszawa, the man had demanded she grace him with an appearance in his private apartment. At night. Alone.

When he wouldn't desist, and had even tried to pussyfoot his way into *her* private chamber, she'd politely informed His Majesty that she was going to require quarters outside the palace lest she set fire to the throne room. Arrangements for separate quarters were granted without resistance or delay. Only now she had *this* to contend with.

The bell rang yet again, annoyingly echoing throughout the vast corridor, reminding them of the crowd impatiently loitering outside. Only this time, the large knocker was being pounded against the door, causing them all to pause and glance toward the bolted entrance.

The butler turned and motioned to the footman. "'Tis best we take precautions. Watkins? Escort the Countess to her room and ensure she remains there until royal guards arrive and disperse the remaining crowd."

"Yes, Mr. Lawrence." Watkins advanced, politely gesturing toward the direction she was supposed to go.

Zosia shifted against the padded crutches digging into the pits of her arms. She was not about to hide in her room merely because one of the men had decided to use the knocker. "Forgive me, gentlemen, but I have no desire for this to give way to a riot. 'Tis obvious you are in need of intelligent leadership and I intend to offer it. Mr. Lawrence, open the door and keep taking their cards until the guards arrive. Mr. Watkins, you will coordinate the line to ensure order. That should provide enough structure to keep the masses from panicking."

The butler sniffed. "Remove her from the foyer, Watkins."

The footman leaned toward her, gently touching her arm in an awkward form of compliance. "Countess. If you would please—"

"No. I will not please." She shifted away and glared at them. "Need I remind you both, gentlemen, that I am not the one getting paid to serve you. You are the ones getting paid to serve me. Now, for the better good of our safety, as well as the safety of those unfortunate souls being forced to wait in that crowd outside, open the door and do as you are told. 'Tis a simple matter of courtesy that will ensure order until the guards arrive."

The butler set his jaw and hastened toward them. "I think it best we take away her crutches, Watkins."

She gasped and clutched at the oak posts holding her up. "You will do no such thing!"

Watkins jerked toward the old man. "Mr. Lawrence. You don't expect me to actually—"

"Do as you are told, boy," the butler commanded in a harsh tone. "Or you will find yourself without a position or a reference. You know our orders. To oppose them is to oppose your own King."

Zosia lowered her chin in disbelief as Watkins sighed, leaned toward her and tried grabbing hold of her right crutch. She jerked away, stumbling against her crutches and tightening her hold, hopped back on her one foot. "This is outrageous! How dare you—I demand to know what orders His Majesty has given and why!"

Watkins grabbed hold of her crutch again and yanked at it, each pull growing all the more firm and insistent. "I will carry you upstairs, Countess."

Her eyes narrowed. "No one ever carries me. I

carry myself. Now I am demanding you disclose your orders."

"Those orders are confidential," the butler supplied in a flat tone. "Now, please—"

"No! I—" She gritted her teeth and savagely held onto her crutches, despite swaying against Watkins's each yank and tug. Since when was it acceptable for servants to assault their mistress in the name of the King, who was supposed to be her protector?

Her bare fingers slid against the smooth oak, her grip loosening bit by bit. Though she didn't need her crutches to balance herself on one foot, her very dignity was being pried away. And while she couldn't physically take them on, unless she planned on beating them with the crutches they were so intent on having, she supposed there was only one way to go about this. She would unleash a weapon no man expected a genteel lady to use. A weapon she hadn't used since she was ten, and one she hoped would also draw the attention of every single man outside.

Sucking in a huge breath, Zosia released a long, piercing scream that pulsed against the respectable silence surrounding them.

Watkins jumped away, releasing his hold on both crutches. His eyes bulged as he snapped up both gloved hands. "Countess! Please. *Stop!* Mr. Lawrence, what—"

A rapid pounding against the door rattled the

crystal chandelier above as a male voice boomed from the other side, "*Open this door!* Open the goddamn door! *Now!*"

Zosia paused, bringing an abrupt end to her charade, and regally eyed the butler, well satisfied with the result it had produced. "It appears we have our very first concerned citizen. I suggest you open the door, Mr. Lawrence, or I will continue screaming and make every man outside think I am in desperate need of assistance. Then it will be *your* safety at stake. Not mine."

Mr. Lawrence's eyes widened. He edged back, then heaved out a sigh and muttered something, his thin lips curling. Swinging his stout frame toward the door, he unbolted the latch and fanned it open just wide enough for her to peer past the opening beyond his shoulder.

Shouts echoed from the street as men frantically pushed and shoved their way up the stairs, holding out and waving their cards. Zosia sucked in an astonished breath, not only in response to the chaos, but in recognizing the man looming in the doorway just beyond the butler.

Lord Moreland.

SCANDAL FIVE

If a lady is descendant from an illustrious family, she should never parade her lineage. Should she be of humbler means, she should never create an air of pretense to elevate her status. A true lady will be able to impress others by what she is, and not the name she holds. ~~I myself value compassion, intelligence and integrity above all else, but sadly, a name, money and a pretty face that is only capable of commenting on music and needlework is all the ton ever clamors over.~~

—*How To Avoid A Scandal,*
Moreland's Original Manuscript

UPON GLIMPSING A NOTABLE sliver of her dashing neighbor, Zosia gripped her crutches so tightly she could actually feel her pulse throbbing against the smooth wood.

Lord Moreland leaned toward the narrow opening the butler had made, his top hat momentarily shadowing his features. "I am requesting an audience with your mistress. 'Tis obvious she is in dire need of assistance and I am here to offer it."

The butler stiffened. "I am afraid she is unavailable. But if you would like to leave a card, sir, I assure you—"

"I don't have a card. But I do have *this*." Lord Moreland rammed his broad shoulder against the door, causing the butler to stumble off to the side as the door freely swung open. Several men waving their calling cards in gloved hands tried pushing their way past Lord Moreland.

"My card!" one of the men shouted, reaching past Lord Moreland's arm and waving his card.

"Ey, now, I was here first!" another shouted, shoving that man, causing Lord Moreland to stumble forward.

Zosia stiffened, expecting a rush through the door, but Lord Moreland whipped around toward them, scooping the clamoring men back and away from the entrance with an impressive sweep of his long arms. *"Step off!"* he boomed, using his entire body to push them back. "Cease this behavior for one breathing moment, gentlemen, and step off."

"I suggest *you* step off," a stockier, round-faced man boomed back, stepping toward Lord Moreland. With riled aggression, he hit Lord Moreland in the shoulder with a solid thud. "We were here first, fancy boy, and if you think—"

Lord Moreland snatched hold of the man by the lapels of his coat and with a violent thrust sent both the man and his hat flopping in full reverse toward the group of men pushing up the stairs. The clamoring crowd fell back with a slur of curses and shouts, buckling beneath the weight of the large man.

Zosia cringed, thankful she hadn't been at the receiving end of that.

Lord Moreland stalked inside and slammed the door with a thunderous bang, bolting the latch. "Fancy boy," he muttered aloud as if it had been the greatest insult he'd ever heard. He turned, sweeping into the foyer and demanded, "What the devil is going on?"

Mr. Lawrence and the footman scrambled toward the door to ensure the entrance had in fact been bolted.

Lord Moreland paused, apparently only now noticing her standing in the vast foyer. Dark, arched brows rose beneath the curved rim of his hat as enigmatic brown eyes swept over her. He captured her gaze and offered a cool, gentlemanly nod.

Her heart ricocheted toward her head and down to her one foot, his presence prickling awareness across every last inch of her heated skin.

He removed his top hat, scattering silky, straight auburn hair across his forehead, and intently scanned the foyer around them. "I heard screaming. Between the crowd gathered outside and no one opening the door…is all as it should be?"

His genuine concern and his earlier display of valiant brawn made her inwardly beam. More impressively, he wasn't staring at her crutches. "Yes. Thank you. I was informed guards will be arriving shortly." She eyed him. "Might I inquire as to why you are here, my lord? Did you come to deliver your card for matrimonial consideration, as well? If so, I may force you to go back outside, *fancy boy,* and stand in line with the rest of my admirers as punishment for avoiding me these past two weeks."

He snapped a gloved finger back toward the entrance. "All of those men are seeking your acquaintance?" he demanded in an exasperated tone. "With a view toward matrimony?"

She grinned and leaned forward on her crutches, wondering if he was jealous. "Yes. And though I have no idea as to how they all came to be here at once, I find it rather endearing to know there are so many fine gentlemen in London capable of recognizing a woman of quality." She stared him down tauntingly. "Unlike yourself."

He lowered his shaven chin against his knotted silk cravat. "Who are you?"

She *tsk*ed. "That is rather rude. I suggest we retire into the drawing room if you seek an introduction."

He hesitated and gestured toward her crutches

with his top hat. "Are you unwell? Did you twist an ankle?"

The butler cleared his throat and turned away.

Zosia glared at Mr. Lawrence, wishing she had the ability to smack him and dismiss him. The impudence of the man to openly mock what couldn't be detected beneath the fullness of her gown.

She scanned Lord Moreland's lean but impressive physique, knowing she might not have the ability to dismiss the servants His Majesty had hired, but she could certainly intimidate them. "Lord Moreland?"

He eyed her. "Yes?"

"If I were to ask you to toss my butler out into that crowd, would you? Not only did the man refuse to execute my orders, he also had the audacity to encourage the footman to assault me. That scream you earlier heard was me politely fending him off."

Lord Moreland's husky features tightened. He swung his large frame toward the butler, who shrank back. "How about I give you a reason to tote your own set of crutches, sir?"

She bit back a grin. "There is no need for that, my lord. If he and the footman don't retire within the next few minutes, *then* you may proceed to break however many legs you want."

Watkins cleared his throat and stepped back.

"Please ring if I may be of any further assistance." He offered a curt bow and scurried down the corridor.

Mr. Lawrence lingered before stoically providing, in an amiable tone, "As it appears you are already well acquainted with the gentleman, Countess, I will permit an hour, despite his visit being unapproved. I hope you will consider my offer generous, as I am going against orders."

She set her chin. "That is very generous of you, Mr. Lawrence. Now, see to Lord Moreland's hat."

"Of course." The butler turned and extended his gloved hand toward him.

Lord Moreland shifted away. "I will not be staying long, thank you."

The butler hesitated, then awkwardly rounded them, veering out of sight.

Hopefully, His Majesty would hear all about her blatant defiance in accepting an unapproved gentleman caller. Maybe it would enrage the fat fellow enough to make him ride out from Windsor. She had a few Polish words for the man regarding the manner in which he was going about finding her a husband. She only needed *one* husband. Not four hundred.

Lord Moreland turned fully toward her and assessed her with the wry coolness she'd encountered the first night they had met.

Her heart raced, knowing he now stood only a few crutch lengths away. No more silly overtures from the window or a passing carriage. The next hour would define whether or not an alliance between them was even plausible. Attraction and banter was one thing. Getting him to understand her cause and genuinely support it, was quite another.

She drew in a shaky breath and let it out, trying to appear regal and confident. "Did you come to talk? Or did you come to stare?"

"Both, actually." His smooth jaw tightened as he closed the respectable distance a man usually offered a woman. He paused and towered directly before her, the tantalizing scent of cardamom faintly drifting toward her from the heat of his body.

She flicked her gaze past the buttons on his gunmetal waistcoat, up toward his face. Tilting her chin upward, she boldly met his gaze. "I do hope you are not overly disappointed to find me supported by a pair of crutches."

"Only all the more intrigued, I assure you." He shifted closer, his leather boots almost touching the hem of her gown. "Who are you? And how is it you know my name, considering we were never formally introduced? Who have you been talking to?"

The man was standing much too close, causing the weight of her amputated limb to weaken the one leg and ankle she did have for support. She actually fought to remain indifferent. "A lady ought never to disclose her sources. That is gossip. All you need know is that I pride myself on knowing everything about anyone I choose to get involved with."

He leaned toward her. "I already have a woman like that in my life. I don't need another one."

"Oh, is that so?" she tossed up at him, cheering herself on to be *bold, bold, bold*. "Are you referring to your mistress?"

The edges of his masculine mouth crinkled. It wasn't a smile, but it wasn't an uncivil snarl, either. "I was referring to my grandmother, who, much like you, revels in violating other people's right to privacy."

She winced. So much for being bold, bold, bold. "I meant no disrespect to you or your privacy, Lord Moreland. I merely sought to know more about you."

"Did you?" He hesitated and lowered his gaze to her mouth without bothering to conceal his apparent interest in it. "What is your name?"

She wet her lips, conscious of the attention her mouth was receiving, and set her shoulders more firmly against her crutches, trying to give herself a more regal stance. "I am Countess Kwiatkowska. But you may call me Zosia."

"Zosia." His brows came together, his attention shifting away from her lips. "Are you Russian?"

She snorted and rolled her eyes. "I would sooner hang myself. No. I am Polish. And as for who I am,

I am the granddaughter of King Stanisław August Poniatowski. Sadly, my poor grandfather was forced to abdicate his throne after Russia partitioned the last of our land."

His dark eyes brightened with keen interest as he searched her face. "Might I inquire as to why a royal descendant from another country would journey all the way to London in search of a husband? Are there no men where you come from?"

Her throat tightened, knowing she had yet to understand why she'd been banished, although she sensed it trailed back four years earlier to the death of her mother. After all, that was when everything had changed. Her cousin, who had become her guardian, had grown cryptic, constantly checking her correspondences both coming in and going out, while forever warning her not to associate with men she didn't know. Which was laughable, since after her amputation even the men she did know didn't want to associate with her. She always had to *force* men to associate with her.

After four annoying years of *that,* Karol had suddenly insisted that an impending uprising was going to endanger her life, since she was a descendant of the former crown, and it was best she relocate. Considering Karol and the rest of her cousins were all royal descendants themselves, yet had all remained in Warszawa without any concern for their own safety, she knew there was far more to the story than was being told. For if her safety was of any concern, guards would have been assigned. And yet…not even His Majesty had favored her with a single one.

She sighed. "In truth, I have yet to understand why I am really here and what is expected of me."

He shifted toward her. "I find that very odd and unconvincing. What little I do know about your grandfather is that he wasn't very popular with anyone, let alone his own people. I imagine someone connected to a man responsible for the demise of an entire country is likely to have a few enemies."

She lifted a brow. "I am impressed you know anything about my grandfather. I always thought you British kept your noses too close to your own coats to ever notice the struggle of others in the world."

"I happen to specialize in history and world politics." He lowered his voice to a lethal tone of seriousness. "Why are you here? Are you in some sort of peril? Answer me. I want to know."

He really was rather serious and imposing in nature, wasn't he? She couldn't decide if he tried to be or simply was. "Peril? No. Not likely. Otherwise I would have been assigned guards, as opposed to annoying servants. As for why I am here…?"

She shrugged against her crutches. "The saints above are only privy to that. Since the passing of my mother four years ago, I have been the victim of broken half truths spooned to me by my overly patriotic cousin. At first, I was told I needed to escape an impending uprising, only to arrive in London and discover I am being forced to wed instead. Though I sought to oppose it, my cousin threatened by courier that I would be escorted to France by summer's end if I did not cooperate. And so here I am, cooperating."

He hesitated. "And what in France are you so opposed to?"

She sighed, dreading the thought of it. "There is a convent in Amiens. Karol wishes to place a habit upon me."

"A habit?" He eyed her. "That is preposterous. A beautiful woman such as yourself deserves to be admired by far more than God."

Zosia let out an astonished laugh, amused by the dry deliverance of his flattery. Usually men offered a cocky stance, a smile or a twinkle of the eye to go along with flattery, but he tossed it at her as if he had just read it in the newspaper. "That sounded rather blasphemous. Is that supposed to be a compliment?"

He held her gaze and purposefully lowered his voice. "Take it to mean whatever you wish."

Her stomach flipped at the simmering heat lacing those words. Why was it that whenever he was around, she wanted to crawl inside his head and understand him in a way she didn't usually care to know a man?

He tossed his top hat off to the side, causing it to roll toward one of the walls. "I cannot have you standing about like this. Come." He slipped his arm around her corseted waist, yanking her toward himself, and then pried her crutches from her fingers, sending each clattering to the marble floor at their feet.

She grabbed hold of the lapels on his morning coat, balancing herself on her one leg and froze, realizing her breasts and her body were pressing against his hard, broad frame in a *very* provocative manner.

His other hand slid around her waist, holding her more firmly against him as strands of his auburn hair fell into his eyes. "There. Better?"

She dared not move or look up into his eyes, lest she forget the words she needed to speak. She hated how vulnerable he was making her feel. "Better for you, I suppose. I am the one at a disadvantage. I am asking you to return my crutches to me at once, if you please."

"You don't need them whilst in my presence," he offered quietly, his face leaning down more toward hers, as if trying to better see her face. "Though I would never advise you to trust me, I am asking you to do so. Do you trust me? Do you trust what it is I am about to do?"

Her breath hitched. "It depends. What are you about to do?"

His hold on her body tightened, causing the buttons of his waistcoat to dig into her gown and skin. "You aren't going to scream as you did earlier, are you?"

She stared awkwardly at the broad chest pressed against her. "And…what would give me cause to scream?"

"You don't trust me, do you?" He smirked. "That is wise. Hold on to me." His other arm slid down from her waist and looped beneath her upper thighs.

Her eyes widened as he yanked her up high into both of his arms in a single, easy swing. She stiffened as the crook of his muscled arm sank past the missing leg beneath her left knee. His hand jumped farther up toward her thigh, to prevent her from rolling. He paused, his brows coming together as he glanced toward his gloved hand that was buried beneath her palomino skirts.

He was obviously expecting a twisted ankle.

Not a missing leg.

"The third of June will mark six years to the day," she confided.

His brows softened as he lowered his gaze to her exposed throat. "I am very sorry to hear it."

She eyed him, hoping to Mother Mary he didn't think she now needed coddling. "There is no need to be. I am alive and quite happy for it. Very few survive the sort of amputation I did."

"'Tis an endearing sentiment to hold. One to be proud of." He turned and carried her through the open doors of the vast, darkened parlor. Heavy curtains covered all the windows, drawn by the servants in an effort to prevent the crowds from peering in.

The heat of his body pressed against hers was overwhelming, causing her breath to quicken. She could feel his large hands digging into her beneath her stays and the soft muslin length of her morning gown.

The continual hum of voices outdoors was the only thing to penetrate the silence. She openly admired the regal side view she had of his chiseled, shaven face. What a marvelous looking man he was.

Despite usually objecting to others carrying her, she felt rather eminent draped in his taut arms. "Would you like to be my own personal sedan? I will pay twenty shillings on the hour if you promise to carry me around for the rest of my life. What do you say?"

He glanced down at her. "Are you always this flippant?"

"Are you always this serious?" she flung back.

"Very little amuses me. Does that answer your question?" Averting his gaze, he effortlessly crossed the expanse of the room, turned and lowered her onto the long, velvet cushion of the chaise. His gloved hands slipped out from beneath her thighs and waist, his eyes meeting hers. He quickly straightened and stepped back.

She shifted, pushing out the breath she was holding, and rearranged her skirts around her leg, trying desperately to ignore how the lower left side of her gown had flattened against the chaise in a most unbecoming manner.

He lingered before her. "Should you be walking without a prosthetic? Do you have one?"

She glanced up at him, giving in to a rare pang of resentment, knowing she would never again stroll about in an elegant, refined manner meant to bring any man desire. Vain as it was, she missed the way men used to fawn over her. But she was grateful for what she did have. Her life. "I prefer balancing myself with simple devices. The prosthetic I had was like walking around with an axe embedded in my stump. It was very painful and very awkward."

Lord Moreland eased onto the chaise beside her. Out of the corner of her eye, she spied him perusing her bundled hair, her clothes and the side of her face.

She eyed him, curling her stockinged toes against the inside of her slipper in anticipation. "Are you here to progress the possibility of a courtship, my lord?"

Please say you are. His Majesty's impatience only festers.

He cleared his throat. "I, uh…no. I actually came to ensure your safety. Large crowds usually denote an unpleasant situation."

Zosia's heart sank. Even after six whole years of being subjected to men awkwardly avoiding her, she kept hoping that perhaps there was one man capable of seeing past her amputation. "I expected as much." She smiled tightly and set her chin, trying to pretend she didn't care. "You are not the first to be intimidated by my missing limb."

He hesitated, then reached out and touched her forearm, his gloved fingers pressing into the pearl-buttoned sleeve of her gown. "I am not intimidated, I assure you."

She lowered her gaze to his large hand, her heart pounding. His hand lingered, resting heavily upon her arm. He gently fingered her sleeve, causing her heart to pound even faster. That soft, meandering touch fell well outside the realm of mere compassion and sympathy. It was very…intimate.

She released a shaky breath, trying not to move, fearing that if she did this moment of unguarded intimacy between them would somehow disappear. Since her amputation, men hadn't even tried to offer her such touches. "I only have until summer's end before I am forced to leave for France," she confided.

"Though I am dedicated to the belief of God, and endlessly respect those that join nunneries, I am meant for greater things and believe our alliance would ensure it."

His fingers tightened, causing the buttons on her sleeve to dig into her skin. "And what is it you think our alliance will ensure? Exactly?"

She swallowed, doubting he would take kindly to what she had in mind. Publicly voicing the concerns of her people by calling for a revolution against the Tsar was not something anyone would willingly agree to support. Which was why, before revealing anything else, she needed to appeal to the man's sensibilities and dig into who he was and what he believed in. "Do you have aspirations, Lord Moreland? Aspirations that compel you to be more than what others expect you to be? Aspirations that—" She froze when he leaned in.

His large shoulder grazed hers as his hold on her forearm tightened. "You smell like cinnamon." He lowered his head toward her cheek, his presence feathering her skin and turning it to fire.

She inwardly melted and refrained from setting her cheek against his lips. She felt dazed by his presence, as if she had drunk too much laudanum and were floating away from her own body. "Yes. I…mix ground cinnamon into all of my cosmetic creams."

"Ah." He released her forearm, but his heat and the

pressure of his shoulder against hers remained. His hand floated up, the tip of his gloved finger touching the end of her chin. He traced the side of her cheek and throat, dragging his finger down toward her collarbone, which was hidden beneath her morning gown.

She wanted to faint from overawareness.

His finger grazed the braided chain around her neck, then slid beneath the collar of her gown, tracing the chemise and skin beneath. "Does that mean if I were to touch my tongue to your skin, I would be able to taste cinnamon?"

She choked on an astonished laugh and leaned away to prevent his finger from wandering anymore. "You are being exceedingly bold considering you are not here to offer on me."

He hesitated and moved his hand, also leaning away. His gaze traveled back toward her face and lingered. "I can only apologize for finding you irresistibly attractive."

He found her attractive? Despite her amputation? How incredible. How…odd. She bit back a smile. "I confess I am looking to be married, my lord. Not flattered."

He edged back toward her, his mouth drifting toward her ear. "You would never survive being married to me. Not one hour, not one night and most certainly not for the rest of your life."

She closed her eyes, vowing to keep her erratic pulse steady. "If I can survive an amputation, I can survive anything. I challenge you to prove me wrong."

He leaned away again. "Do not encourage me or this."

She reopened her eyes and shifted toward him. "Are you insinuating you *can* be encouraged?"

"You have no idea what you'd be getting involved with."

She lifted a brow. "What would I be getting involved with?"

He captured her gaze. "A man incapable of any self-control."

She let out a most amused laugh. "Does that not describe every man in existence?"

He smiled. "Yes, I suppose it does."

She smiled, in turn, and set her palm on the cushion of the chaise between them and slid it back and forth against the smooth, upholstered surface. She wondered what else she should say to this man who appeared to be gifted with more than the usual wit. She liked him.

He shifted and set his thigh firmly atop her roaming hand, not only stilling it, but trapping it beneath the smooth wool of his trousers and the warmth of his muscled leg. "Enough."

Her heart thumped, her gaze darting up to his.

"It was annoying me," he said matter-of-factly.

She eyed her hand which was still wedged beneath his solid thigh and decided not to move it so as to make a very valid point. "So instead of informing me of your annoyance, you thought it necessary to assault my hand?"

He grinned tauntingly, and without moving his thigh, casually draped a long arm across the back of the chaise, his gloved fingers brushing her outer shoulder. "Are you objecting to my methods, Countess? Or are you objecting to my touch?"

She yanked her hand out from beneath his thigh and shifted away. "Both."

His extended arm on the chaise skimmed around her shoulder. "So I make you nervous?"

She feigned a laugh, heat creeping into her cheeks. Yes. Yes, he was making her *very* nervous. "No. Not at all."

"Liar." His fingers gripped her outer sleeve and her heart popped as he jerked her possessively toward himself, pressing the side of her waist and thigh against the side of his own.

Grabbing her hand from between them, he yanked it up and crushed it in his hand, causing her to gasp against the unexpected pinch and aggression. He pressed her fingers harder against the warmth of his expansive hand, until her nails dug deep into the black leather, indenting it.

He tapped her hand rigidly against his lips, as if resisting the urge to eat it and everything else attached to it. "I should warn you. Lucifer often appears in the guise of a gentleman."

Despite his merciless hold and the fact that he was locking her body against his, she had no fear of him or the blatant domination he sought to impose. In truth, she had long ceased fearing much of anything.

Having her leg removed with both blade and saw by surgeon Monsieur Lisfranc, who had boasted to her the day before the procedure that he could amputate a foot in less than a minute, had cured her of ever thinking there was anything more to fear in life again. "I have met Lucifer, Lord Moreland, in the form of a French surgeon who removed my leg with great brio, and you and he bear no resemblance at all."

His savage grip tightened. "What is it that you really want from me? Be honest."

Her fingers and wrist throbbed from the relentless pressure of his hand, but she refused to give him any satisfaction in knowing she could be intimidated. In some way, she sensed she wasn't really giving this Moreland his due. Maybe he was a revolutionist at heart. He certainly had the grip of one.

"I have plans," she confessed with staid calmness, still holding his gaze.

"Share them," he whispered.

She could feel heat radiating not only from his body but her own. She tried to focus on her thoughts and her words, but it was becoming increasingly difficult to ignore how close his face and his lips and body really were. "It is my hope," she confided softly, "that you would..."

He lowered his gaze to her lips. "That I would... what?"

She swallowed. "That you would allow me to use your seat in the House of Lords, as well as your connections as a Marquis, to rally support for the return of Poland to its rightful state. To a state free of Russia."

His eyes widened as he sucked in an audible breath. Releasing her shoulder and hand, he stumbled to his feet, moving away from her and the chaise. "That is hardly something I—"

He paused and swung away, trying to button his morning coat in an effort to prevent her from seeing what she already seen: a well-defined bulge pressing against the flap of his trousers.

She bit her lip, pretending not to notice, but was shamelessly flattered all the same. It meant that despite her amputation, he still found her attractive. Imagine that.

He swung back and cleared his throat. "Even if this progressed enough for me to offer matrimony, I could never support such an endeavor."

"Why ever not?"

"England is on neutral terms with Russia and has been for years."

"England and France used to be on neutral terms, too."

"No, no. That is completely different."

"Oh? And how is it different?"

"Aside from you Poles being Roman Catholics, every last one of you ceased being popular with the Brits when you up and supported Napoleon. And Napoleon, by the by, if you didn't already know this, slaughtered almost every last one of our soldiers. Supporting Poland won't go over well with the masses here in London, I assure you. As a woman and a Pole, you have *no* concept of what you seek to get involved with. None."

She narrowed her gaze, sensing a battle ahead. "I am not non compos mentis. As a woman *and* a Pole, I know exactly what I am getting involved with."

"I doubt it."

"Six years ago, Lord Moreland, I watched a group of Russian soldiers burn my neighbors' home to the ground. 'Twas a beautiful and grand home bearing three generations of possessions. All of it gone in a few short hours, merely because Count Bilowski was involved in a patriotic organization the Emperor did not approve of. I lost my leg whilst trying to assist his family, and that is all too symbolic of what is happening to my country."

She slapped her left thigh just above her amputation. "We are all being amputated one by one, by pompous noblemen who are more dedicated to pleasing the Tsar than to the basic rights of their own people. Even our own council, our *sejm,* has been holding sessions in secret out of fear of being dismantled by the Emperor. Although, yes, you British were all in an uproar when we supported Napoleon, he was the only one lending us support against the Russians. What did you British ever support us in? You all clapped your vile little hands as Austria, Prussia and Russia pranced in and partitioned every last piece of what was rightfully ours. My mother's last breath was dedicated to seeing a Poland free of Russia, and I intend to make her proud by doing my part and becoming a voice for that cause."

He stared at her for a long moment, and then slowly shook his head. "You are a child if you think a marriage between us would return Poland to its rightful state."

She glared at him. "Is comparing me to a child supposed to be an insult? Children believe in the very things we as adults lose sight of, like hope against all odds. I may not be able to do much more than be a voice, but even *that* is far more than what is being offered to my people, who have lost everything, including their basic rights to speech and press. None of the resolutions that have been set by the Congress of Vienna are being respected by the Tsar, and I intend to inform the world about it by rallying support."

He swiped a hand over his face and huffed out a breath. "You are going to get yourself killed."

She shrugged. "If my death brings attention to the cause of my people, I will gladly embrace it. The real question is, are you valiant enough to support me in such a cause?"

The lines in his brow deepened as he dropped his hand back to his side. "And what reason would I have to support such a cause? I am an Englishman. Not a Pole."

"And what does an Englishman believe in?" she prodded. "God. Liberty. Parliament. Justice. It is the same thing we Poles believe in. Only we do it in a different language and under a different church."

He snorted. "I am looking for a wife. *Not* a cause."

She rolled her eyes. "A wife *is* a cause. And if you believe otherwise, you know nothing of a woman's worth. Admit it, Lord Moreland, you are no different from the rest of your pompous British peers. You seek an ornament, not a wife of any worth, and are only dedicated to yourself."

He shrugged his broad shoulders in mock resignation. "I cannot even claim that much. I am dedicated to no one. Not even myself."

"You expect me to believe that? *You?* A man of great wealth and privilege upheld by a freedom you cannot even begin to appreciate? A man who knows nothing of true strife?"

He angled toward her and growled, "Is that what you believe? That because I am born of wealth and privilege, I know nothing of strife? I suggest you cease choking on your own assumptions."

Sensing she had finally vexed him, Zosia met his piercing gaze, challenging him to be the sort of man she desperately needed. "If you are more than you appear, my lord, I challenge you to prove me wrong. I have no need for self-loving cowards and pretty words. I seek a valiant man capable of being honorable toward me and my cause whilst making the world tremble in his effort to support me and that cause. You obviously are not that man."

His nostrils flared. "You know nothing about me or what defines me as a man."

"I know what has been conveyed to me by a most reliable source."

"Which means you know absolutely nothing." His cold tone was laced with impatience and disapproval. "Gossip is the root of misconception, Countess."

She *tsk*ed. "Gossip can also be the root of tainted truths one must merely wade through. From what I was told, you lead a very private, regimented life and despite your amiable disposition and being respected and admired by many, you have no friends outside of superficial associations that are tied to Parliament and your fencing club. According to His Majesty—who I dare say is a very reliable source, for is he not your grandmother's cousin?—you strive to be the perfect gentleman by leading a perfect life. Which means, you, my lord, are a perfect farce."

His eyes darkened. He edged toward her. "And how am I a farce?"

"You told me in your own words the night we formally met that you play the role of a gentleman for a reason, and that it has *nothing* to do with respectability. Which leads me to conclude that you are hiding behind the illusion of perfection you create for the sole purpose of misleading others. Because there is no perfect life, my lord. Just as there is no perfect gentleman. Lie to yourself and to those who feast on your illusion, but do not lie to me."

A muscle quivered in his jaw. "You think yourself clever."

"At times."

They held each other's gazes in fierce silence.

Zosia could practically feel the air between them pulsing. "Am I wrong in my assessment?"

"No." His voice was fading. "In that, you are not."

She softened her tone, sensing his vulnerability. "You need not play a role for me, Lord Moreland."

He set his hands behind his back and offered coolly, "There are times one must play a role to avoid complications. That is the only role I play. I care nothing for what others may or may not think of me. I am what I am."

"I think you care a lot more than you let on or you would have already disclosed what role you play and why."

He lowered his chin. "I suppose there is only one way to go about this, Countess." Removing his morning coat, he tossed it onto the chaise beside her and stepped toward her. "'Tis obvious you will not desist unless I make you desist."

She stared up at him, her palms moist, and shrank back against the chaise. Why was he undressing? Why was he—

SCANDAL SIX

No matter how fearless we believe ourselves to be, there will always be something capable of causing every heart to quake. Recognizing one's fears and facing them will not necessarily eradicate those fears, but it will gift the soul with a renewed strength to enable it to survive. ~~My greatest fear is finding a woman of beauty and worth, whose soul I connect with, only to discover that my morbid need for the blade will keep her from not only understanding me, but accepting me for what I am and what I have always been.~~

—*How To Avoid A Scandal,*
Moreland's Original Manuscript

ZOSIA FROZE.

Lord Moreland yanked up the sleeve of his white linen shirt, leaned in and leveled the bare length of his outer forearm just below her chin. "Go on. Look at it."

She blinked and stared at his solid forearm covered

with endless white, raised scars. Some were thick and jagged. Others were thin and angled, set almost side by side. It was apparent by the patterns, and the number of scars covering the length of his forearm, that they were not accidental.

Her eyes widened as she glanced up at him. His face hovered close above hers, causing her to drag in a breath and lean back. *Boże.* "Who did this to you?" she whispered, almost unable to say the words.

He straightened and yanked the sleeve down, covering his arm. "It is my doing. It is my vice. It is the strife you claim I do not have due to my privileged upbringing. I am indeed a farce, Countess. Bravo."

She blinked up at him, her chest tightening. "You…did this to yourself?"

He stared at her. "With a razor."

She gasped. "With a razor? But why? Why would you carve yourself like that?"

"As if you care." He sidestepped back toward the side of the chaise and snatched up his morning coat. Pulling it back on, he adjusted it around his frame and waistcoat. Not meeting her gaze, he veered away. "Now that you have had your share of entertainment, I take my leave."

Zosia leaned forward on the chaise, his dismissive tone luring her to try to understand him. Something very sad tortured this man for him to have done that to himself. It was something she wanted to touch and lull to peace. "Please stay, Lord Moreland. I ask you cease assuming that I taunt you. For I do not."

He paused but did not turn.

"Stay," she insisted. "I do not want you to leave."

He turned, his brown eyes darkening with a visible raw emotion that silently conveyed that he wanted that and more. "You want me to stay?"

"Yes."

"Even after what I just showed you?"

"Yes."

He drew closer. "Why?"

Because I see a part of my own wounded soul in you, she wanted to say. Instead she offered softly, "You fascinate me."

"I fascinate you," he repeated tonelessly.

"Yes."

"The way an insect fascinates a child before it crushes it, out of curiosity and disgust?"

Sensing his mounting vulnerability and the edge in his voice, she responded, "No. Not at all like that. You fascinate me in the way a woman is beguiled by a man she yearns to kiss."

He lifted a dark brow. "You yearn to kiss me?"

Her cheeks grew hot, realizing she had blurted out a bit too much. "I apologize."

"For wanting to kiss me?"

She let out an awkward laugh. "No. I simply have an annoying tendency to not censor myself. 'Tis something, I fear, intimidates most. Both men and women alike."

He said nothing.

She might as well get to the point. "Given these scars, are you at all capable of offering a woman a relationship?"

He snorted. "What a question. Of course I am capable. But I highly doubt you'd want to associate with a man who…" He hesitated.

She waited for him to define himself. When he didn't, she offered, "It appears you have already decided what I am or am not capable of accepting in a man. We cannot pursue anything of worth, Lord Moreland, if you assume I am incapable of offering you my understanding."

He eyed her. "A most valid point."

She drew in a breath. "Might I inquire more about…"

"My scars?" he casually provided.

She lifted her gaze to his. "Yes."

After a long moment of awkward silence, he slid his gloved hand into his coat pocket and retrieved a slim brass case. He fingered it and then held it up, rattling its contents. "Most of them were made with this."

She drew her brows together. "What is it?"

He plastered it against his palms, as if trying to

her. "I also have a penchant for whips. Though it is more of a soft fancy than a necessity."

She inwardly cringed. "Neither sound pleasant."

He shrugged. "Champagne cannot please everyone."

"Champagne? Whatever does champagne have to do with pain?" She blinked. "Aside from rhyming, that is?"

The edge of his mouth lifted. "'Tis a metaphor I use in understanding myself. You see, champagne has this flavorful, stinging zest that is similar to what a blade does for me. That initial burn is crisp and sharp and almost unbearable to swallow, but it is soon followed by a soothing, sweet euphoria that makes one swallow more. I have always found it bizarre how champagne tastes the same no matter who you are in this vast world, and yet there are those who do not hold any value in its taste at all. Similar to how no one holds any value in what my blade does for me. Why do you suppose that is? Why is *my* tongue so different from *yours?* Or anyone else's, for that matter?"

Utterly fascinated, Zosia stared up at him. "There is an astounding intelligence rooted in your sentiment. One I cannot help but genuinely admire."

His lips parted as he dropped his arms to his sides and stepped back. "Are you…complimenting me?"

She shrugged. "Would you rather I condemn you

keep her from looking at it anymore. "My raz
case."

Her throat tightened. "You carry a razor?"

"At all times."

"You slice yourself that often?"

"I haven't done so in almost a year."

"But why would you even…?"

He shrugged. "'Tis a form of comfort I discovered in my youth. One that I confess will always be a part of me, regardless of whether I do it or not." He shoved the case back into his pocket, a lethal calmness settling over his features. "Do you still yearn to kiss me, Countess? Or should I leave?"

She stared at him. "I apologize if I am digging into your personal thoughts too much, but how is it you find comfort in carving yourself? There is no comfort in pain."

He sighed and slowly crossed his arms over his chest, causing his well-fitted morning coat to strain against his arms and shoulders. "Let me ask you this—do you find comfort in the support your crutches offer you?"

Her eyes widened. "That is hardly an acceptable comparison. My crutches enable me to walk."

"Exactly. And morbid though it may be for you or anyone else to understand, my blade enables me to walk." He dropped his arms to his sides and eyed for something you are clearly ashamed of and struggle to accept in yourself? That would not be very sporting of me, would it?"

He swiped a hand across his face and shifted from boot to boot. "Christ, you are not of this earth. Everything about you is so——" He winced and after a moment blurted, "I think it best we not associate."

She drew her brows together, trying to better understand him. He seemed to swing from one way of thinking to the next far too quickly for her to decipher his meaning. "Why ever not? Do you not like me?"

He feigned a laugh. "Oh, I like you. I like you a bit too much. And therein is the problem."

She refrained from tossing up her arms in exasperation. And here she had thought her missing leg would be a deterrent. "And what is so very wrong with liking a woman?"

He raked a hand through his hair and blew out a pained breath. "I am…how shall I word this? Overly passionate."

"Overly passionate?"

"Yes."

"And that is…?"

"Bad."

"Bad?"

"Yes. Bad."

"How so?"

He cleared his throat. "I have a tendency to rile

myself into becoming the sort of man I try to avoid. The sort of man you do not want to ever meet or know. And this…you…between your hardship and mine, what could we ever truly offer each other? Aside from this attraction. Nothing. Absolutely nothing. Given your condition, you need a reliable man. And I am not reliable. I am but a queer, who if provoked, can take a blade to himself at any given moment. *That* is a fact."

The conviction in that husky voice overwhelmed her. She understood this man better than he realized. And in acknowledging that, an agonizing weight settled upon her soul. It was a weight she hadn't felt since that morning she had first discovered a bandaged bloody stump where her knee used to be. That shapely, nice little leg with its ankle, foot and toes she'd taken for granted had ceased to exist and no amount of sobbing would ever bring it back. Sometimes at night, even after six years, she still thought it was there. Only to fall straight to the floor, realizing she had only one leg, not two.

With the guidance of her mother, whom she missed dearly, she had learned that she didn't need a leg to survive. What she needed was to have her mind in the right place. It was obvious this Moreland had yet to embrace that way of thinking himself. "Do not mislead yourself into thinking we could never offer each other anything. A one-legged woman will probably be able to understand a man who mars himself in a way a two-legged woman never could. It would seem you and I are queers in our own right. And we queers, Lord Moreland, should stay together. We will judge each other less."

He turned toward her, his dark eyes capturing hers. "You are making it very difficult for me to walk away."

A smile curved her lips. "Good. Because I need you for a noble cause I could never accomplish on my own. I am not intimidated by you, your scars or what you have disclosed. Despite that razor case, I find you to be surprisingly rational. Why is that?"

"I have no idea. I ceased trying to understand myself years ago."

"You should never abandon understanding yourself, Lord Moreland. One is only ever worth as much as his own opinion of himself."

"You are a woman of astonishing depth. Do you realize that?"

She bit back a smile. "You appear to be a man of astonishing depth yourself."

He shrugged, but said nothing.

She drew in a soft breath. "Might I offer you a bit of advice?"

"Advice? About what?"

"About yourself."

"I am well aware of my flaws, Countess."

"I mean well."

"Do you?"

"Yes. I suggest you cease carrying that razor case and replace it with something more meaningful. Something that will empower you, as opposed to tempting you into doing the very thing you clearly abhor."

"I see." He tugged at the snug leather of his gloves, stripping them from his hands, and tucked them into his coat pocket. He closed the space between them and lingered before her, his long legs brushing the fullness of her gown, which draped the chaise. "Are you suggesting I replace my inherent need for the blade with an inherent need for you?" he asked in a low, taunting tone.

She lifted her gaze to his and released a shaky breath. "I would never be so bold as to presume I could meet all of your needs. But I can try."

His dark eyes dominated hers. "I can easily control a blade and how deep I want it to cut, where I want it to cut and when I want it to cut. But I cannot readily control you should you decide to gouge out the last of my heart. Can I?"

A knot rose in her throat. "I would never hurt you. That is not who I am or what I seek to do."

He leaned toward her, his ungloved right hand unexpectedly drifting to her face. "And what is it that you seek to do?" he whispered.

She swallowed. "I…"

Warm, calloused fingers touched her skin and gently traced the entire curve of her chin, causing her breath to hitch. With a firm, guiding nudge, he tilted her chin upward, forcing her face up to his.

He edged closer, the smoldering invitation in those unwavering dark eyes making her entire body feel heavy and warm. He paused, his lips hovering above hers. "Close your eyes."

Without question, she closed them, anticipating the feel of his mouth against hers and praying it would erase everything that had ever come before him.

"Am I to be the first to ever kiss you?" he asked softly, his fingers delicately tracing and retracing the sides of her face.

She swallowed, knowing he wasn't the first. Her Russian was. But perhaps one day, she would be able to forget who had been the first and why. Perhaps *he* would make her forget.

With eyes still closed, she leaned forward, trying to connect her own mouth to his in a desperate effort to erase a past she childishly clung to.

She connected with…cool air. Her eyes fluttered open, realizing Lord Moreland had already stepped back and away. She heaved out a disappointed breath.

He yanked on his gloves, molding them against his large hands and fingers, but didn't meet her gaze.

"You didn't answer my question pertaining to your level of experience. Why?"

Heat crept into her cheeks. "Admitting to having kissed a man while attempting to kiss another is rather awkward. Would you not say?"

He glanced up. There was a distinct hardening in those eyes. "Who was he? And what was the extent of your involvement?"

Seemingly simple questions, yet his tone was laced with raw accusation. He wanted more than just a name. He wanted details. "I know nothing about him except that he was Russian."

He stepped toward her, his stance rigid. "Were you assaulted?"

She sighed, shaking her head. "No. It was nothing of that nature. Do you wish to know more?"

He shook his head and glanced away. "No. I have imposed long enough."

"You graciously bestowed your confidence unto me, Lord Moreland. Allow me to return the sentiment. My association with this man goes back to when I lost my leg."

His gaze snapped to hers with a pulsing intensity. "Go on."

Awkwardly, she cleared her throat. "I was…assisting the Bilowski family to scavenge for any remaining valuables left from their burnt home. It was a sad, arduous task, sifting through debris with thick leather gloves. I remember the sky above me was a brilliant blood-pink with hues of blue and black as the sun descended from the sky. I often wonder if it was a warning from God that I did not heed. My mother appeared, after one of our servants had informed her I had snuck out of the house to assist in scavenging. She demanded I retire, insisting I was too respectable to be rummaging through debris like a peasant. I thought her reasoning to be shallow and unfounded so I ignored her by moving into a section of the house I had yet to explore. I spotted a silver jewelry box hidden beneath a beam, reached down to dig it out, when a crack resounded and I was instantly buried beneath a wall."

She closed her eyes, giving in to the twisting memory of pulsing sounds, acrid smells and torturous agony that would forever haunt her. "I could hear my mother screaming for assistance over my own panicked breaths and sobs. That was when *he* appeared."

A faint smile touched her lips as she reopened her eyes and reveled in the adoration she knew she was cursed to feel until her very last breath. "His carriage had been riding past when the wall collapsed. He dashed out to give aid without hesitation, and climbed through mounds of charred rubble, pulling everything out of his way to get to me. After several attempts, he lifted the beam that had splintered every bone in my left leg. Though he was Russian, he lovingly spoke to me in Polish, insisting I only look at his face. He wouldn't let anyone, not even my mother, touch me as he unraveled his cravat and secured a tourniquet on my leg. He then carried me into his carriage, shouting for directions to the nearest doctor."

She swallowed at the memory of seeing her own blood smeared all over his masculine hands and face. A face with sharp features and striking green eyes. His evening attire had been ruined from his efforts and his wavy black hair had been dusted with soot and ash.

"Both he and my mother," she went on softly, "held me through each agonized scream until we arrived at the home of a doctor known for treating severe wounds. Everyone was instantly commanded to leave the room, as all of my clothing had to be removed. That is when this Russian seized me, cradled me against him and kissed me. It was not a chaste, sympathetic kiss, either, but one delivered with a breathless passion meant to excite the soul. He kept kissing and kissing me until the doctor was forced to remove me from his hands. My mother was livid, claiming he was some vile Russian libertine who obviously did not care if I lived or died, but I felt as if…as if he had been willing me to live."

She drew in a shaky breath and let it out. "Though I will never know. He disappeared and it was as if he had never been there. I became obsessed and could think of nothing but him, even as the best surgeon in Europe was rushed to Warszawa from France to amputate my leg, which had yielded to gangrene. My mother eventually submitted to my demands of posting monetary rewards for anyone who might have known him, but nothing ever came of it. Who he was, I know not, and despite him being Russian, much to my mother's own horror, I fell in love with him and everything he represented."

She shrugged, sensing perhaps she was revealing too much. "I live because of him." She pinched her lips, forcing herself not to yield to emotion, knowing she had never been given the chance to even thank him.

Lord Moreland's tight features had long been softened as he continued to stare at her. He searched her face. "That was not what I expected. At all." He hesitated. "Was he the only one to ever touch you?"

"I am still a maid, if that is what ails you."

He lowered his chin. "You had better be. Because that is a requirement for whatever wife I take."

She rolled her eyes. "You men place so much value on being first in everything. What if women were to place that same value upon men? I dare say, society would be at a loss and God would have to send forth another Adam and Eve. Do tell. How many women have *you* kissed in your lifetime? And how many more have you bedded?"

He glanced away and shrugged.

She leaned forward, waiting for his response, yet he still said nothing. "Are you still counting?" she prodded. "Is that it?"

"Of course not," he drawled. "I happen to think this conversation crass."

"Crass? We are merely being honest with each other. Since when is honesty considered crass?"

He stared at her. "You want to know?"

"Yes. I want to know. How many women have you bedded and kissed?"

He cleared his throat and smoothed his waistcoat against his chest. "A few. All of which I regret. I have had the misfortune of attracting eccentric, older women in my circle who never held an understanding of what it is I truly want."

She hesitated. "And what is it that you want?"

"A relationship."

Zosia blinked in astonishment and scooted toward the edge of the chaise, shifting her leg. "I dare say, you truly are respectable."

He looked away, the muscles in his jaw flicking. "There is no need to mock me."

"I was not mocking you. In my opinion, there are far too many seasoned rakes debauching poor, unsuspecting virgins for their own sport. 'Tis rather endearing to actually meet a gentleman chasing after…a relationship."

He smirked. "I wouldn't have minded chasing a virgin, but I knew the sort of seasoning I would have required from a virgin would have probably led to my arrest."

Zosia burst into laughter, then smacked a hand over her mouth, squelching her reaction. "Forgive me. That was exceedingly rude."

"I am not without humor." A smile softened his lips. "I meant to make you laugh. And you laugh beautifully, by the by."

She bit her lower lip and nodded, fidgeting her fingers against the fabric of her gown. She really liked this Moreland. Despite his bizarre leanings toward pain, he was incredibly witty, intelligent, rational, handsome, not in the least bit annoying and, above all else, he was a Marquis who held a seat in the House of Lords.

She could only demand so much from the reality of her situation. It was him or the men His Majesty kept insisting on. "I like you, Lord Moreland."

He grinned, the edges of his eyes crinkling. "Do you?"

"Yes. I like you well enough to pursue this. That is…if you are interested in pursuing this."

His grin faded. He shifted toward her, his brows rising a fraction. "You wish to pursue this?"

"Yes."

"As in a relationship?"

"Yes. With a view toward matrimony."

"Even after everything I told you?"

Yes, she'd lost the last of her mind, but it wasn't as if her nameless rescuer would ever sweep her off her one foot. With every noble cause came noble sacrifices, and compared to all the other strange, British men she'd met thus far, this one who sliced himself was without any doubt the most appealing. Which she supposed didn't say much for British men.

She shrugged. "I sense there is far more good in you than bad, and that is all I could ever hope for in a husband. If you vow to assist me in publicly voicing the rights of my people, I will accept an offer of matrimony."

He let out a low whistle. "Are you being serious?"

"I am."

Amusement flickered in his dark eyes as he scanned her entire body with renewed, raw interest. He set his hands behind his back, widening his stance. "So my scars and my penchant for whips and blades do not intimidate you?"

"Not even the Russians intimidate me, Lord Moreland."

"Ah, but you won't be bedding the Russians, will you?"

She let out a laugh. "Heaven forbid."

He hesitated. "I have yet to convey a commentary on your cause. If I may say, I admire what it is you seek to do for your country. More than you realize."

She was almost too startled to say anything.

He gestured toward her. "When one thinks of a patriot, a woman never comes to mind. And that may, in fact, grant you favor. There are ways to illuminate your plight without causing riots, and I would be willing to offer you the support you require if you would be willing to offer yourself to me."

Her pulse skipped. "Are you offering marriage?"

He cleared his throat. "No. Not quite yet. I would require more substantial proof of your character first. Stunning though you appear to be, you cannot expect me to commit to spend the rest of my life with a woman I just met. And through a window, no less."

She laughed. "No. Of course not."

"I am so pleased you agree."

"So what sort of proof would you require?"

"Something a bit more…intimate in nature."

Her eyes widened. "Are you insinuating that we—"

He *tsk*ed. "Let us keep this respectable, shall we? For your sake. Not mine."

She blinked, her cheeks heating. "Forgive me."

"I was more flattered than offended, I assure you."

He smiled. Stepping toward her, he swept up her bare hand, pressing it into the heat of his own hand and bent toward it, kissing it. He glanced up, rubbing her fingers against his own. "I am requesting you send me a missive before you retire tonight."

She tried not to linger on the way his large fingers continued to rub her hand, which seemed so small compared to his. "A missive?"

"Yes."

"And what exactly am I to include in that missive?"

His fingers tightened. "It is to be a very *intimate* missive describing what it is you think of me."

She swallowed. "How intimate?"

He leaned in closer, his eyes drifting down to her lips before drifting up and meeting her gaze again. "So intimate, it would be considered indecent if society were to ever glimpse it. I am also asking that you leave your bedchamber curtains open tonight so that I may look upon you as I read it."

She gasped and yanked her hand out of his and leaned back. "I suppose you will expect me to watch you whip yourself through the window next?"

He rumbled out a laugh and straightened. "Don't give me any ideas."

"I suggest you leave, Lord Moreland. Before I grow another leg and kick you into Russia where you belong."

"So you are passing on the opportunity I am offering?"

"I happen to think it vile and pointless. For all I know, you will use my own words against me."

He smirked. "I am not playing the role of a lecher. Such a missive would simply allow me to determine the sort of woman you truly are. What do you define as being indecent? Hmm? That is all I want to know."

Her lips puckered in annoyance. She supposed a man who had a penchant for whips and blades would require more than the usual set of passions and was about to test her own. Heaven forbid. "And what if I decide not to write the missive?"

He held up both hands as if admitting defeat and slowly stepped back. "Then we are both at a loss. For if you cannot entertain one indelicate missive, I doubt you will ever be able to entertain me."

He offered a respectable bow of his head. "I have imposed long enough." He turned and strode out of the parlor.

An exasperated breath escaped her lips. It would be far easier to bed the man and prove herself that way, than to write about it in a language that wasn't even her own.

He paused in the corridor.

She glanced toward him, expecting him to say something more on the matter, when to her astonishment, he gathered her crutches, which still lay strewn across the foyer floor.

Turning, he strode back in, toting a crutch in each gloved hand. "I still hear the crowd outside. I'll depart through the servants' quarters. If there are no guards tending to the crowd, I will have my footmen fetch the authorities and will remain outside until they arrive. Until then, promise me you will stay inside."

Zosia could hardly find the words to disclose how incredibly touched and astonished she was, given the conversation they had just finished. *"Obiecam."* She winced and amended, "I promise."

She had actually slipped into Polish. Whatever happened there? She *never* slipped when speaking any of the five languages she knew and applied herself to. "I will remain inside. Thank you."

He nodded. Without meeting her gaze, he set the crutches together against the chaise within her reach. "If I don't receive your missive before I retire—which is always a quarter to midnight—I will assume we are no more. Whatever you decide, I'll not harbor any ill feelings. It was a pleasure, Countess. And I do mean that."

He turned and strode back out. Retrieving the top hat he'd earlier tossed, he disappeared, his firm steps echoing down the corridor of the house.

Zosia eyed the crutches he had so gallantly

remembered and brought the hand he had kissed up to her own lips. She had always believed there was a reason why she had survived an amputation that should have killed her. She was meant for greater things. Things meant to change the world. And to change the world, she was going to need a powerful alliance. An alliance such as this one.

Any other rational woman would have recognized that a man who sought to revel in pain was not a man who would make for a good husband *or* a good lover *or* a reliable associate to assist her in leading a cause against the Russians. Despite that, there was still something breathtakingly endearing about a man who remembered to tend to a woman's crutches as he marched out the door.

SCANDAL SEVEN

There are many rebukes that never require a
single word. With a certain glance, or a certain
stance, one can condemn another soul to suffer
an emotional lashing felt for days. Be wary
of such vicious rebukes. Whilst society may
tolerate a superficial ~~bitch~~ *lady who revels in*
being superior to those around her, in truth,
there is nothing desirable, genteel or refined
about crushing others.

—*How To Avoid A Scandal,*
Moreland's Original Manuscript

ALMOST A DOZEN ROYAL GUARDS on horses wove
their way through the crowded square, their fixed
bayonets and commanding shouts slowly dispersing
the men around them.

Tristan rounded back toward the scattering crowd,
determined to figure out what the hell had brought
all of these men to Zosia's door in the first place. The
urge to physically protect the most incredible woman
he had ever had the pleasure of meeting pounded

through his veins with every breath and every step he took.

He stalked toward a well-dressed gent pushing his way in the opposite direction of everyone else. Tristan jerked to a halt and held out a gloved hand, blocking the man from proceeding. "Sir. Might I pose a question?"

The man swung toward him, shoving a newspaper beneath his arm, and met his gaze from beneath the rim of his top hat. "If you must," he replied in a bored, flat tone.

Tristan shifted toward him, trying not to acknowledge that this young man of about twenty was good-looking, with sharp, noble features and prominent brown eyes. He couldn't help but be agitated knowing that this man was only one of hundreds seeking matrimony from Zosia. "Is there a reason why you and so many other men are gathered outside this young woman's door? 'Tis very offensive to her good name."

The man slipped out the newspaper from beneath his arm and pointed it tauntingly toward Tristan's head. "A righteous one in the crowd, I see."

Tristan shoved the newspaper away from his face, refraining from shoving the man along with it. "I don't appreciate having anything waved in my face when I have given you no cause. Now, please. Answer the question."

The man rolled his eyes and sauntered around him. "Go flog the bishop. I have an appointment and have already wasted half my day."

Oh, flog the bishop, was it?

Tristan jumped toward him and grabbed hold of the man's morning coat, knocking the man's hat from his dark head with a solid shake. Jerking him closer, Tristan seethed down at him through his teeth, "Why is a self-righteous bastard such as yourself seeking matrimony from a respectable woman you don't even know? You have six seconds to answer before the razor in my pocket ensures you cease to breathe."

The man froze, his eyes widening. He snapped up the folded newspaper. "I was merely…responding to an advertisement."

Tristan released him. Snatching the newspaper from the man's hand, he unfolded it and scanned the rows of ads. But there were far too many for him to decipher which one he needed to look at. "Where is it? Show me. Which one?"

The man hesitated, leaned in and pointed a gloved finger toward the bottom of the page. Edging away, the dandy turned and sprinted in the opposite direction, without bothering to pick up his own hat, which had rolled out into the street. His boots thudded against the pavement, his wool morning coat flapping around him as he rounded the corner and disappeared from sight.

Tristan smirked, rather amused that the man found him *that* imposing, snapped the newspaper straight and read.

Wanted, a gentleman of good income and respectable breeding with a view to matrimony. The lady is 23 and presumes her manners and appearance will recommend her to all. £5,000 will be awarded upon engagement and £10,000 upon matrimony. No interviews will be considered or granted without the deliverance of a calling card. All cards will be accepted for one day and one day only, at 28 Grosvenor Square on the 13th of May.

Tristan sucked in a breath and glanced up, jerking toward the crowd of men still struggling to push out of the square. With the promise of fifteen thousand pounds, every criminal, bogtrotter and Captain Queernab in London was going to apply. Was Zosia even aware of what was going on?

He paused, squinting at the royal guards milling through the dwindling crowd of men. Why the devil had the royal guards come out? Royal guards never dealt with public crowds. Not unless...

Tristan refolded the newspaper and slapped it against the palm of his hand. How utterly fascinating. His Majesty did indeed appear to be involved in her personal affairs. Well, well, well. For once, luck appeared to be on his side after all.

AFTER MUCH THOUGHT and internal grumbling and procrastination, Zosia set aside her misgivings and dipped the tip of her quill into the inkwell before her, ready to yield the most provocative set of words known to humanity.

Dear Lord Moreland,

She paused, edging her quill away from the words. That was not a very provocative opening, was it? She huffed out a breath and pushed the parchment off the desk, letting it flutter to the floor. Angling a new piece of parchment before herself, she hesitated and commenced again.

To the man I hope to make my lover (once he is my husband, that is, and most certainly not sooner),

Feeling more confident, she dipped her quill again.

I have already had the privilege of seeing you fully undress, so I will agree that there is no need for me to be coy. I am most impressed. I will say no more. I certainly hope you have proven to be more of a gentleman than I have proven to be a lady and that you have not been using your spyglass in the same manner I have been using mine. I will graciously leave my curtains open for you tonight, in honor of your request, and will sit before the window for your viewing pleasure. Should you require my words to be more amorous in nature, I fear not only are we both at a loss, but so is my dear Poland.

Ever hoping,
Zosia

She set her quill aside. There. Let him do with it what he will. That was about as indecent as she was capable of being.

TRISTAN FELT LIKE A DAMN CHAP about to embark upon his very first tryst. Only, without any doubt, this was far more soul-consuming. Setting his robed shoulder against the frame of the window, he held up the sealed letter, silently informing Zosia that he had indeed received her missive.

She leaned toward the window, propping her elbows upon the sill, and stared out at him across the expanse of the square.

Tilting his head, he slid a bare finger along the smooth surface of the folded parchment, wishing it was the curve of her throat, the curve of her breasts and the planes of her stomach his finger was tracing and touching.

Was it possible he had finally found a woman capable of accepting him for what he was? He gently broke the wax seal and unfolded the letter. His brows rose as he scanned her words. "You devil."

The written word, he knew, conveyed as much about a person as any form of conversation. If not more. He methodically scanned the letter. Given her very pretty penmanship, perfect alignment and lack of smearing, she demonstrated a sound, focused mind. Her words and their tone conveyed what he had already assessed throughout their conversations. She was witty, intelligent, respectable, agreeable without being submissive and, above all, held an unrelenting self-respect, despite her dire impediment.

By God, he couldn't help but be smitten.

He refolded the letter and drew in a fortifying breath before letting it back out. Inclining his head toward her, he held up a forefinger, requesting she wait, and veered out of sight toward the writing desk in the corner of his bedchamber.

Tucking her letter into one of his favorite books on Roman history, he leaned over the desk. He took up his quill and slid a piece of parchment toward himself.

He hesitated, then wrote.

Fear not for your dear Poland, my beautiful Countess, for she has found a friend in me. Allow me to call on you tomorrow so we might further discuss matters.

Yours,
Moreland

He smiled. Folding the parchment, he melted the end of the wax and dripped it onto the overlapping flap. Grabbing up his seal, he pressed it into the wax. He tossed the seal with a clatter back onto his desk and snatched up the parchment.

Ringing the service bell, he wandered back over to the window and held up the sealed letter, informing her she was about to receive a missive.

Passing off the letter to his footman with instructions that it be delivered with discretion, he returned to the window and waited.

Minutes later, she was opening his letter. He could see her dark head bowing over his words. She paused and glanced up.

He inclined his head one last time to gallantly bid her a good night when a movement on the other side of the square gave him pause.

A broad-shouldered figure, saddled upon a horse, dressed in full military attire, suggestively lingered beneath Zosia's window. Tristan could make out little of the attire, which was dimly illuminated by the surrounding gas lamps, but could see it was not of British rank.

The man circled his horse beneath Zosia's candlelit window as if settling into a position to watch her.

Why the blazes would a foreign military officer be—

Tristan's pulse thundered. Christ. Zosia wasn't safe. Jogging over to his dressing chamber, he grabbed up his riding boots and shoved his feet into them. Not giving a spit that he was still wearing his robe, he flung open his bedchamber door and quickly made his way along the corridor, down the stairs and into his study.

Yanking out one of the rosewood boxes he kept on the bookshelf in the study, he retrieved his best pistol. Though there was little candlelight to guide him, he managed to methodically prime the pistol. Grabbing the ramrod, he loaded the lead ball and shoved the rammer back into place.

"Remain by the entrance and await further instruction," he yelled out to one of the footmen, who was extinguishing candles.

"Yes, my lord." The footman hurried out into the corridor and disappeared.

Cocking the pistol, Tristan stalked to the entrance door and opened it, signaling to the footman to remain where he was. Crossing the square, Tristan focused on the horseman, who quietly continued to linger beneath Zosia's window. The occasional soft snort from a restless horse rustled the night air.

Keeping his stride quiet but steady, Tristan drew closer until he was able to make out a broad back and dark hair tied with a red ribbon that peered out beneath a large, feathered military hat.

Tristan paused, remaining within the shadows, and pointed his pistol. "Dismount!" he called out, his voice echoing around them. "Dismount or, by God, you will swallow lead."

The man's gloved hand jumped to the sword at his side, but otherwise he did not attempt to turn himself or his horse.

"Toss your saber!" Tristan moved closer, keeping his pistol steadily pointed at the center of that back. "Toss it! Do it. *Now!*"

The man held up both hands in the air, as if demonstrating his ability to fully cooperate with the request, then carefully unsheathed his sword and tossed it toward the cobbled street. The sword clanged with a resounding echo in the silence of the square.

"Now dismount!" Tristan commanded.

The man swung a booted leg from over his horse and in a single thud dismounted, the feathers on his hat swaying. He turned and fully faced Tristan, the rim of his hat shading most of his face.

Ensuring that the man had no other weapon on his

person or attached to the saddle of the horse, Tristan drew closer, never once lowering his pistol.

"Lord Moreland?" Zosia's voice echoed around them from above, through the open window where she was now leaning out. "Whatever are you—"

"You will retire until this matter is resolved!" Tristan yelled up at her, never once averting his gaze from the target standing before him.

The man boldly stepped forward and said in a very low, heavily accented tone, "Do not speak to her in so vile a manner."

Tristan squinted, tightening his hold on the pistol. Was he Polish? "Who are you?"

"A friend."

Tristan moved closer until he was an arm's length away. The blurring shadows slowly revealed a young, shaven face and striking green eyes. "Whose friend?" Tristan demanded. "*Hers?* Because you most certainly are not mine."

"I am not *your* friend." The man intently stared at him. "I have been watching you, Lord Moreland. I have been watching you very closely."

Tristan refrained from snorting. "Oh, have you, now? So you take great pleasure in lingering beneath my window, too? Shall we let the authorities settle this matter? Before I do?"

The man narrowed his gaze. "From this night forth, you will cease any and all association you share with the Grand Duchess. You are overstepping your bounds as a gentleman and I will not tolerate it. I suggest you offer the very last words you wish to share and retire."

With that, the man strode past Tristan, toward the sword he had earlier discarded. Tossing it up, he angled it and casually sheathed it in a single sweep. He then strode back to his horse and mounted it with pompous bravado.

The gentleman glanced up at Zosia, who still leaned out the open window, garbed only in her nightdress. A grin overtook the man's lips as he offered her a bow of his head. *"Dobra noc."* There was an adoring reverence in that low tone that made Tristan want to pull the trigger on the pistol he still held.

Zosia hesitated, as if astonished by his words, but softly offered, *"Dobra noc."*

Steering the horse away, the man trotted past, fiercely holding Tristan's gaze. "The Duchess is already spoken for. Heed that. If we meet again, I assure you, it is *you* who will be at the end of *my* pistol." Kicking his booted heels into the sides of his horse, the man pushed his white stallion into a clattering gallop and disappeared out of the square into the night.

Tristan lowered his pistol and heaved out an exasperated breath. What the hell was that about? How had *he* become the villain in this? He glanced up at Zosia, who still gazed in the direction the man had gone.

Tristan strode toward her window, determined to know why there appeared to be a territorial Polish military fop on the loose laying claim to her. Noticing that her thoughts were still with the man, he cleared his throat obnoxiously. "I haven't quite left, dearest."

She drew in a notable breath and glanced down at him, as if suddenly remembering he did in fact exist. "Hmm?"

He knew that lost look in a woman's eye. It was a look he had yet to earn. "Do you know him?" he prodded, unable to hide his agitation.

She hesitated. "I was unable to make out his features well enough to say. The brim of his hat shadowed his face far too much."

"Allow me to rephrase the question. Is it *possible* you may know him?"

She shook her head, sending her long braid swaying. "No. I suppose not."

"So why is it he knows you?"

She shrugged. "Many know of me. I am, after all, the granddaughter of a disgraced king."

He shifted his jaw, unable to push away this fierce, gnawing jealousy overtaking him. "Are you already spoken for, Zosia? As he said?"

She rolled her eyes. "I would know if I were spoken for. I assure you, I am not."

"Then why did he say you were?"

"I have no idea."

"He called you Grand Duchess."

Her brows rose. "He did?"

"Yes. Were you not privy to the entire conversation?"

"Some of it."

"Are you in fact a duchess?"

"No. He is clearly delusional."

"He didn't appear delusional to me. He also said something to you. What did he say?"

She lowered her chin. "Why, Lord Moreland. Are you jealous?"

"What if I am?" He tossed his words up at her. "Have you not been wooing me all this time? What is this? Some sort of sport? Leading me to believe one thing when in fact it appears to be quite another."

She leaned further out the window, her golden locket falling out of her nightdress and swaying. "I have been forthright with you, my lord, from the moment we met. It is up to you to decide whether you wish to submit to a childish form of jealousy that has clearly overtaken the last of your senses. You have not even offered on me, therefore what right do you have to make demands? None."

It would indeed be his luck that some damn gallant

would appear in the dark of night on a white steed just as he was about to get on his knee. He seethed out a breath. It was inevitable. There was no sense fighting it anymore. She wanted it and he wanted it. And he'd best do something before someone else wanted it.

He glanced down at the pistol he still held and inwardly winced. This was not how he envisioned proposing to any woman. He cleared his throat. "I wish to ask a few questions I expect answered in earnest before I will even allow myself to submit to this."

She rocked against the sill. "You may ask however many questions you want. When do you intend to call with these questions?"

"Now."

"Now?" She scanned the square around them and lowered her voice by a whole octave. "What if the neighbors should hear?"

Oh, now she cared. "I doubt our neighbors will mind being privy to the latest in gossip." He dragged in a breath and let it out, knowing he was officially stepping on the path toward matrimony. "First question."

Doubts slowly edged into his thoughts bit by bit, keeping him from focusing on the question he wanted to ask. Hell, he knew he *wanted* and *needed* a woman like her in his life. An incredible, beautiful and intelligent woman who sought to understand him and make him feel as if he deserved far more out of life than he'd been able to give himself. But he also knew that she herself deserved far more than him. She deserved a self-assured, reliable and dashing gallant on a steed with a saber at his side. Not a queer with a razor in his pocket and a leather whip at his bedside.

She blinked. "Did I miss the question, Lord Moreland?"

He sighed. "No."

"Oh, good. I was worried I had somehow missed it."

Ever cheeky and ever brilliant. Damn her. Damn her for making him want her!

She rolled her hand. "What is the first question?"

He huffed out a breath. "Will you be marrying me solely to support a political agenda?"

She quirked a brow and primly lowered her hand. "Of course not. I do, in fact, like you. Very much."

A sense of pride drummed through him, knowing he had somehow gotten this stunning woman to like him. "Next question." He met her gaze. "Would you ever place your country before the needs of your own husband?"

She scrunched her nose. "I should hope that the

needs of my husband do not exceed that of millions of people."

He rolled his eyes. "I am being quite serious."

"So am I."

"Perhaps I should rephrase the question."

"Perhaps you should."

"What is more important to you? Your country? Or your husband?"

She played for a moment with the tips of her fingers. "In truth, I would seek to make them of equal importance."

Good answer. "Next question. Do you find me attractive enough to bed?"

Her eyes widened. She blinked down at him several times. "Why…yes. Of course."

He squinted up at her. "Why did you hesitate?"

"Because I thought it was obvious, given my letter. Did I lead you to believe otherwise?"

He shrugged. She had yet to see the full extent of his scars. They covered more than just his forearms. They also covered parts of his chest. Something he'd stupidly done in his younger years, when he had first started cutting. Something he regretted, for it wasn't in the least bit attractive, even to him, and he doubted she would find it so.

He fingered the pistol, wishing it weren't in his hand and in her presence. "Can you see yourself submitting to me?"

Their gazes locked.

"As in loving me," he added.

The edge of her mouth quirked upward. "If I find you worthy of it."

Was he worthy of having a woman love him? Sometimes he thought he was. Sometimes he hoped he was. And sometimes, damn it, he didn't think he was worthy of love at all.

The mounting weight of new expectations awaiting him as a husband made him glance away. "My final question." He awkwardly scanned their surroundings and dropped his voice to ensure it didn't travel too far. "Are you willing to entertain my penchant for whips?"

She snorted. "No."

"Why not?"

"Neither of us are horses."

He glanced up at her, his throat tightening. Horses. The devil take him. He supposed she thought him deranged. "I assure you, it isn't that sort of whipping. It is more a form of play."

She lowered her voice to a mere whisper. "If I allow whips, my lord, heaven only knows what you will insist on next. Will it be paddles and ropes?"

His breath hitched as he gave her a raking gaze. "Paddles and—"

"*Shhhh!* There is no need to repeat it!" She

glanced about the square in exasperation. "Do you have any more questions for me?"

He cleared his throat, still flustered at the thought of her and paddles and ropes. "No. Not at the moment."

"Are we formally engaged now that I have answered your questions?"

He cleared his throat again. Though he wasn't the greatest of romantics, he was not about to reduce his proposal to this. He was going to do this civilly. The way she deserved. "I would like another week before anything more is said or done."

She huffed out a breath. "A week. Of course. Good night, my lord." She leaned back inside.

"Wait, wait." He held up a quick hand, ensuring it was not the hand that wielded his pistol. "Let there be no misunderstanding between us. I merely wish to go about this respectably."

Her features softened. "If that is indeed your intent, I wholeheartedly submit to it."

"It is indeed my intent."

"I appreciate that intent. Good night."

"Good night? Oh, no, no. We are not quite done."

She paused but did not lean back out. "What more do you want, Lord Moreland?"

"Don't you have any questions for me?"

"No."

"No?" he echoed in disbelief, stepping closer toward the railing lining her home. "Do you not want

to know me more? Before we proceed to a—a…life-long commitment?"

"We have the rest of our lives to better understand each other, my lord. If I ask all of my questions now, there will be nothing left for us to discuss and we will only bore each other."

He bit back an exasperated laugh. "Yes, but—"

"Good night," she added.

"Wait. So be it. Might I at least ask another question?"

"Does it involve more whips?"

"No, my dear. That it does not."

"Then you may."

He eyed her. "Were you at all aware of the advertisement that was placed in *The Times* today?"

She angled back out, her arched brows coming together. "Advertisement? What advertisement?"

It appeared he had yet another matter to resolve before he could offer on her. "Good night."

"Good night?" She gestured toward him. "But what of this advertisement you were referring to?"

"It is of no consequence as of this moment. I intend to look into the matter myself."

"Oh."

"One last question. Who am I to call upon for your hand when it is time?"

She smiled, tilting her head. "His Majesty."

His brows rose. "As in England's Majesty?"

"Yes. As in England's Majesty."

He let out a low whistle. "I only hope the man still likes me." Stepping off the pavement and onto the cobblestone street behind him, he set the pistol against his side and offered a sweeping, gallant bow. "Give me a week, Countess, before we proceed to a formal courtship."

She grinned, her face brightening. "I will breathlessly await you." Still grinning, she pulled the window shut and latched it.

They were getting married. And the worst of it? He was going to have to announce it to his grandmother, whilst praying that His Majesty liked him well enough to approve.

SCANDAL EIGHT

Everyone carries at least one secret they slip into the pocket of their souls and quietly tote about in a desperate effort to protect themselves from the world they believe will grant no understanding of who they are. While this is your right, eventually, someone you trust will slip a hand into your soul and hold up your secret for the world to see. It is the way of things. It is why we are not born alone. If a secret must be kept, a woman had best acknowledge she cannot trust anyone anymore, not even herself. ~~Secrets also create horrid burdens. Should I ever be fortunate enough to purge myself of the shame I often feel for reveling in the touch of a blade, I will ardently embrace it. Will I ever recognize the opportunity when it presents itself? Probably not, but one can hope.~~

—*How To Avoid A Scandal*,
Moreland's Original Manuscript

WITH *THE TIMES* STRATEGICALLY folded and tucked into his outer coat pocket, Tristan strode into his grandmother's ornate dining hall. He rounded the oversized walnut table lavishly decorated with fresh linen, gardenias and the best silver and crystal, despite there being no one at the table other than his grandmother.

She glanced up from her unfinished supper and paused. Astonishment momentarily flickered across her pale features. She elegantly set her fork and knife aside and smiled. Gathering up the linen-and-lace napkin laid across her lap, she dabbed the corners of her mouth with it and regally set it alongside her plate.

He paused beside her chair. "Forgive the intrusion."

She peered up. "Moreland." Her voice held a wry tone of amusement. "Have you taken leave of your senses? It isn't Tuesday."

"I know." He cleared his throat, well aware that he would never hear the end of this. "Might we speak without an audience?"

"Of course." She glanced toward the footman and waved toward her gold-rimmed plate. The footman approached and removed it dutifully from the table. She then waved toward the rest of the servants around the dining hall. "Leave. All of you."

The footmen gave curt bows and one by one

breezed out of the dining hall, their boots clicking in unison.

Tristan grabbed hold of the closest chair and yanked it up and out, setting it with a clatter beside his grandmother's. He angled it toward her just a bit more and then settled himself into it. Tugging at the tips of his black leather gloves, he stripped each one from his hands and tossed them both onto the table.

He leaned all the way back against the chair, the newspaper sticking out of his coat pocket and rustling its little reminder. "I would like to begin by apologizing for my behavior when last we spoke. I was overly agitated and had no right to be. I also wish to apologize for not calling on you these past two weeks. I have been rather preoccupied with…matters."

"Apology accepted. Let us move on."

"Thank you." He cleared his throat. "So. How have you been since I last saw you?"

She shifted toward him, her silk orchid skirts bundling around her corseted waist. "I doubt if you came all this way to inquire about my health, Moreland. Get to the point. What do you want?"

He rested his elbows on the curved arms of the chair. "I am in dire need of assistance."

She chuckled. "You?" She chuckled again. "In dire need? Assure me you have not squandered your entire estate in some ghastly card game."

He rolled his eyes. "No. It concerns my neighbor."

"Your neighbor?"

"Yes. Countess Kwiatkowska." He drew in a breath and let it out. "Things between her and I have progressed rather rapidly. So rapidly, that in fact, if I do not go about this civilly, it may result in whispers I prefer to avoid. I understand that her ruling guardian is in fact my ruling King, who also happens to be your cousin. So I was hoping you could assist me in acquiring a private audience with His Majesty as soon as possible."

Her eyes widened as she edged away.

He lifted a brow. "Is that a no?"

She blinked several times and glanced away.

He shifted in his chair, sensing her unease. After his grandfather had vilely and repeatedly accused her of being her cousin's whore, she was rather sensitive about anything relating to her relationship with the King. "I am not seeking to meddle in your affairs. Understand that it would simply take me twice as long to acquire an audience with His Majesty on my own, and given the urgency and the nature of—"

"Moreland. Please. I don't think it wise."

"Fair enough. I understand and do not wish to impose on your association. I will arrange it all myself. But I will insist on one thing. 'Tis a question I need you to pose to His Majesty. One of importance." He yanked out the newspaper from his pocket, snapped it open and set it onto the table directly before her. He tapped at the advertisement he'd earlier circled with his quill. "I want to know who placed this advertisement in *The Times* and why."

His grandmother stared down at what he'd been pointing to, her bosom rising and falling more heavily, as if she were now having difficulty breathing.

He leaned toward her, his stomach squeezing, and touched her elbow. "Are you unwell? What is it?"

"Moreland, I…" She closed her eyes and sighed heavily. "I placed the advertisement."

He choked, his hand jumping away from her. *"What?"*

She reopened her eyes but said nothing.

Oh-ho. Now he knew why she'd been so quiet these past two weeks. It wasn't because she was sore about their argument or his storming out. It was because she'd been orchestrating a bloody siege!

Grabbing the armrest of her chair, he leaned toward her and demanded, "What the blazes have you been doing since I last saw you? Do you have any idea the amount of chaos this advertisement created? Hundreds of desperate men flocked into my own goddamn square, milling around for hours. I've never seen anything like it. Hell, over a dozen royal guards had to be brought in! What—"

He paused, his mind suddenly connecting the royal guards to His Majesty and His Majesty straight to…

his grandmother. He stared at her. "Last we spoke you knew nothing about my neighbor and sought to fully investigate her. And now you are well involved in her affairs, taking out advertisements in her name? What the devil is going on?"

She set her chin and eyed the newspaper before her. Reaching out a trembling hand, she pushed it away. "I was tasked to assist His Majesty, that is all. He rarely makes demands, so when he does, it is my duty as his cousin and his loyal subject to submit. Hence the ad."

Tristan snorted and pushed away from her chair, settling back into his own with a solid thud. "You expect me to believe that?"

She heaved out a sigh. "'Tis true, Moreland."

He snorted again. "You expect me to believe that the King himself casually asked you to place an advertisement in *The Times* to give away a woman's hand—*a woman descendant of royalty, mind you*—to any random dangler off the street for an astounding fifteen thousand pounds? What sort of *fruit* do you take me for?"

"Do not raise your voice to me."

"What choice have I?" he boomed, gesturing in exasperation toward her. *"You aren't making any goddamn sense!"*

She winced, leaning away.

Blowing out a ragged breath, he eyed her, knowing

he shouldn't have raised his voice. Not given her years with his grandfather. "Forgive me," he whispered, swallowing hard. He reached out and rubbed her shoulder affectionately. "I will refrain from raising my voice again, but I do expect you to explain. Understand that this involves the well-being of a respectable woman who deserves far better than this. What have you gotten yourself involved in and why? I want to know."

She lowered her gaze to the folded napkin set beside the newspaper and vacantly stared at it. "Much has taken place since we last spoke."

He grunted, pulling back his hand. "Obviously."

"You will be pleased to know that I was at long last hanged by my own folly."

"Oh? And how did that happen?"

"I commenced a series of inquiries pertaining to your neighbor the day you left."

He lowered his chin. "After I asked you to refrain."

"I can only apologize, Moreland. I was only—"

"Yes, yes. Nothing to be done about it now. Set it aside. So what happened?"

She glanced away. "Barely three days after I commenced those inquiries, I received a scathing letter from my cousin demanding I desist. Apparently, royal spies assigned to the girl had informed him of my interest. As punishment for meddling into her personal affairs, I was therein charged to find a generous selection of marriageable men outside of the aristocracy. Since I never leave the house, nor do I know of any gentry, I had a servant place an advertisement, along with an incentive. His Majesty was well pleased with the idea, as it created a wider selection of men for him to present to her. She is apparently very selective and has refused every man His Majesty has set before her."

Yet she hadn't refused him and, in fact, insisted on him. Oddly, it made him feel...of worth. "Might I ask how she came under the protection of the crown to begin with?"

His grandmother turned toward him in her seat and sighed. "She was offered assistance in honor of an old private agreement her grandfather made with Britain during times when revolts threatened the Polish crown. My cousin would have never deigned to honor it, as it held no worth, except he has always had an annoying fondness for assisting foreign women in need. And you and I both know the sort of fondness I am referring to."

Tristan tapped a rigid fist against his thigh in growing agitation, suddenly feeling the need to protect Zosia from his own damn crown. "Is there anything else I ought to be aware of regarding her situation? Anything of importance at all? Because now would be the time to disclose it."

She lowered her chin, her dark eyes never once leaving his gaze. "And why is that?"

"Because I intend to make her my wife. Does that oversized pompous ass, who dares calls himself King, think he has any right or claim to toss the well-being and happiness of a good woman in so vile a manner?"

Her eyes widened. "Moreland. I can understand your concerns, but for heaven's sake. You cannot offer on her."

"Whatever do you mean I *cannot?* I most certainly *can.* And I will."

She shook her head, her gathered white curls swaying against the movement. "Moreland. You cannot marry her. Dearest God, you cannot. You have no idea what you'd be getting involved with."

He sighed. "I understand that a foreigner and a Catholic is going to raise over a dozen brows, including your own, but the woman is very respectable. She is also descendant of royalty. It will all wash itself clean. You will see."

She gasped. "Wash itself clean, indeed! That is hardly amusing." She leaned toward him, her chest rising and falling in a panicked state. "I forbid this match. Do you understand? *I forbid it!* I will *not* have you getting involved in this—this…debacle! Forget you ever met her, Moreland. Forget you even care!

She does not exist. Do you hear me? *She does not even exist!*"

Abashed, he fell back against the chair. His grandmother rarely gave in to an irrational panic unless it was related to men or leaving the house. He lowered his voice, hoping to calm her. "Why are you panicking? What are you not telling me?"

She leaned back into her own chair and released a shaky breath. She eventually set her chin, resuming a calm, regal facade. "There are far too many burdens attached to her name, Moreland. Far too many. Even my poor cousin was under the delusion she was but a pretty face of no consequence. That is, until a high-ranking officer from the Ministry of the Tsar's Imperial Court arrived in London with a group of soldiers and announced that by decree she was his."

Tristan froze. An officer? No. It couldn't possibly be the same man who— "A Russian military officer, you say?"

"Yes. His Majesty was in quite a flurry about it, for he knew nothing of the matter, and immediately consulted not only with her guardian but also England's Russian ambassador, demanding answers from both sides. It was then her *real* identity was revealed."

She *tsk*ed. "The ways of this world are indeed wicked. Her guardian pleaded to my cousin she be kept from Russian hands. His Majesty agreed and decided a husband of no consequence would best settle the matter and bury her identity. Hence the advertisement. His Majesty intends to remove her from Europe, so as to silence this matter. Which means that whoever he awards her to will be expected to take the girl to New York and marry her under the laws governing that state. Which is only one of many countless reasons as to why you cannot get involved. 'Tis a snake pit, Moreland. A snake pit that will only result in all sides fighting over who bears claim to her."

Tristan swiped a hand over his face, a headache now pinching his skull. Had Zosia lied to him? About everything? About who she was? About this officer?

He shifted in his chair and refrained from altogether sweeping everything off the dining table. "The Russians don't seek to harm her, do they?"

His grandmother glanced away. "You already appear to be very attached to this girl. Are you?"

He swallowed hard and fisted his hands, digging them into his thighs. Yes. Yes, he was already madly attached to Zosia. How could he not be? Everything about her was so damn—

"I am indifferent at this point." Lie, lie, lie, but better that than to openly admit that he had been duped.

"Good. 'Tis best you remain indifferent. You don't want to marry into a mess like this one." She reached out and plucked up the glass of wine set before her. Bringing it to her lips, she tilted it back and swallowed until every last drop of red wine was gone.

He blinked in astonishment. The woman was never one to swallow *that* much wine in a single sitting. He leaned toward her and rasped, "Who the hell is she? Does she even know?"

His grandmother set the empty glass on the table and said in a distant, troubled voice, "No. Her mother saw to that. Both women were erased from all public records, though each for very different reasons."

"Christ." Tristan momentarily closed his eyes, dreading what Zosia didn't even know about herself or her mother. People weren't erased from public records unless they were a serious liability to those in power.

Reopening his eyes, he heaved out a breath. "Tell me what this is about. I want and need to know."

"Moreland." She reached out and grabbed his hand, pulling it toward her chair. "I will only tell you if you promise not to get involved. 'Tis black scandal involving very powerful people. Surely you don't intend to—"

"Enough." Tristan yanked his hand out of hers and rose, pushing back his chair. "I don't appreciate how you always seek to control the decisions I make. Am I a man in your eyes or a child?"

Whoever Zosia was, and however it was going to

affect and complicate his life, it couldn't possibly be worse than condemning himself to the superficial life he'd led all of these years. Always pretending to be ordinary, when he was anything but.

The sizzling connection between himself and Zosia was real. That much he knew. She sought to understand him, not judge him. It was breathtaking coming from a woman who not only understood anguish herself, but had miraculously risen above it. That alone made her a rare breed of woman he would marry within a breath.

Rounding his grandmother's chair, he headed toward a side table laden with silver platters of fruit, tarts and decanters of wine. He snatched up one of the decanters and made his way back toward the table.

Leaning in, he refilled his grandmother's glass just below the rim, set aside the decanter and pushed the wineglass back toward her. "Who is to say whoever His Majesty awards her to will treat her with any respect once that fifteen thousand is in hand? Do you remember the way you were treated by your own husband once *you* were in hand? And grandfather was considered respectable. Imagine putting her into that same situation. I will not have it. I simply won't. I am too fond of her and intend to resolve this matter by making her my wife. You can either support me in this or you can be a thorn in my thumb I will only seek to remove."

His grandmother blinked rapidly, tears now glistening against her dark eyes. Her full lips trembled as a lone tear slowly trailed its way down her pale cheek. She glanced up at him. "Moreland," she pleaded softly. "What if these Russians seek to eliminate you in an effort to retrieve her? Have you given thought to that?"

His chest tightened. Setting aside those heavy words, with the way that Russian officer had addressed him, he had no doubt they had elimination in mind. But what truly moved him in that moment was seeing his own grandmother cry. He'd never seen her cry. Not even when her own son, his father, had slit his throat out of blind grief in being unable to protect his mother.

He sometimes forgot how much she'd done for him. It was his grandmother who had been the iron fist to see him through the black misery of being orphaned at fifteen. She and she alone had seen him through his first days of cutting, not even a week after being in her care. Despite many months of restraints, harsh words, punishment, hiding sharp objects and even threatening him with bedlam, only to find he still always found *something* to slice himself with, she'd finally accepted what he was. A queer.

It was then she compassionately taught him how to

tend to his self-inflicted wounds with brandy, confiding how she herself had tended to many of her own wounds whilst married to his grandfather.

Tristan reached out and smoothed away the tear from her chin. "You cannot protect me from everything. You do realize that, don't you?"

Her hand rose to his and she pressed them shakily against the warmth of her face, releasing a sob.

He placed his other hand to her face, leaned toward her and kissed her forehead twice. "I love you, grandmother dear. And no one and nothing will ever come between us. And most certainly not some damn Russians."

Another sob escaped her as she grabbed hold of his arms and yanked him toward her, burying him against the soft warmth of her neck. The lulling scent of rose water surrounded him.

He held her for a very long moment, smoothing her soft curls with his hands. "I intend to marry her," he admitted against the curve of her shoulder. "She is stunning in so many ways and has a rare understanding about life that humbles me. I want to get to know her in a way only a husband can. And unlike other men— " he teased, dropping his voice "—I will not cower in fear, but enjoy whatever blade or lead ball may strike my flesh in her honor."

An anguished laugh escaped his grandmother as

she pushed away his hands and waved him off. "You have no pity for my sanity, do you?"

He straightened, biting back a smile. "None."

She swiped away her tears, sniffed and took up the glass he'd earlier filled. Taking a few lingering sips, she set it back on the table and glanced up at him. "Do you truly seek to wed her? Is that what you want for yourself?"

"Yes."

"Knowing that it may endanger your life?"

He sighed. "I have the financial means to permanently disappear. No one will ever touch her or me."

"Yes, but is she worth such sacrifice?"

Zosia's mesmerizing gray-blue eyes flashed within his mind. He drew in a satisfying breath and exhaled, nodding. "Yes. I won't ever find another woman like this. She stirs every last part of who I am and who I wish to be."

"You would have to leave England, Moreland."

He shrugged. "Then I will."

"To go to New York?" she cried in exasperation. "To live amongst horrid, uncivilized Americans who know nothing of gentility or good breeding?"

He let out a laugh. "You exaggerate. New York is very progressive."

"Yes, you also think Catholics are very progressive." She groaned and swiped back several misplaced curls from the sides of her face. "If you leave to New York, what will become of me? We would never be able to see each other. Even worse, I would never have the glorious opportunity to hold my own great-grandchildren. Is that what you truly want for me? Do you seek to be so cruel?"

He cocked his head, rather amused by her dwindling arguments and the fact that she was even mentioning great-grandchildren. That was a first. "Come with us. You can terrorize Americans with your overbearing opinion of gentility and good breeding. Of course, it would mean you'd have to step outside of this house and board a ship."

She brought a hand to her throat, clasping it gently as her chest rose and fell more notably. "I haven't left this house in years, Moreland. You know that. I have tried. Believe me, I have. Irrational though it may be, for I am old and gray, I am terrified that my appearance into any circle of society will result in men calling on me. And after your grandfather, I... no. As for boarding a ship?" She shook her head. "I would rather drink prussic acid."

He leaned closer and nudged her gently. "Come. Come with us. We will create our own little family. The sort of family you and I deserve."

She dropped a limp hand onto her lap. "My life is here, Moreland. This is all I know and all I wish to know. Understand that."

He half nodded. "So be it. But don't expect my life to be here with you. I know I have not made the best decisions for myself, and that you have seen the worst of me, but I am a man of eight and twenty now and stand beside you asking that you treat me as such. Will you support me in this or not?"

Smoothing her skirts against her lap, she glanced up at him from where she still sat and nodded. "You will have to acquire His Majesty's permission and strictly adhere to all the requirements pertaining to your duties as her husband."

He hit the table with a renewed sense of purpose that rattled all her crystal and china. "Done."

She sighed. "It won't be quite that simple, Moreland. Acquiring an audience with His Majesty will prove difficult. He is in seclusion at Windsor and will see no one. But as you know…he and I are very close."

She paused and met his gaze. "Bring this girl to me tomorrow. During calling hours. I want to meet her. If I find her to be amiable, I will inform His Majesty of your intent and recommend the match. I am quite certain His Majesty will be pleased to have the girl off his hands, even if it results in the loss of a seat in Parliament. I can only hope another Catholic won't be replacing you. You marrying one is enough to make all of our Protestant ancestors gag on the earth that covers them. Of course…you will have to get the girl to convert if you mean to marry. Otherwise no church will recognize you."

"I will convert, if need be. She and I will discuss what needs to done when that time comes. Now, as for you offering up assistance, I find it promising, except for two things—you don't ever find my choice in women amiable, and how am I supposed to deliver her to you? I don't want to offend His Majesty by imposing myself upon his protégé whilst also publicly sullying her reputation."

She feigned a laugh. "Worrying about her reputation and whether or not His Majesty will take offense is pointless if you are both going to New York. I would worry more about her servants. For that will prove to be far more daunting than trying to save her reputation."

His brows came together. "Whatever do you mean?"

"By order of the crown, her servants have been tasked to keep her within the bounds of her home at all times. No exceptions, unless ordered by His Majesty. Which means you will have to find a way around them if I am to meet her. Shoot every last one of them for all I care, and whisk her out into the night on your steed. I hear women these days love that sort of romance."

He laughed. "Your idea of romance will see me hanged."

She glared up at him. "The situation in which you are about to involve yourself is what will see you hanged, not I. But you have always enjoyed the point of a blade against your own skin, haven't you?"

He rolled his eyes. "Isn't there another way to—"

"No. I want to meet her before I could ever recommend the match. Your only other option in this, aside from my generous intervention, would be to ride out to Windsor and wave your coat of arms outside His Majesty's window. I highly doubt *that* will make him any more fond of you. Especially after you opposed his political stance by supporting the Catholics having their own seats in Parliament."

Tristan sighed. She had to remind him of that. "If I find a way to bring her to you tomorrow, do you promise to treat her with respect?"

She squinted at him. "I am not a savage, Moreland."

"I have known otherwise."

"Bah. That is your opinion. I am far more civilized than *you* ever will be." She waved him off. "I bid you a good night. Go. Leave. Before I change my mind and insist His Majesty marry her off to the Russians instead."

"All threats aside, Grandmother, you and I are not quite done." He set a hand against the table and eyed her. "Tell me who she is. I need to know if I am to protect her and myself. More importantly, she needs to know. It is her right."

She tilted her face up toward him. "Sadly, Moreland, my cousin insists she remain oblivious to that history. If you mean to marry her, you must accept never knowing who she is."

"The devil you say. Out with it."

"I am sworn to secrecy, Moreland. Accept it."

He shifted toward her chair. "You will tell me."

"No."

He leaned closer, growing agitated. "Tell me."

"*No.* Now go. We are done."

He stared her down. "Do you want me to carry you out of this house and into the night? I will."

She feigned a laugh. "That is hardly a threat."

He smirked. "I haven't even threatened you quite yet. *After* I carry you out of this house and into the night, I will inform every widower of the ton that you desperately desire another husband. Your wealth will be quite a draw."

She froze and glanced up at him. "You wouldn't dare."

"Wouldn't I?" He forcefully yanked her chair back from the table, causing her to yelp as she clutched the armrests. He leaned toward her again. "All of these years locked away from the pleasures of the world has probably left you quite in need of a man."

She gasped as she sank back against the chair. *"Moreland!* How dare you—"

"You have five seconds to tell me. One. Two. Three. Four." He stared her down as viciously as he knew how, trying so desperately to pretend he was very, very serious and that he *would*. Even though he knew he would never hurt her. "For your sake, don't let me get to five." He lowered his voice in warning and jerked her chair toward him. *"Five."*

"Oh, cease already!" She narrowed her gaze and snapped up a manicured finger, shaking it at him. "I will only tell you if you vow never to disclose it to her. You *cannot* tell her, Moreland. She is overly patriotic and may very well run off into the world in an effort to destroy herself. Is that what you want for her?"

His jaw tightened as he stepped back. Of course that was not what he wanted, but how could he keep her from her own identity? He'd be betraying Zosia before she was even rightfully his. "No, of course not. But I cannot possibly promise such a thing. She deserves better than that."

His grandmother lowered her hand. "She requires protection from herself, Moreland. Very much like *you* require protection from yourself. Hardly a suitable match, if you ask me." She feigned a laugh. "The both of you would make Romeo and Juliet's suicide look like a happy ending."

Why the hell did nothing ever come tied with a pretty satin bow? He blew out a breath. Who was going to enforce his promise? No one. He and he alone would decide when the time was right. And he would. "I swear she will never know."

She eyed him dubiously and pointed up at him. "Swear it upon your father's grave. For that I know you will honor."

She knew him all too well. Of course…his father would understand it was far more honorable to disclose a truth than to withhold it. He set a hand against his chest and tried to look genuine and honorable. "I swear upon my father's grave."

"*That* I will believe. 'Tis obvious you are protective of this girl. Which is good. It means you won't wag your tongue." His grandmother stood, rearranging her skirts around her feet. "Come into the library." Turning, she swept out of the dining hall, her heeled slippers echoing.

Why did he suddenly feel like he was placing his very name and entire fortune on a card table seated with cheats? Tristan pushed himself away from the table and strode beside her down the vast candlelit corridor toward the library in the east wing of the house.

They eventually veered into the massive room. He paused in the middle of the library, which was lined with hundreds of books from floor to ceiling.

Books he knew his grandmother selectively removed
and replenished with new editions every three years
after she'd read them all. It was her most cherished
room and one she had dedicated her entire life to.

She settled before her painted French writing
desk, lit by a standing candelabra, and gathered up
a stack of folded letters. Sifting through them, she
pulled one out and tossed the rest onto the desk. She
turned and held it out with the turn of a wrist. "This
is only one of several letters I've shared with my
cousin over these past two weeks. It has everything
you need to know pertaining to her situation. And
I do mean everything. After you read it, I will burn
every correspondence in my possession bearing her
name, and her past will cease to exist for the both of
us. Are we in agreement?"

Tristan hesitated, his chest tightening. The moment
he took that letter, he would officially involve himself
in Zosia's life and all of her personal affairs. Affairs
she herself knew nothing of. It was a very dark and
very twisted situation to be placed in.

His desire and fondness for her compelled him to do
this, to submit to this, but the idea of keeping her blind
to her own identity, even for a short while, was a different sort of blade he was not accustomed to handling.
This could cut very deep. But if he walked away now
and allowed her to marry another, Zosia would remain

blind to who she was for the rest of her life. And that he would never allow. She needed him.

"Yes. We are in agreement." He strode toward her and snatched the letter.

His grandmother patted his arm reassuringly before crossing the room, her skirts rustling with each smooth step. She turned and eased into a gilded chair. "You will forgive me, Moreland, but I intend to ensure my letters don't leave this room or this house. I will burn everything the moment you read it."

"I understand." Tristan turned and made his way to the writing desk. Dragging out the chair, he sat and unfolded all four tediously long pages of parchment.

He leaned toward the candelabra to attain better light against the shifting shadows around him and read.

Dearest Cousin,

It is quite fitting, I suppose, after having endeavored upon so many adventures of the heart with no care as to the consequence of my own people or my poor family, I should find myself protecting the most astounding affaire de coeur to have ever graced these ears. For what I entrust in ink is vile scandal I do not wish to be associated with. 'Tis only my admiration for the girl that keeps me from flinging her out the door. In response to your incessant pestering, I will reply in earnest with all I know. Sadly, much like her deceased mother, she is but a ghost. Her mother, Anna Petrovna, had the great misfortune of being the daughter of the Empress of Russia and her Polish lover, Count Poniatowski. Her birth was recorded to have taken place in Saint Petersburg in 1757, followed by her death not even fifteen months later. Despite that recorded death, according to the Poniatowski family, Anna's death was in fact staged. It would seem the Empress had sought to remove every last association she had with Count Poniatowski, whom she was planning to make King in the hopes of tucking all of Poland into her reticule. Where Anna had disappeared to after her supposed death, and what became of her, was unknown until decades later. Apparently, the Empress confided to her grandson about a long-lost aunt in Warsaw and presented him with a sealed parchment he was to personally deliver to that aunt. Before he was even able to make his journey from Saint Petersburg to Warsaw, however, the Empress unexpectedly died, making that letter the only contact she ever had with her bastard child. However, that bastard child was no longer a child but, in fact, a woman of nine and thirty. Anna Petrovna had since flourished into a Catholic, a Polish patriot and a sworn spinster who had lived her entire life thinking she was Maria Hanna Kwi-

atkowska, the daughter of a widowed scholar. In
learning of her heritage from the letter the Empress
had written, which called upon her to return to the
Russian Court, she avoided her duty and became
all the more sympathetic toward her fellow Poles.
And herein my words blacken. That grandson, Alexander the First, former Emperor of Russia and
godfather to our own Princess Victoria, fell in love
with his estranged aunt. Learning of her patriotic
tendencies from spies he had sent ahead, when he
arrived to deliver the Empress's letter to his aunt,
Alexander was so smitten he never disclosed who
he was. Instead, he assumed the name of Feodor
Kuzmich, claiming to be nothing more than a
Russian royal courier. Despite already being married,
he pursued his aunt for years, visiting Warsaw often
and in disguise, even long after becoming Emperor.
Although Anna resisted, she eventually became his
lover, and at the astounding age of nine and forty,
she gave birth to her first and only child, Zosia
Urszula Kwiatkowska. Shortly after Zosia's birth,
Alexander revealed his identity, wanting to bring
both mistress and child into Saint Petersburg. That
is when a vicious war ensued. Alexander's own wife
and the entire Russian Court refused to recognize
the explosive heritage of both mother and child,
whilst Anna was horrified that her lover turned
out to be her own nephew. She chose to raise

Zosia alongside the Poniatowski family, instead, who offered support. All contact was eliminated and to the relief of the entire Russian Court, the Emperor was forced to accept that the relationship was over. Zosia's mother died in 1825, and nineteen days later, so did the Emperor, bringing a tragic but romantic close to their relationship. Only now, four years after the death of both her parents, the Russians have rekindled their interest in making Zosia Grand Duchess. An officer from the Tsar's Imperial Court has appeared, claiming she is his rightful bride, promised to him by the former Tsar after he heroically rescued her whilst stationed in Warsaw.

Tristan tightened his hold on the letter, crinkling the parchment. He stared unblinkingly at the scribed words, refusing to acknowledge that this Russian was not only the same Russian who had saved Zosia's life and stolen her heart with a single kiss, but was, in fact, the same man he'd confronted with his pistol last night.

Tristan swallowed and forced himself to finish what little remained of the letter.

Despite the decree, I do not wish to expose her to two generations of scandal at the cost of her own sanity. As Grand Duchess of both Polish and Russian heritage, she would be expected to represent both sides of one coin under one nation. Though I know she would argue for an opportunity to represent Poland within the Russian Court, the weight of it would only dismantle the poor girl. She is still under my protection, and as such, I have decided to inform the Emperor of my decision to turn away her title. I intend to create a match that will ensure she becomes a pawn to no one, not even herself. Due to your crass meddling into this unfortunate girl's affairs, you will assist me in finding her a husband of gentry or, by God, I will unfrock you. She needs a sizable selection of men if we are to offer her the sort of happiness I never knew as King. You have two days to inform me as to how we should go about finding these men. Oversee my command and respect her right to a better way of life. She deserves it.

Your Loving Sovereign,
George

Tristan refolded the four-page letter and tossed it onto the desk before him in disbelief. This was… The devil take him. There was no word for what this was.

What if Zosia discovered she was the very thing she had been cultivated to hate? And what would she—as a woman, not even as a Pole—do if she were to discover that the nameless hero she had been searching for was no longer nameless, and that, in fact, the man sought to make her his wife?

The woman he had hoped to make his wife, his lover and his friend would run without a blink from the freak who mutilated himself and dash straight into the arms of her long lost hero. Even if Zosia no longer loved her Russian, there was no doubt she would, in fact, marry her Russian. After all, why settle for a mere British Marquis, when she could marry into the Russian Court itself and become an even stronger voice for her people?

He would never see her again.

He would never know her touch.

He would never know *her*.

It was over. All of it. It was over before his chance at happiness had even begun. Tristan drew in a long, slow breath and edged it out, fisting his hands. No. Damn it, no. It wasn't over. He was not about to give her up. He was done with life maliciously snatching everything away from him, whilst he sat in a corner gouging himself, trying to retain his sanity. He had to stop expecting life to grant him the sort of favors it never did.

If he wanted Zosia, it was up to him and him alone to claim her, and he was not about to give her up to anyone. She was his now. She wanted to be his and had agreed to be his, and as such, he would ensure she remained his.

Despite what His Majesty thought, Zosia had the right to know her history and had a right to continue to be a voice for her people. And he would ensure it.

Tristan rose to his booted feet, knowing full well what needed to be done. Zosia had to be removed from London as quickly as possible. Before this Russian up and lost whatever patience he had with His Majesty and took her by force.

He turned to his grandmother, who continued to observe him from across the room. Drawing in a steadying breath, he announced, "I can't bring her to you during the light of day. I've already met this Russian of hers and he was anything but fond of me. Should he hear of me parading about his intended, it will be like me throwing down the glove before all of Russia."

She hesitated. "I agree. Bring her at night, when eyes are less likely to see. Shall we say…tomorrow at eleven?"

"No. People will still be returning from festivities." He paced. "I'm going to need well into late evening on the morrow to settle matters pertaining to my estate. Whatever I cannot settle, which I fear will be more than half of what I am worth, I will allot to you." He swung back to her. "Of course, it will only be on loan until I have time to oversee it from abroad."

His grandmother arched a silvery brow. "It isn't necessary for you to settle your entire estate quite yet, Moreland."

"That is for me to decide."

She sighed. "When should I expect her?"

"Tomorrow night at two."

She gawked at him. "You intend to bring her at two in the morning?"

"Yes."

"Oh, no, no. That is crass, even if we are stooping to temporarily kidnapping my cousin's protégé due to passions you cannot control."

He strode toward her. "Seeing that you do not wish to go to New York, it is either two in the morning or not at all. Whatever you decide, you'll be tasked to inform His Majesty three days from this night that it is with much regret your grandson has gone indefinitely to New York with his protégé. I have decided not to wait for his approval. It would only complicate matters."

She gasped, her eyes widening as she rose to her feet. "Moreland! You cannot oppose your crown like this. You must await approval."

"To hell with approval. Do you think His Majesty will approve of my marrying her? *Do you?* 'Tis obvious he seeks to sever her way of life and her ability to assist her own people. And that is wrong. I intend to remove her from his so-called protection and take her to New York. New York is conveniently liberal and would be far more supportive of her views than England ever will be."

"Dearest God." She brought the tips of her fingers to her lips. "You mean to actually support her irrational patriotism by publicly campaigning against the Russians? *In New York?*"

"Her patriotism is not in the least bit irrational. Ambitious, yes. But not irrational."

"Why do you always seek to punish yourself like this, Moreland? Why do you never allow yourself the sort of peace and happiness you deserve?"

He glared at her. "I am not punishing myself. In fact, I am honoring myself by submitting to what it is *I* want and what it is *I* need. I'm bloody tired of circumstance controlling every aspect of my life. If I want her, I have to take her. Now, what is your answer? Do you want to meet her before we leave for New York or not?"

She dropped her hand to her side and said in a suffocated whisper, "Bring her. I will do my best to keep His Majesty from demanding your head. I only hope that she is well worth the mess you are intent on creating."

"She is that and more."

He would ensure Zosia knew everything, including who she was and why he was doing what he was doing. And together, they would fight for everything she had ever wanted, including her dream of seeing a free Poland.

And perhaps one day, though he knew not when, he would be able to forgive himself for submitting to a deceitful form of greed by never telling Zosia the one thing he knew would destroy his chance of ever touching happiness. She could never know her beloved hero had at long last found her and sought to marry her. Because he was never letting Zosia go. Not now. Not ever. She was going to be his from this night forth and nothing and no one was going to stand in his way. Not the Russians and not even the King himself.

SCANDAL NINE

There are dangers in permitting even a kiss prior to matrimony. Though seemingly romantic, allowing such a thing is no different than inviting the devil to dine at one's table. Whilst, yes, the devil may be a gentleman the first time he sits and may partake in very little, if his desire to taste what you have served should ever arise again, he will keep returning until there is nothing left at your table to serve. He will then strut off without a backward glance and dine at a new table offering better delicacies, leaving you to starve in shame. Try to remember that when you serve up a kiss. Try to remember that before you offer a man bliss. I genuinely fear for whatever woman allows me to dine at her table. For I know without any doubt that I will set up both boots and feast so heartily, she will wish for the devil over me.

—*How To Avoid A Scandal*,
Moreland's Original Manuscript

DESPITE STAYING UP well past the hour of sleep, Lord Moreland's windows on the other side of the square had remained black as pitch all evening. Oddly, he hadn't returned after leaving uncivilly early in the morning. Unless she had somehow missed the return of his carriage.

Her concern for him had induced her to actually sit by the window most of the day and well into the night, hoping all was well. Exhausted, Zosia drew the curtains shut, ensuring she didn't yank them off the rod again, and veered her wicker chair away from the window. With several pushes of the large spoke wheels, she rolled toward the bed and kicked out her bare foot to stop herself beside it. Leaning far forward, she yanked back the plush coverlet and smoothed the linen beneath it.

Wheeling herself closer to the side table, she hoisted herself up onto her leg, hopped a turn away from her chair and leaned against the upper end of the mattress. Leaning back, she gathered up her night-dress from around her foot, swung up her leg and rolled herself onto the mattress, plopping herself onto it.

Gathering up the coverlet and pulling it up, she leaned toward the side table and blew out the lone candle lighting the room. Everything disappeared into a curling wisp of darkness.

She snuggled against the pillow, turning once,

then twice, as she always did before settling in, and closed her eyes. As time passed and passed, and she drifted ever so slowly toward the outskirts of sleep, she sensed her bedchamber door creaking open. She opened her eyes and blinked against the fuzzy darkness.

Had she imagined it?

A click within the lock met her ears, as if someone had turned the key from inside the room. Zosia bolted up in bed, eyes wide, and snapped toward the sound, but could only make out shadows pressing against shadows. "Mrs. Wade?"

"No," a deep voice provided with faint amusement from somewhere beside the door. "'Tis me. Moreland. Forgive the intrusion."

Her eyes widened and for a moment, she couldn't move, let alone find her voice. Moreland was in her house? And in her room?

The floorboards creaked against the weight of boots and she could sense his presence drawing closer. The crisp scent of leather tinged with cardamom drifted toward her, and she knew he was standing beside her bed.

She tightened her hold on the linens as panicked breaths escaped her lips. "Lord Moreland?"

"Yes?" His voice was soft and alluring.

She swallowed. "Is that really you?"

He hesitated. "Were you hoping for someone else?"

She was not going to swoon. She wasn't. She wasn't, she wasn't, she wasn't. "No…I…however did you get in?"

"Getting in was simple enough," he casually provided from within the darkness. "Dealing with your servants, on the other hand, was not. Hang me for trying, but what a bloody mess. One of my footmen got assaulted, so we had to rope up every last one of your servants. I can only apologize for that."

Zosia choked, gawking in the direction of his voice. "You roped up all of my servants?"

"It's only temporary. Until we get out."

"Out?" she echoed.

"Yes." He cleared his throat. "I was hoping you could join me for a coach ride. 'Tis a pleasant evening. Not a cloud in the sky. Would you honor me?"

She squinted at the darkness, wishing she could see him, but the shadows all blurred into each other. "A coach ride?"

"Yes."

"Now?"

"Yes. Now."

She shook her head and kept shaking it. "No. Absolutely not. Setting aside this rancid business of you stealing into my home and tying up my servants—*who had every right to assault your footman for trespassing*—we are not even engaged, and as such, I cannot and will not permit any of this. Now, leave."

"Whatever do you mean we aren't engaged?" A tender playfulness emerged in that low tone. "We *are* engaged."

She inhaled sharply, wishing she could look into his eyes and get him to say it again. "Since when?"

"Since now."

She huffed out an agitated breath. This was *not* how she envisioned him proposing. "I worry about your overall lack of thought in this."

He leaned against the edge of the mattress, toward her, the outline of his broad frame barely visible. "I beg for your forgiveness in being smitten beyond my control."

She rolled her eyes. "I suggest you cease being a court jester and return tomorrow afternoon during more respectable calling hours. Try to put more civil effort into this, will you? Bring me a pretty bouquet. I prefer violets, not ropes." She waved toward wherever his voice was coming from. "Now, go. And untie all of my servants on your way out or I will inform His Majesty of this nonsense and you will never see me again."

A throaty laugh escaped him. "I will ensure you get those violets. But I am not leaving." He patted the mattress beside her, then hopped onto her bed with a thud.

She gasped and yanked the coverlet up to her chin, as if that would somehow protect her from whatever he had in mind. "*Co ty*...what are you doing?" she amended in English.

"Sitting on your bed. Why?"

She snorted. "Will you cease being so nonchalant? We are not sitting on a chaise in the parlor. Now, remove yourself from my bed at once!"

He snorted right back at her. "I don't intend to ravage you." He tauntingly lowered his voice. "Not yet, anyway. I was hoping we could talk. Might we?"

"Talk? In the dark? And in my bed? What is amiss with you? Are you bright in the eye?"

"Of course not. I only had one glass of brandy before crossing the square."

"That glass must have been the size of a barrel. For you are not behaving like the Lord Moreland I like and know. Lord Moreland would never tie up my servants so he could crawl into my bed and...*talk*."

"Perhaps the Lord Moreland you think you know isn't the Lord Moreland you deserve to know." He settled closer, shifting the pillows around them. He behaved as if it were the most natural thing in the world for a man to climb into the bed of a woman he wasn't married to and arrange all of her pillows.

He hesitated. "You don't sleep in the nude, do you? You aren't…nude right now, are you?"

Her cheeks burned, and despite the tremble overtaking her hands, she somehow managed to keep her voice steady. "No. I do not sleep in the nude. I always sleep in a nightdress."

He feigned a laugh. "A pity. I was envisioning something far more exciting for myself."

She offered her own mock laugh. "'Tis obvious what you were envisioning, and I assure you, I require matrimony first. One does not slaughter the cow before collecting the milk. Now, remove yourself from this bed and from this house before I—"

"For God's sake, Zosia. I am *not* here to ravage you. I came here to discuss a very serious matter with you."

"Return during calling hours, my lord. Not sleeping hours."

He shifted toward her, his agitation pulsing toward her in the darkness. "Would you prefer I stand in the farthest corner of the room and turn myself toward the wall? I can do that if it will appease your damn virginal propriety."

Zosia jerked toward him, her brows coming together. He actually did want to talk? Now? Like this? This couldn't be happening. Or could it? She poked his shadowed but very solid shoulder with a finger. "Are you even here?"

He blew out a breath and leaned closer, the heat of his body now unnervingly close. "Zosia. Since I last saw you, I have uncovered an astounding amount about your life. I am still trying to grasp everything I have learned. 'Tis an involved history your own mother has kept from you since birth. One you deserve to know. Now, before I say anything more, did you ever suspect something was amiss? Did you ever suspect that perhaps your mother may have been hiding something from you? Something important? Like who your father was?"

Zosia snapped back her hand in disbelief and hesitantly touched the locket around her throat. Her fingers gripped the locket, the metallic smooth edge pinching into her skin, as a voice within her soul whispered that what she had known all along, but had refused to accept, was in fact true. Her best friend in all matters, her own dear mother, who had seen her through everything with the brightest of smiles and intelligence, had hidden something very important from her.

Zosia had always known the locket was part of a secret. It was an empty locket her mother had always worn, its portraits long stripped. Her mother had refused to reveal its history, though in time she had admitted that it had been a gift from Zosia's father. Despite that admittance, her mother never did disclose anything more on the matter. She had asked to die with his name buried within her soul, claiming it was shame enough to have ever loved him. It was something Zosia had never understood.

Her stomach squeezed. "Are you saying you know who my father is?"

A large hand gently touched her thigh. "I know that and more."

She pinched her eyes shut, her shaky fingers digging into the hard edges of the locket, and willed herself not to succumb to years of pent-up emotion. Somehow, he had uncovered the greatest secret of her life.

She reopened her eyes. "Tell me. Please tell me. I have been wanting to know all of my life."

"I will tell you," he whispered, drawing away his hand. "But not right now and not like this. There is far too much to tell and time we do not have. I came here to offer you far more than your own history, Zosia. I want to be with you and protect you and assist you in all matters, including voicing your concerns for your people. It is my hope that by offering you all of this you might…marry me."

Zosia drew in a tremulous breath and smoothed the linen around her waist, all too aware of how close he really was. She didn't realize anyone could ever be *this* intent on overseeing all of her wants, needs and dreams. She had learned to repeatedly climb over others to reach her own desires. It was beyond endearing to know she was not alone anymore and that someone not only cared for her but sought to watch out for all of her needs.

Angling herself toward him, she let out a breath and strategically offered, "Propose in a gentlemanly manner and I will accept, momentarily disregarding that you tied up my servants and crawled into my bed."

He leaned toward her, his shoulder grazing hers. "Are you giving me permission to propose?"

"Yes. You may, in fact, propose."

He leaned in even closer. "I *propose* we remove your nightdress."

Zosia gasped and hit the muscled shoulder closest to her all the same. Hard. "I *knew* it would come to this!"

He let out a gruff laugh, his large, leather-gloved hand grabbing not only her fist, which had swung out at him, but the side of her thigh hidden beneath the coverlet. "I wasn't going to insist."

She froze, realizing her wrist and thigh were still in his full possession. The frantic thudding of her heart made it almost unbearable for her to breathe. She swallowed, knowing if they stayed in this position it would progress into far more than she was willing to entertain.

She pried her wrist from his grasp and pushed off

his hand. "Try it again. Only without slaughtering the cow."

"I will try. Don't move."

She froze.

He leaned in, placing his hand back onto her outer thigh, and ever so slowly, he slid it up past her hip, toward the waist of her nightdress. "Marry me, Zosia," he murmured against her cheek. "Have me. I do not wish to know a life without you and it is my hope you feel the same about me."

A strange fluttering overtook her stomach as he slipped his other hand around her shoulder and pressed her against the heat of his muscled frame. She felt the room sway in the darkness, his solid warmth pressing harder against her. She held her breath, anticipating lips, but…he didn't kiss her.

His hand trailed up toward her breast, grazing her nipple, making her suck in a sharp breath. But his fingers did not rest there. Cool, gloved fingertips brushed up past her throat, before cupping her face gently.

He turned her face up toward the fuzzy outline of his own face, which she wished she could fully see. "Your life is about to change," he whispered down at her. The tantalizing movement of every breath escaping his lips feathered hers. "But I promise, by the blood of all that I am, it will be for the better. I will ensure you have everything you could ever want or need."

She melted against him and wrapped her arms around his broad shoulders, feeling more adored than she ever thought possible. "I feel as if I have been pushing you toward me against your own will from the very first moment we met. Are you certain this is what you want? Forever is a very long time."

"Forever will ensure we do it all," he murmured, his fingers skimming the curve of her throat. "Including properly fall in love."

She swallowed against the hot ache growing within her throat as his fingers wandered toward her mother's locket. She had always wanted to fall in love. To truly fall in love with a real man, as opposed to a man who simply did not exist.

"Can I kiss you?" he whispered.

She could barely breathe. "Yes."

His fingers dug into her and his weight pressed her harder against the mattress beneath her. His shadowed face lowered and warm, soft lips brushed against her own, causing her heart to skitter.

After a lingering, heart-pounding moment, he pressed his mouth harder against hers, his tongue sliding between her lips and forcing them open. The tantalizing zing of spiced brandy transferred from his tongue to hers as he deepened their kiss, erotically probing her tongue, her teeth and the roof of her mouth. The taste of him magically awakened not only her body but her soul, making her want him so much more.

His large frame shifted against her body as his mouth crushed against hers savagely, snatching away whatever breath she had left. He slid her further down on the mattress, yanking her beneath him. He groaned, sending low vibrations into her mouth as the buttons on the flap of his trousers and his erection buried beneath them rubbed slowly against her lower half, each rotation of his hips growing more urgent.

She reveled in tasting his hot tongue, letting her hands mindlessly travel across the length of his smooth greatcoat, down, and back and up again, the material bunching beneath her fingertips.

He suckled her tongue into his mouth and shifted slightly off to the side, trailing a gloved finger down toward her stomach. He skimmed the smooth material of her nightdress until his finger paused between her thighs. Gently, he cupped the area, rubbing it through her nightdress with the tips of his fingers, spiking stomach-tightening but thrilling sensations up the length of her body, causing her breasts to tingle.

She gasped against his mouth, her fingernails digging into his shoulders as she desperately tried to keep herself from thrusting against his hand.

He tore away from her lips, his chest heaving jaggedly against hers. "Do that again."

Her cheeks stung as she realized her nails had excited him. She swallowed and smoothed her hands against the fine wool of his greatcoat, molding it against his shoulders. "No."

"You milksop," he growled.

"Better a milksop than a fool."

"And a fool I am." He slid away from her body and heaved out a pained breath. "Christ. Here I go." The mattress shifted as he jumped off the bed with a thud.

She blinked. "Where are you going?"

"Wait here." The floorboards creaked as he crossed the room. She heard the click of the door as he unlocked it and pulled it open. He hesitated as if he were searching the darkness for something. "Benson," he hissed out into the corridor. "Benson, where are you?"

"Coming, my lord!" Quick, heavy steps and approaching dim light appeared, swaying and shifting against the shadows of the yellow-wallpapered corridor. A young, strapping footman carrying a lit lantern in one hand and an oversized carpetbag in the other appeared in the doorway. Coiled hemp ropes looped around each broad shoulder of his livery as he glanced around like a thief about to carry everything out of the room.

She yanked the coverlet up to her chin in exasperation. "Assure me those ropes are not for me."

"Of course not." Moreland's illuminated broad frame turned. "Pack whatever you can, Benson. Do it. *Now*."

The footman darted toward the other side of the room, set down the lantern beside the carpetbag and yanked open her large wardrobe dresser. Grabbing gowns by the armful, stays and chemises, he stuffed them all into the open bag.

Her heart felt like it was going to leap out of her chest. "Why is he packing my clothes?"

Moreland rounded her bed and pushed her wheelchair out of the way, causing it to roll toward the window. He paused beside her. "We are leaving London tonight."

Her eyes widened. "Leaving London? Whatever for?"

"I will explain in due time." He hesitated. "Do you trust me? Do you trust me to oversee what is best for you and for us?"

She swallowed and told herself she could trust him. She could. Couldn't she? "I...yes."

"Good." His rugged features were half-hidden in the shadows, but she could make out a small smile on those lips. "My footmen have already gathered sixteen of your servants. Are there any more? Or is that it?"

She really shouldn't be encouraging any of this. It was madness at best. "There are seventeen. Not sixteen."

"We'll hunt down the last servant before we leave."

She hesitated. "Why are you so intent on rounding up my servants?"

"I cannot have anyone informing the authorities or His Majesty of our departure. From this night forth, you are under *my* protection, Zosia. While His Majesty has yet to agree to the match, I know in time he will. He has to."

She blinked up at him, her gut tightening. *That* was why he was tying up all of her servants. He was going against his own crown, who obviously didn't approve of him if he had to resort to... Oh, no. *She was being kidnapped!*

Zosia resisted her own panicked need to cross herself. She tried not to give away that she was onto him. Instead, she steadied her breathing and said in a most impressive, rational tone, "Though I want to trust you, Moreland, I sense something is very wrong. I cannot leave until you explain why you are opposing your own crown. What are you not disclosing?"

He hesitated. After a pulsing moment, he sighed and leaned toward her, his gloved fingers brushing aside a loose strand of hair that had unraveled from her long braid. "Zosia. There are many things I wish

I could say right now. But I can't. Not yet. I will. I promise, I will. But what I can say now is this—I have unearthed far more than your history. His Majesty is seeking to marry you off to a man of no consequence who will be paid to keep you blind to your own history for the rest of your life. You also won't be able to pursue advocating for the rights of your people if you marry whoever His Majesty intends. The idea is to permanently remove you from anything that might give you a voice. Is that what you want?"

She eyed him, sensing he was telling the truth. "How is it you know of His Majesty's plans?"

"My grandmother and he are cousins, remember? They are very close and share everything, including things that I sometimes wish to God they wouldn't. I am taking you to meet her right now. She has great influence over His Majesty, and it is my hope she will be able to convince him to give his blessing in this."

She couldn't help but be extremely flattered the man was going through all of this effort. *For her.* But...why? Heaven only knew. Maybe it involved whips. She giggled at the very thought. "Are you going to expect a form of payment in the guise of my whipping your backside? Because I really am not at all too keen on that."

He jerked down toward her and growled, "I am announcing that I am going against my own king in your name and you have nothing to offer me but insults?"

"I was only—"

"Have I somehow misunderstood what it is we share? If I have, Zosia, you had best tell me now before I carry you out of this house and into my life. Because there is no changing this once it is done. There is no changing it."

Her grin faded. She could barely think or breathe beneath the sudden weight of expectations he was placing upon her. She was confused. So confused. About him. About this. About what he wanted. About what he needed.

She shifted toward him. "Why are you doing all of this? What is it that you really want? Why are you—"

"Because *you* matter to *me*," he insisted in a grudging tone. "I know what I want out of a woman, and you are that woman. The question is, do you know what you want in a man? Am I that man? Will I ever be that man? Because I want to be."

Her lips parted as she stared up at his taut, heated features that silently awaited her reply. Her pulse thundered as she pieced everything together bit by bit by bit. A man didn't go through this much effort for a woman unless there was a form of personal gain. What could be gained by a British Marquis whose own grandmother was cousin to the King?

Nothing. Which meant… "Are you in love with me?" she blurted.

He hesitated and eyed the footman who had long packed everything and was now lingering in the doorway, listening. "Move into the corridor, Benson, and at least pretend you're not listening."

The footman bowed and hurried out into the corridor.

Moreland leaned toward her and whispered, "I am sacrificing *everything* for an opportunity to make you mine. Does that answer your question?"

Zosia sucked in a breath of astonishment. Though he didn't say it, the intense deliverance of those words indicated he *was* in love with her. *Her*. A woman who would never bear any grace and would forever wheel herself about in a chair like a horse pulling a carriage. "How can you be in love with a one-legged woman?"

He smiled. "How can I not be? There is no woman like you. And I have met quite a few."

Her belly was turning to liquid fire, and though she knew she would never be able to do the sort of things she sorely wanted to do and missed, like walking and running and dancing, in that moment he made her feel as if she *could* walk and *could* run and *could* dance.

Without thinking—for she wanted to give in to *feeling*—she whispered, "Yes."

He searched her face. "Yes, what?"

"Yes, you are what I want and need in a man."

He slowly grinned, his husky features brightening. "I will never let you take back those words. Not ever." He leaned closer, his gloved hands slipping beneath her thighs and back. "Grab onto my shoulders. We're leaving."

She scrambled to sit up as he dragged her across the mattress and rolled her out of bed and into his arms in a single toss. She squeaked, grabbing onto his neck and shoulders as her one bare foot dangled outside her nightdress, which was riding up. "I should probably dress. I most certainly cannot—"

"We are not attending a ball, my dear," he drawled, turning with her in the darkness and heading toward the door. "You can dress more appropriately once we arrive at my grandmother's."

As he quickly moved them into the darkened corridor and past his footman, she patted his solid shoulder frantically, trying to convince him otherwise. "But I am not even wearing a stay! I cannot—"

"You can wear my greatcoat so *I* don't have to notice you aren't wearing a stay. Benson. Move ahead of us."

"Yes, my lord." The footman scurried around them, dutifully bathing the corridor in light.

A female scream pierced and echoed through the corridor behind them. Moreland swung both himself and Zosia toward Mrs. Wade, who had stumbled back against the wall, her nightcap tipping to one side, exposing a section of her bundled gray hair.

"Seventeen," Moreland announced matter-of-factly.

Zosia held up a hand and waved it toward Mrs. Wade. "Mrs. Wade! Please. There is no need to shatter every skull in the corridor. This is not as vile as it appears. This is Lord Moreland. He is a friend and means to assist me."

"More than a friend," Moreland provided gruffly, glaring down at Zosia. "I am here to marry you. Or did you already forget?"

She winced, knowing whatever they said would sound completely absurd. "Would you prefer I announce we are lovers?" she hissed up at him. "Let us not upset the poor woman more than is necessary."

"Considering all that I am doing," he tossed back, "do you really think I care who the hell I upset anymore?"

Mrs. Wade pushed away from the wall and edged toward them, glancing from Moreland, to her, to the footman. "Sir. She is under the protection of His Majesty."

"Not anymore," he said, his hold tightening.

Mrs. Wade edged steadily closer, as if she were approaching a feral beast. "She is an invalid, sir, and requires better care than this."

Zosia gasped and glared at Mrs. Wade. "I am not an invalid."

"Tie her to a bedpost, Benson," Moreland grumbled. "Show her what an invalid *really* is and use every goddamn rope you have. When you're done with her, meet us by the carriage outside."

"Yes, my lord!" The footman tossed the carpetbag and set down the lantern, jogging around them.

Mrs. Wade let out a piercing scream and darted in the opposite direction, her robe and nightdress flapping around her. The footman dashed after her, yanking ropes off each shoulder, his boots thudding against the floorboards in an effort to keep up.

Zosia grinned as Moreland toted her down the corridor. She grabbed his lightly stubbled chin with the tips of her fingers, leaned in and kissed his warm cheek soundly. "*That* is for defending my honor."

He tightened his hold on her and glanced down at her as they reached the candlelit stairwell. "I will never let anyone disrespect you. That I vow."

A part of her was already madly in love with this man and everything he was. She kissed his cheek again, only more tenderly, nuzzling her lips across his prickling stubble. "Thank you. Now remove me from this house. I am well and done with His Majesty. I have found myself a new protector. One who actually knows what he is doing."

He grinned. "I am yours to command." With that,

he carried her down the length of the stairs, his steps and his hold proud and strong.

Rounding the bottom of the staircase, he quickly headed through a long corridor, which deposited them in an empty kitchen. A footman held open the servants' door leading out, waiting for them to pass through.

Moreland carried her out into the night. The blast of cool, coal-tinged, murky London air made her take in a deep, savory breath as if it were the best air she'd ever had. And in some way, it was. For this was the beginning of a new life.

SCANDAL TEN

Imagine a person being called upon by all of society to speak a language they have never even heard of. Imagine that same person being told they must speak this language or lose all they hold dear. It is neither fair or realistic, in theory, and yet, such is the role women play when becoming wives. Though love may not always assist a woman in speaking the same language as her husband, it will offer assistance in one of the most demanding roles known to humanity. Honor love, even if your marriage is one of convenience. I know nothing of such roles or of being a woman, but I have seen these parts played by the best. To this day, I believe love was the only thing that kept my father happy throughout my poor mother's horrid last year, when she suffered from a melancholy no quack could cure. To be sure, there is no greater gift or curse than love.

—*How To Avoid A Scandal,*
Moreland's Original Manuscript

MOONLIGHT BATHED the small terraced courtyard in a haunting, fuzzy gray glow as Moreland swiftly steered Zosia out toward the coach house and through the open gates. He paused before the open door of an unmarked, black-lacquered carriage whose outside glass lanterns remained unlit.

Moreland leaned toward the young footman who held the door and instructed in a low, quiet tone, "We wait for Benson. After we depart, you will stay here with the rest. Don't untie any of the servants until morning. That will give me enough time to be well out of reach. Come morning, return to the house. My secretary will call with fifty pounds in hand for each of you. I will not be informing you of anything more. That will keep you and everyone else out of harm's way should the authorities get involved. Tell them you know nothing and you were only following my orders. My barrister will oversee the rest."

The footman bowed his dark head. "Yes, my lord."

Moreland leaned away, adjusting her weight in his arms and added, "When Benson arrives, knock. I will knock, in turn, for you to signal to the driver to depart."

"May God see you through your journey, my lord."

Moreland offered a curt nod. "I thank you for those words and your service."

Turning her sideways, Moreland guided Zosia gently into the coach, leaning forward just enough to place her onto the cushion of the seat inside.

Stripping his greatcoat, Moreland cloaked her with its heavy, soothing warmth. She inhaled the scent clinging to it, which smelled just like him: cardamom.

He stepped up and into the upholstered space, falling back into the seat across from hers, causing the entire carriage to sway. He snapped his fingers and the footman folded up the steps and secured the door.

Moreland gestured toward her. "Lean back against the seat. I don't want you falling."

She smiled and tapped her one bare foot against the cold floor of the carriage assuredly. "All I need is one foot to uphold myself." She drew his greatcoat tighter around herself, snuggling inside it, feeling as though she were snuggling against him.

There was a knock on the covered window, announcing Benson's arrival. Moreland leaned forward and thudded his gloved fist against the side door. He sat back as the carriage clattered forward, swaying them and the small, lit lantern above their heads, which appeared to cast more shadows than light.

She scooted toward the window. Lifting the drawn curtain, she peered out as the coach house disappeared and they turned onto the main street. Except for random passing lampposts, she could make out little else against the darkness.

"Keep the curtains drawn." Moreland's terse tone indicated it was a command, not a suggestion. "The coach is unmarked and we ride without lanterns for a reason."

Her fingers instantly released the curtain, letting it fall into place over the window. She glanced toward him.

His fist kept tapping his upper thigh as if he were counting fast to a hundred or waiting for something to happen. Something of a sinister nature.

She stared at him. "Are we in some sort of peril?"

"No. Not you. I."

Her heart pounded. "*You?* How so?"

He shrugged, still tapping his gloved fist against his thigh. "His Majesty could very well strip me of everything I own—including my title—for doing this. But it's the only path I know to take that will ensure you don't live a lie and that I don't lose you to another man."

A soft smile tugged at her lips, his words flinging away whatever doubts she might have had. There was nothing more gallant and daring and romantic than a man risking everything for a woman. "You are unbelievably courageous and bold to oppose your own King in my honor."

He grunted. "Stupid is what I am. But we won't go into that."

She laughed. "Allow me to express how endlessly grateful I am for your stupidity."

He shifted his jaw, not in the least bit enthused, and kept on tapping and tapping and tapping that rigid fist.

She cleared her throat. Perhaps it was time to refocus their conversation. Pulling her long braid down over the front of her right shoulder, she fingered its length, following the threaded grooves of soft hair. "Will you tell me?" she hinted softly.

He paused from tapping his fist. "Yes. Tomorrow morning. When my mind isn't so muddled. Will that be agreeable?"

She half nodded. What was one more day after twenty-three years of not knowing? She shoved her braid back over her shoulder and eyed him. "So what are your plans?"

"Plans?" he echoed.

"Yes. *Plans*. I imagine you have some daring scheme, considering we are practically fugitives."

He shifted against the seat and glanced down at his hand, which was now picking at the knee of his trousers. He drew in a pained breath and huffed it out. "We won't be staying in London. We can't."

"Yes, I suspected as much. So where are we going?"

His hand stilled on his knee. The dim lantern light above their heads swayed light and shadows across his face as he met her gaze. "New York."

Startled, she sat straight up in the seat and jolted against the movements of the carriage. "New York? New York, as in America?"

"Yes. New York, as in America."

She shook her head and kept right on shaking it. "No. Oh, no. No, no, no. Take me anywhere in this vast world *but* America."

He leaned toward her. "You have no choice in this. I have already chartered a ship."

She glared at him. "You obviously thought I was going to submit to anything and everything you had in mind. A bit conceited, are you?"

"No, of course not. That isn't—"

"Despite my willingness to place faith in everything you are saying and doing—*which I am*—I have no intention of neglecting my cause or my people. Not for you or for anyone else. You had best remember that."

His features tightened. "I am not telling you to abandon your cause or your people. You will simply have to tend to your cause and your people in New York for a small while."

"But I cannot preach the rights of freedom to a nation that has no concept of freedom! Americans believe in slavery. They keep colored people uneducated and do unspeakable things to them for their own vile gain. How am I to preach to that?"

He intently searched her face. "His Majesty wants you situated in New York and I intend to honor what little of his requests I can in the hopes of appeasing him. I vow to support you through every breathing moment of whatever you have in mind, but it will have to be done in New York for a while. We can relocate later, after a few months, if that is what you want."

"I am *not* going to New York. *Or* America."

His nostrils flared. "Would you prefer I return you to His Majesty and allow *him* to oversee all of your patriotic plans? Because I can do that. I certainly don't want you feeling like you're being roped off to America by some blade-loving savage. That is not what I want for you. That is not why I am doing this."

She sighed, knowing full well His Majesty would sooner place a habit on her than allow her to dip her hands into political waters. "You are no savage, Moreland, and should never speak of yourself as such." She sighed again. "I suppose if I am forced to go to New York to appease His Majesty, then I will simply have to assist preaching for colored people, too. Because I certainly cannot voice the freedom of one people and ignore the rights of another."

Heaving out a breath, he glanced over at her.

"Though assisting colored people is a very noble, and indeed a worthy cause, you cannot take up every battle you come across."

"And why not? Our wealth and status give us privileges few in society have. We have a responsibility to ensure more than our own voices are being heard. As my mother used to say, *'Leaders must be reminded that their duty and their morals do not serve them, but their people.'*"

He snorted. "Yes, and your mother knew all about duty and morals to have birthed you out of wedlock and then kept you blind to your own history. Who was that serving? Not you, to be sure."

Zosia swallowed against the tightness clenching her throat. She had no right to be infuriated by his words. Because he was right. Her mother had indeed lost sight of herself, her duty and her morals to have gone against everything she had preached. But that would never change her own love for her mother.

She fought the tears stinging her eyes. "Regardless of what my mother may have been guilty of, her strength and her wisdom saw me through everything. *Everything.*"

She pointed rigidly to her amputated thigh buried beneath his greatcoat and choked out, "Do you think I was always at ease with my physical state? I sought to *die* knowing I would forever be a cripple and that, with the loss of my dignity, I also lost so much more.

You should have seen my coming-out in Warszawa two months before that wall fell and destroyed my life. I admit to being vain in those days. I was. It was very easy for me to be vain for I was hailed as a beauty. Men lined the hall for hours waiting for an opportunity to dance the Polonaise with me. Only they all disappeared the moment my leg did. And though those men meant nothing to me, it was all too symbolic of what I had been left with. *Nothing*. Or that is what I thought. It was my mother who resurrected me each and every time I wanted to take my last breath. It was my mother who reminded me of my worth. And nothing you or anyone else has to say about her will ever change that truth for me."

Moreland's shadowed eyes and face held so much anguish, there was no doubt it reflected her own. Very softly and apologetically, he offered, "I had no right to impose upon the memory of a woman I never knew. Forgive me."

Zosia nodded and blinked rapidly, pushing back whatever tears remained. She set her chin, struggling to compose herself. "She meant everything to me. I cannot imagine her being...deceitful."

He lowered his gaze. "I understand," he whispered. "I will tell you about your father."

She shook her head. "No. Not now. Not yet. I...I am not ready to hear it."

He kept his gaze on his gloved hands. "All you need do is ask."

She sniffed, trying to lull herself back into a state of peace, and nodded. "I will."

They sat without speaking. The thundering clatter of the wheels rotating against the cobblestone overtook all sound.

She hated the way he kept staring at his hands. She also hated the pause in their dialogue. It only allowed for bad thoughts to fester. Needing to push out the tension and the last of the emotions still coiled within her, she released a shaky breath. "Forgive me for having bowed to my emotions in a manner that might have induced you to believe that I am not at all grateful for all that you are sacrificing in my honor. Might we commence our conversation anew? As peers?"

He glanced up. "Are we not more than peers?" His voice was notably cool and distant.

She swallowed, sensing his displeasure with the thought of them being mere peers. "Yes, of course we are. I only meant in conversation."

"Did you?"

She smiled, trying to show that she was no longer affected by her earlier display of emotion. "I was merely hoping you and I might partake in the sort of conversations men and women do not usually engage in."

His eyes and his face softened. "And what sort of conversation were you wanting?"

"One involving...politics."

"I should hope you could converse with me about anything. Especially politics, Zosia."

"Thank you." Her smile widened. "Given your years in Parliament, if you were to offer an underling, such as myself, any advice pertaining to my plight, what sort of advice would you give?"

He eyed her pensively, rubbing his fingers against the length of his set jaw. Hefting out a breath, he dropped his hand heavily onto his lap. "I would advise you to remember that a person can only do so much. Choose one battle at a time, not a dozen. The more battles you dedicate yourself to, the less effective you will be. I should know."

He leaned forward, as if trying to better convey his words. "I went into the House of Lords at the age of four and twenty thinking I would conquer the world, only to discover I couldn't even conquer the votes of fifteen people. I assure you, Zosia, New York will offer you a far bigger platform than you think. The city is quite progressive in its freedoms. Americans are also fascinated by the aristocracy, which will fall in our favor. In New York, you will be a celebrity preaching for a just cause. Whilst here? You would be nothing more than a damn blow book. Something to look at, then forget."

She blinked. "A *blow book?* Forgive my ignorance, but what sort of nonsensical British word is that?"

He winced and leaned back. "Forgive me. That was not a respectable analogy for me to have used."

She lifted an inquisitive brow. "So the term *blow book* is crass in nature?"

"Yes. Very."

"And is a *blow book* an actual book, as the term itself insinuates?"

"Yes." He cleared his throat. "Now please. Stop saying *blow book*. It doesn't sound right coming from you."

A crass book that was an actual book? Well, it was obvious what it had to be. She leaned forward. "Are you insinuating it is a compilation of indelicate words and pictures?"

"Yes, Zosia. Yes. Now please. I would rather you not—"

"You compared me and my cause to a *blow book?*" she huffed out in exasperation. *"Moreland!"*

"Curse me for breathing." He shifted his entire body against the seat and looked away, seething out a heavy breath. "Do you have to be so sensitive about the subject of your land? I do believe I am lynching myself merely for being British."

She blinked, noting how adorable and agitated he was trying to maintain peace between them. She let out a laugh. "Forgive me. I will strive to be less sensitive."

"That would be much appreciated."

"I still cannot help but feel that you are far more riled about this whole subject of blow books than I am about my own people. Why is that?"

He shrugged but said nothing.

"Is it because you know quite a bit about blow books and do not wish to expose me to your own vice? That would certainly explain how a whip-yielding, virile man such as yourself ever survived in respectable society. You must have handled yourself quite a bit throughout the years. Every night, would you say?"

He glared at her. "And how would you—*a virgin*—know anything about a man handling himself?"

She smirked. "My cousins have informed me of all that goes on in the privacy of a man's bedroom." Leaning forward, she lowered her voice by a whole octave. "And I do mean all."

A small smile teased Lord Moreland's masculine lips. He leaned forward as well, closing the space in the carriage between them. "You find yourself amusing, don't you?"

"Yes. I do." She grinned and leaned back against the seat. "So how many blow books do you own? Let there be no secrets left unsaid between us.

Two? Ten? Or are we scandalously veering into the hundreds?"

"I have *no* intention of answering that," he drawled, leaning back against the seat. "We'll be arriving at our destination in forty-five minutes. I advise you to refrain from any more talk about blow books, or it will end with you in my lap and my mouth over every last of inch of your body. Is that what you want for yourself? Keep talking. I will ensure it."

Her heartbeat throbbed in her ears at the thought of her in his lap and that mouth skimming the curve of her throat, her breasts, her stomach, her—

The very thought froze her brain—she was more intrigued by his threat than intimidated.

Against her own better judgment she playfully tossed out, *"Blow book, blow book, blow book. Wherefore art thou, blow book? Do you sit at Moreland's bedside or do you hide within his desk? Blow book, my dear blow book, I genuinely fear he loves you best."* She smirked and eyed him. "Do you intend to punish me by taking me into your lap now?"

Moreland lifted a dark brow. "Perhaps we really should send you to a convent. You appear to be far more devious in nature than I."

She laughed. "Unfortunately, my dear Moreland, you cannot dispose of me now."

He tilted his head slightly to better observe her,

sending longer strands of his auburn hair into his eyes. "I would never dispose of such an incredibly beautiful woman," he commented in a low, husky tone.

Her pulse skittered. How was it that in this dashing man's eyes her one leg had become two? "Do you truly think me to be beautiful?" she whispered.

"Yes," he murmured, half nodding. "And selfish bastard that I am, I am looking forward to making you mine. All mine." He averted his gaze in a quiet way that hinted just how much he reveled in knowing that she was indeed going to be his. All his.

She had never felt so beautiful in her entire life. Not even when she had two legs and could dance. Mentally, she was already caressing his jaw, his brow, his hair, his shoulders. She was already indulging in his touch and his body and in turn letting him indulge in hers. She was already his, all his, but the way he continued to keep his eyes averted from her own, she knew if she did nothing in that moment, *nothing* would happen. And so it was time she do *something*.

She nervously bit her lip and strategically lowered the greatcoat to her lap, hoping the outline of her un-corseted breasts through her nightdress would inspire him without her having to do much more.

He paused, his gaze flicking toward her breasts.

"What are you doing?" His attention lingered on said breasts, his jaw tightening.

She shrugged ever so innocently and arched her back enough to ensure her breasts were pressing more firmly against the material of her nightdress. "Making myself comfortable, is all." *And ardently hoping you will show me how beautiful I truly am.*

He cleared his throat. "For heaven's sake, woman, I can see your—" Fisting both hands, he glanced away. "Cover yourself."

'Twas sad, knowing she was failing at something as simple as seducing him. Weren't breasts supposed to inspire a man into passionately seizing a woman against her will?

She chewed the inside of her cheek, knowing she ought to invite him outright to kiss her and touch her. How else was he supposed to know what she wanted?

She angled herself more toward him and offered in a casual, conversational tone, "I enjoyed our earlier kiss. Very much."

He shifted in his seat, avoiding her gaze. "Did you?"

"Yes. Did you?"

"Probably more than you did," he muttered.

She wet her lips, doubting that. "Would you at all be interested in…"

He jerked his gaze back to hers, a vivid intensity

etched into his rugged features. "Interested in what?" he asked in a husky tone that indicated he knew *exactly* what she was insinuating but wanted her to announce it.

Her cheeks burned as he continued to possessively hold her gaze. Mother of heaven, she was begging him to slaughter the cow before milking it.

He lowered his chin, as if warning her. "You don't want this, Zosia. I know you don't."

She blinked. Was he denying her? "I think I know myself well enough to know what it is I want."

He shook his head slowly from side to side as if deeply disappointed in her. "No. You are convincing yourself that this is what you want, because you feel obligated toward me. I can assure you, you needn't feel any form of obligation."

She gasped. "Is that what you think? That I would stoop to barter my virginity to you or any man out of mere obligation? What sort of woman do you take me for? Forgive me, but it is becoming rather obvious that *you* do not want this or me."

"I can barely *breathe* out of my own damn want," he said in a harsh, clipped tone. "But I am not about to ravage you in a carriage like a dog in need of a quick pump. You deserve better than that."

Zosia's brows rose slowly in disbelief. He had actually been sitting there the whole while refraining from pouncing. Imagine that. The poor man had played the part of a gentleman for much too long and it was up to her to make him understand that when a man's intentions were noble and dedicated, he could kiss and fondle and partake all he wanted. Whenever he wanted. Wherever he wanted. And if there was anyone who had earned it, it most certainly was him.

There was only one way to go about settling this. She tugged the shoulder of her nightdress off her entire right shoulder and eyed him, challenging him to resist.

"Zosia," he growled through his teeth.

"Do not make me fully undress," she taunted. "I have no idea how to go about doing this. But I do know men love breasts."

His jaw tightened as he tugged at his black-leather gloves, loosening them from his fingers one by one by one. His dark eyes remained fixed on her as he stripped them from his hands, tossing each glove on the seat beside him with the flick of his wrist. "Are you certain this is what you want? Here? Now? Me?"

She tugged the sleeve of her nightdress farther down, until her bare right breast and dark nipple peered out. She eyed him again. "Does *this* answer your question?"

"You are officially damned." He pushed himself off the seat and whipped his great cloak off her lap, throwing it to the floor between them. He knelt before her and stared her down as his fingers effortlessly unbuttoned the flap of his trousers. Shifting toward her, he shoved his undergarment and shirt out of the way. His erection fell heavily toward her, thick and large.

She sucked in a harsh breath and slapped her hands against her face in disbelief that she had actually seen the entire length of his—

"Oh, now you wish to play coy, do you?" He hitched up her nightdress to her knees, causing her to gasp at the unexpected exposure of both her one leg and stump. "If you don't want this, you'd best start yelling right now because I don't plan on playing the part of a gentleman anymore."

He grabbed hold of her exposed thighs and hoisted her up and onto his lap so quickly her hands fell against his chest in an effort to balance herself.

Her heart hammered, realizing she may have riled him a bit *too* much. She glanced nervously toward the curtained windows, ensuring they were still hidden from the world and the night. Which they were.

He leaned back against the seat, adjusting her to straddle him, further jerking up her nightdress so that her entire lower half was exposed.

Her hand jumped awkwardly to her stump, a raw sense of shame overwhelming her.

He roughly pushed her hand away, forcing it behind her back. "Never hide from me."

His hand possessively rounded her scarred stump, rubbing it with his fingers and his palm, before he reached up and grabbed the sides of her face with both hands. He forced her lips down onto his, thrusting his tongue forcefully into her mouth.

His overly demanding tongue melted away not only her shame but the sway of the carriage, the night and the world around them. She closed her eyes, giving in to his hot, velvet tongue as it tauntingly slid out of her mouth. He licked her lips twice, leaving them moist and cool, then licked one cheek and the other, then the entire length of her throat, leaving everything wet as he repeatedly christened her with his tongue.

"Show me how much you want this," he whispered in a strained voice. He slipped one of his fingers into her mouth, pushing it in deep. "Show me how much you want me."

She sucked on the saltiness of his skin, which was still scented from the leather gloves he had earlier stripped.

He groaned and slid his finger against her teeth and tapped it before pulling it back out and pressing it hard against her lips. "Show me what you feel. Bite it. Do it for me. I need to *feel* you."

The intensity of the moment and the desperate need that resonated in that deep, commanding voice made her slip his finger back into her mouth. She bit down so hard, she could feel his skin giving way beneath her teeth, the bone of his finger keeping her from clamping down any more.

"Again," he hissed out raggedly. His thumb and fingers pressed against her chin harder, as he stilled the forefinger that was still clamped between her teeth.

She didn't know why she was allowing him to take over her mind like this, but it felt so strangely wonderful, tasting him and giving him what he so obviously and desperately wanted and needed. It was only her teeth against his finger. That she could do without great harm. She clamped down even harder until her jaw ached with the rest of her.

He sucked in a harsh breath as his other hand skimmed across her breasts and trailed down between them. He grabbed hold of his large erection and rubbed and jerked its length. His fingers grazed her skin as he slid the moist, rounded tip of his hard cock against the curve of her stomach. He kept sliding it back and forth across her stomach, occasionally digging into her with it until not only his chest heaved but her own.

Desperately wanting to touch him and feel him, she released his finger from between her teeth and mouth and started unknotting his silk cravat from around his throat.

His hands jumped to hers. He grabbed both of her wrists and yanked them away from his cravat, his chest rising and falling unevenly. "No. Not now."

She pried her wrists free and *tsk*ed down at him. "You can yank my nightdress up to the waist, but I cannot so much as expose your throat? *I think not.*" She slid her hands back toward his collar, her fingers unknotting the strip of silk.

His hands grabbed her wrists again, only more savagely, his fingers pinching into her skin. *"No."* His voice had become savage and unfriendly. "If you insist on seeing me right now, this ends."

She froze and met his blazing gaze, suddenly fully understanding his resistance. His scars. Dearest heaven. They were not limited to his arms. "Just as my amputation does not define what you think of me, your scars do not define what I think of you. *You* define what I think of you, Moreland."

"I don't want you to see them. Not now."

She swallowed. "I understand. I will not insist."

His features softened. He released her and set his forefinger against the curve of her throat, nudging the chain on her locket. "I want this moment between us to be perfect and untainted," he murmured, watching his own finger. He trailed the tip of that finger down past her collarbone, down past the fabric of her nightdress, skimming across her breasts hidden beneath, down onto her exposed stomach, until it paused on the curling hairs between her thighs.

Her breath hitched.

Lifting his gaze to hers, he slid his finger down into her wet folds. He rubbed his finger slowly but firmly, probing and flicking.

She gasped against the rippling sensation that spread throughout her body.

Spreading her with two fingers, his forefinger flicked the top of her folds. He met her gaze again as clenching sensations shot up through her thighs, stomach and womb.

He trailed his other large hand around her waist, holding her firmly against the heat of his erection which pressed harder against her thigh. He readjusted his fingers, leaned into her and kept rubbing faster and faster, not even giving her a chance to breathe or think.

She edged closer and closer to a pleasure she wanted to swallow whole and burst from. It was incredible. *He* was incredible. She moaned, shockingly loud even to her own ears.

"Are you thinking of me as I do this?" he asked hoarsely, rubbing faster. "Are you thinking of me as you moan?"

"Yes," she breathed out, riding his hand harder.

"There will never be another, will there?"

"Nie. Nigdy."

"English, dearest," he drawled, his finger bringing her to a heart-pounding peak. "I'm not as intelligent as you."

"Never," she gasped. "You are all I will ever want and need."

"Say it again."

"You are all I want and…need," she choked out, almost unable to say the words against the movement of his finger.

"Am I?"

"Yes."

"I will never let you go."

"Never let me go."

"You are mine now. Accept that you are mine and will always be mine."

"I do. Willingly."

His fingers stilled. He grabbed his erection and positioned it against her wet opening. "Take me into you. Do it. *Now.*"

On his command, she pushed down hard, sliding his thickness deep into her. The pinch and the unexpected stretch snatched her breath. She tightened her hold on his shoulders and steadied herself against the blinding pain that jarred her back into reality.

The dream she'd harbored since she was seventeen was no more. She no longer belonged to a dashing, nameless man. She was a woman of three and twenty and belonged to this dashing man who had a name.

Moreland. Her Moreland. He was everything she could ever want in a man and she knew that with him at her side, she would never yearn for anything more. Not ever again.

SCANDAL ELEVEN

In moments of vulnerability, all that defines a lady may very well cease to exist. Or rather... her maidenhood may very well cease to exist.
—*How To Avoid A Scandal,*
Moreland's Original Manuscript

TRISTAN THREW BACK HIS HEAD, an anguished groan bursting from his lips as Zosia's tight, wet heat surrounded him so perfectly. He slid even deeper, until the crown of his cock was being pushed back by her womb. In that moment, he knew he had an escape no blade or whip could ever bestow upon him. His finger still throbbed, its pulsing heat matching the pulse of his heart, edging him to thrust his length into her.

He reveled in knowing that she had never shared herself with anyone but him. Whatever restraint he thought himself capable of fleeted.

His fingers and palms dug into the smooth waist of her soft nightdress. He inched out and then savagely jerked himself deep up into her tightness as far as he could go.

She gasped, tightening her hold on him, and stiffened.

It wasn't a gasp swelling with pleasure. But pain.

He froze, tightening his own hold on her waist as he raggedly breathed in her melting scent of cinnamon and powder. "Did I hurt you?" he whispered up at her, keeping perfectly still.

"Yes," she choked out.

He swallowed, his chest tightening from an agonizing guilt growing within him. He was hurting her. He was hurting her due to his own stupid, selfish and beastly need to possess her. And worse yet, he was ravaging her in a carriage like a lecher taking a whore in between destinations. She was a lady and a virgin who deserved far better than this. She deserved far better than him.

"We need to stop," he whispered, shifting against the seat, trying to lift her off his aching erection, which was still buried deep within her.

"No." She leaned her head against his shoulder, pressing herself against him. Her arms tightened around his neck, the sleeve of her nightdress brushing his chin. "No, 'tis a…pleasurable pain. Though I do not wish to confess such a thing to you. I do not ever want to encourage what you do to your body."

How could he not love her?

He smoothed his hands up the length of her slim back, wishing he could take away whatever pain he had caused her by swallowing it himself. His fingers slipped into the silken strands of her braided hair and brought her warmth and softness even closer, as he slid his tongue down her exposed throat toward her full, uncorseted breasts. Tiny granules of ground, earthy cinnamon flavored his tongue, causing him to pause and let out a gruff laugh against her skin. "Hell, you really do taste like cinnamon. I suggest a little less cinnamon in those cosmetic creams."

She smacked his shoulder, laughing softly against him.

He kissed her breasts through the fabric of her nightdress, enjoying the softness pushing back against his lips. He fought the raging urge to thrust himself against the tight heat that still held his thick, throbbing cock.

He was such a selfish bastard for letting it get to this. They would be arriving quite soon. "We really shouldn't be doing this," he rasped, drawing his lips away from her. "You deserve better than this. You deserve better than me."

"Shhhh." She brought her hands up to his face and raked her nails gently down to his throat, hidden beneath his cravat, causing his jaw to tighten from the zinging pleasure. "Honor yourself, Moreland. Always honor yourself. You need not convince me of your worth. I know of it. What we do now is not a sin but

a contract between our souls as we make our way to the altar."

He swallowed. Her words were so sweet and promising, but would it change when she realized that—

"Will you always be mine?"

She kissed his forehead. "Always. Now, make me yours. For I am yours." She pressed her entire body against his and forced her tight heat down harder onto him.

Gritting his teeth, he slowly pushed into her, lifting his hips to enable him to penetrate deeper. Heat-laced sensations rippled through him as he slid back out and in. He tried to keep his movements steady and slow, but his need to reach that peak of pleasure was overtaking the last of his tense body and mind. He bit back a loud groan, his throat tightening. "Damn, but you are your own whip."

She moaned against him, in turn, clutching his shoulders. "Moreland, I—"

He yanked her down hard onto his length again and again, pounding into her as deep and as fast as her body would allow, giving in to her need and his. Moisture beaded his brow from the pressure and bursting energy of unfulfilled years being driven into this one incredible moment. He blew out short, sharp puffs of breath, trying to withhold the urge to spill seed into that tight wetness.

She suddenly released a well-pleasured moan,

her entire body quivering against him. *"Boże,"* she choked out, rocking against him.

He knew she had reached her pinnacle, for she was fading into her own native language. And he, for one, was glad for it. Thrusting one last time, the world around him expanded into a bliss he had never thought possible.

He threw back his head and fiercely held on to her as he pulsed out thick seed deep into her. His body coiled against the blinding perfection of that moment until everything faded, leaving nothing but the frantic pounding of his heart and his desperate need to be held.

Tristan wrapped his arms tightly around her for a long moment, cradling her slim frame against himself. His right hand slowly slipped down the short length of her left thigh and rubbed the uneven but smooth, soft edges of her stump. It was like touching a part of her soul.

This was what loving a woman was truly like. So extraordinary and intoxicating. She was perfection to behold, after banishing himself into believing no one could ever truly understand him or find him attractive or value his worth after what he had done to himself throughout the years.

He had been wrong. Though his newfound happiness was coming at a price. He was violating her trust. And if she ever found out—

Tears stung his eyes, unexpectedly overwhelming him as he struggled to push away his emotions. He squeezed his eyes shut and buried his head in the curve of her soft throat, gently rocking her. He hadn't meant to claim her this soon. He hadn't. Not before she was his in name and honor. And though he knew she had yet to love him, at least one thing was certain: her body was now his. All his. And he hoped that one day her heart would be his, too.

ZOSIA FELT SO DELECTABLY dazed she couldn't move. Moreland slowly lifted her, sliding his ebbing erection from deep within her. He kissed her forehead and then lifted her off his lap, turning her just enough so he could set her gently beside him on the seat of the carriage.

He buttoned the flap of his trousers and cleared his throat. "It appears you are a virgin no more."

She let out an awkward laugh and paused, realizing her lower half, including her stump, was still exposed. She cringed and frantically yanked her nightdress down to cover herself. She could feel his moist, warm seed beginning to run down her inner thighs and wondered if she would be blessed with a babe after only one try.

Moreland's hand jumped out toward her and stilled her hands as she covered the last of herself. "Wait."

She glanced toward him, hoping he didn't expect her to remain uncovered throughout the rest of their ride.

Lowering his gaze, he reached into his right coat pocket and yanked out his razor case. Sitting back against the seat, he flicked open the brass hinged lid. The metallic lid fell away with a *tink,* hanging off the rectangular case as it revealed a folded ivory-handled blade sitting atop a piece of creased, frayed yellowing parchment. A snowy white handkerchief lay neatly tucked beside the blade.

She froze, her breath hitching. He didn't plan on actually "What are you doing?"

He plucked out the handkerchief and shook it once, unfurling it as he snapped the case shut. "It's clean."

Shoving the case back into his coat pocket, he leaned toward her and tucked it into her hand. "Whenever I used a handkerchief to wipe the blade clean, I always immediately burned it and replaced it with a new one." He tapped at her hand. "This is a new one. Which, mind you, has remained untouched for quite some time."

She blinked down at it, her grip tightening on the soft, white handkerchief that had only moments earlier been nestled against his blade. It was eerie to touch his world in so intimate a manner. It was a world she had yet to fully understand. "Why are you giving this to me?"

He wrapped his arm around her, pulling her tightly against himself, and whispered, "Do you want me to do it for you?"

"Do what?" She tried not to panic as she leaned away.

"Shh." He yanked her back forcibly against himself. "Here. We will do it together."

She watched as his large hand drifted toward her knee. Gathering her nightdress, he lifted it, edging the fabric back up above her stump until it was well above her waist. She stiffened as his other hand cupped her hand that held the handkerchief. Gently, he guided her hand toward the inside of her thighs hidden beneath and nudged them apart. Ever so softly, he moved her hand and his handkerchief toward the moisture on her inner thighs and wiped everything that clung to her. He dabbed at the sore flesh surrounding the folds of her sex and the dark curls around it.

She bit her lip, heat spreading into her cheeks. Her heart pounded in response to the unbelievably bold, but most endearing gesture. Despite feeling awkward, she didn't stop him. Instead, she silently allowed him to finish, the knuckles of his large, guiding hand grazing her skin with each sway of the carriage, making her feel cherished in so intimate a manner.

"There." He paused, releasing her hand and tugging the handkerchief away. He smiled. Crumpling it, he leaned into her as he shoved it into his coat pocket.

Zosia yanked down her nightdress back over her stub and leg, shifting against him to ensure everything was covered. "Thank you."

"But of course." Still keeping his arm tightly wrapped around her, he reached across the seat before them and grabbed his greatcoat. He draped her with it, tucking it around the contours of her body so that it covered her from neck to toe.

She leaned into his solid warmth, feeling so loved and cherished. How was it he could offer so much tenderness and affection to her yet not to himself? Something must have started him on the path of cutting. But what? "Moreland?" she whispered.

"Hmm?" He sounded so content and at peace.

She glanced up at him and rubbed his chest, her fingers grazing the silver buttons on his waistcoat. She didn't want to break the reverie of that peace, but how else was she ever going to understand him and truly connect with him? "When did you first… cut yourself? And why? I want to know more about it. I want to know more about you."

He hesitated, his brows coming together. He stared off somewhere before him, but eventually nodded and replied in a soft, distant voice, "It wasn't something I had ever knowingly given in to. It simply…happened. I was fifteen. I was young, stupid, bitter and angry. I wanted to rip everything around me apart and one day I childishly gave in to the way I felt by yanking a mirror off the wall and shattering it in a single sweep. The moment that mirror shattered, it was as if the person I knew drifted from my own body and never returned. I sat on the floor, picked up one of the countless shards of glass from the mirror lying all around me and, without even thinking, sliced my forearm for the first time. It was oddly comforting to see and feel my own torment being pulled out from within me."

He sighed. "Only after I did it did I panic. I knew what I had done to myself was demented. So I bandaged it and tried to hide it from my grandmother. But one of the servants had informed her about finding blood on one of my shirts. She confronted me and I confessed. I'd never seen her so livid. She threatened me with bedlam if I ever did it again. I promised I never would, and I meant it. But after I healed, I wanted to do it again. And again. And again. She and I were forever at ends about it."

He tightened his hold on her shoulder. "I didn't start using a razor until I was seventeen. That was when I sought to control what I was doing to myself by limiting my urges to only one object and only doing it if I desperately needed to. Prior to that, I submitted to doing it whenever I felt like it. In fact, most of the scarring on my arms and chest are from those first two years. And I regret it. For it isn't something that can be undone."

Zosia swallowed hard, her throat aching and tight. She nestled herself closer against him, wishing she had the means to erase everything he had done. "What made you so angry?" she whispered. "What happened?"

"I…" He lowered his gaze. "Please. Not now."

She pinched her lips together and nodded, pressing her head against his chest. Trying to offer him whatever comfort she could give, she whispered back, "I will always be here for you, Moreland. I will always be here to listen. Know that."

He tightened his hold, but said nothing.

They sat in silence and said nothing more as they moved side to side against each other with the constant pitching of the carriage. Despite resisting the need to close her eyes, which were growing heavier with each passing moment, Zosia eventually drifted off and escaped to nothingness.

"Zosia." A LOW MALE VOICE edged into the darkness she had somehow floated into. "Dearest. Wake up."

Her eyes fluttered open. Soft candlelight flooded her vision to reveal a beautifully ornate blue-and-gold sitting room angled on its side, which had magically replaced the carriage she had just been in. A silver-haired woman bearing aged but refined porcelain features, which whispered of great beauty in youth, sat elegantly poised in a gilded chair barely an arm's length away. She was exquisitely dressed in an emerald lace-and-satin evening gown, its full, bouffant sleeves stitched with floral patterns. Her black eyes were soft and compelling as she quietly observed her with notable curiosity.

Zosia stiffened, realizing her head and shoulders were actually resting on Moreland's lap. They were both on an embroidered velvet sitting couch, his great cloak still covering her body and nightdress.

She bolted up, ensuring she yanked his greatcoat up with her to cover her breasts and all the other appropriate places. She didn't even remember being carried. "Please forgive me," she offered, sliding her leg off the length of the couch and down to the floor where it belonged. "I did not intend to arrive in a nightdress *or* in a state of slumber."

Moreland rubbed the length of her back assuredly. "Given the hour and circumstance, Zosia, there is no need for you to apologize." He gestured toward the elderly woman with an ungloved hand. "My grand-mother. Lady Moreland."

The woman set her chin upon introduction and glanced toward him. "Her English is rather impres-sive." She swept a pale, veined hand toward the open double doors to her right. "Leave us, Moreland. No interruptions and no listening. This is between her and me. Respect that."

Moreland leaned toward Zosia and swept up her hand. He gently kissed it, not once, but twice. "Her forked tongue hides an angelic heart, I assure you."

Lady Moreland's gaze lingered on the hand he was still paying homage to, before flicking away. "You will only be gone for twenty minutes, Moreland. Not twenty years. Now, off with you."

Zosia bit back a laugh as he released her hand.

Moreland rose and pointed down rigidly at his grandmother. "Mind yourself." He then heaved out a breath and strode past them, through the vast double doors, disappearing from sight.

When his footsteps had faded into the distance, the woman angled herself toward Zosia and announced in a cool, flat tone, "I have very little to say to a woman I do not know. But what I do have to say, heed. For if anything happens to my grandson whilst he is in your care, I will hold you responsible and ensure that you and everything you hold dear bleeds until dead."

Zosia's smile faded, those words scraping against her very soul. It appeared she had officially stepped into the lair of a very protective lioness. A lioness who reminded her very much of her own mother.

"Moreland is far more fragile than he will ever

let on." The woman stared at her as if intent on penetrating her thoughts. "He had the great misfortune of having a mother who was very loving and very kind but very lost unto herself. A woman who in the last year of her life repeatedly attempted to destroy herself, as she'd fallen into a disturbing form of melancholy. My son refused to lock her away in bedlam where she belonged and took on the responsibility of caring for her himself. Though only fourteen at the time, Moreland supported his father's decision, and without even being asked, became obsessed with securing every room in the house and locking away anything she might use to hurt herself. Needless to say, it warped his young soul into carrying a burden that was never his to carry."

Zosia pinched her lips together and clasped her hands in an effort not to fight the squeezing emotions that demanded release. Even then, Moreland sought only to protect those he loved. Even at the cost of his own sanity.

Lady Moreland sighed. "Despite their efforts, she succeeded in destroying herself all the same. My son, upon discovering her lifeless body, lost the last of his mind. He bolted her bedchamber door, where he'd left her body untouched, dismissed the servants for the day and then sent Moreland to fetch a doctor, claiming his mother wasn't feeling well. In the short time it took for Moreland to fetch a doctor, my son scribed one last letter to Moreland and destroyed himself with a razor." She closed her eyes and shook her head. "What he did to Moreland was unforgivable. I loathed my own son for it. I still loathe him for it. He destroyed that boy."

Lady Moreland reopened her eyes and sighed. "Though I repeatedly asked to see the letter that his father left behind for him, to this day Moreland refuses to share it. I relented many years ago, with the understanding that it was meant to be kept between him and his father. 'Tis a letter he keeps protectively tucked in his razor case and carries with him at all times. My advice is that you never touch that case or that letter. Do not even ask him about it. He will only resent whatever good intentions you may have. If in time he does let you touch his case or if he ever opens it in your presence, it is only because he trusts you not to violate what is his. Do you understand?"

Tears burned Zosia's eyes, blurring the room as she fought the sob clinging within her chest. She finally understood the burden Moreland carried and why he was the way he was. Knowing he had already opened his razor case in her presence, even if it had been only to offer her his handkerchief, meant he trusted her without question. It was a trust she hoped to never violate.

A tear spilled forth, grazing down her cheek. She swiped at it with the tips of quivering fingers and set her chin, trying to remain composed despite feeling anything but.

A sad smile graced Lady Moreland's full lips as she tilted her silvery head slightly. "You appear to be very compassionate. That is good. He needs compassion. That is probably why he is so drawn to you. You seek to understand him, not judge him. Few know how to set aside their own views. Even I have a tendency to judge him, and he is my own grandson." She hesitated, glanced toward the doorway and met her gaze again. "I take it you already know about what goes on with the razor case he carries?"

Zosia nodded. "Yes."

"He will never be cured of it. He will always have the need to carry that razor."

Zosia leaned forward and stared at her. "Do you have so little faith in him, Lady Moreland, to think he is incapable of change? I, for one, firmly believe that if I asked him to, he would set aside his razor for me. I know he would."

Lady Moreland's dark eyes brightened. "You have yet to understand Moreland, child. Ever since he was old enough to toddle about on his own, he never did anything unless *he* wanted to. He is ruthlessly stubborn and passionate to a fault. Much like me. But there is great danger in being overly passionate and stubborn. For when Moreland *does* want something, nothing will keep him from it. Not even reason. Why

do you think you are sitting here? Because *he* wills it.
He is going against his King, his morals and his own
common sense because he wills it. Nothing you or
I say will ever matter. Moreland has to want to stop
carrying his case on his own. And it is not something
he is prepared to do. Obviously. He may never be
prepared to let it go. And that is something you will
have to accept."

"I will not accept anything but the best for him.
And allowing him to carry that case is not best for
him."

Lady Moreland rose from her chair and breezed
toward her, sitting elegantly beside her. Grasping
Zosia's hand with her soft, strong one, she squeezed
it assuredly and leaned toward her. "I have shared
too much of the bad. There is so much more to my
Moreland than the blade." Her mouth curved with
humor. "He is quite the wit. He may never reveal
this to you, for it will offend his male sensibilities,
but he enjoys dabbling with the quill. He wrote the
most poetic commentary on etiquette and courtship
ever to grace the shelves. It was appropriately named
How To Avoid A Scandal."

Zosia's lips parted. The book. The red leather-
bound book Moreland had sent her. The one written by an Unknown Author who in fact had been
known to her all along. Her throat tightened in regret.
She had tossed that book aside without ever once

considering its worth. She had thoughtlessly tossed a piece of Moreland. She never would again.

"Love him unconditionally," Lady Moreland insisted quietly. "That is all I ask."

Zosia's heart squeezed. She nodded and swept up the woman's hand. Bringing it to her lips, she kissed it. "I will. I promise."

"Thank you." Lady Moreland's hand trembled against her own. She nodded. Glancing away, she withdrew her hand and rose, waving her off. "You may leave."

The woman must have forgotten her predicament. Zosia lifted her one leg up off the floor, lifting Moreland's greatcoat along with it. "I fear I will be as dependent upon Moreland as he will be upon me."

Lady Moreland paused, her tight features softening. "I will fetch him for you." She turned away and then hesitated, glancing back at Zosia from over her shoulder. "I sense you and he will be very happy and it is far more than I could have ever hoped for him." She nodded again, then turned and walked out of the room with a smooth, beautiful grace and sashay Zosia couldn't help but admire and long for.

Oh, but to have two legs again! How she did miss it. Moreland would have fallen all over himself had he known her when she still had two legs. She would have waltzed around him at every turn.

She smiled at the thought and glanced down at

her one bare foot set against the cool, marble floor, suddenly wanting and needing to greet Moreland like the young debutante she once had been.

Zosia hesitated, then swept aside Moreland's great-coat and pushed herself up onto her one leg and off the couch. She teetered for a moment, using her arms to balance herself.

Her one leg was very strong. She had ensured it by standing on it quite often throughout the years, to enable her to stand without assistance for long periods of time. She had simply grown lazy these past few months.

Biting her lip, she lifted the hem of her nightdress above her ankle and hopped toward the middle of the room, pausing every now and then to balance herself. Now standing directly before the door, she angled herself strategically toward it, dropping the hem of her nightdress down to her foot.

Quickly unbraiding her hair, she raked it loose and brought it forward over her shoulders, ensuring it framed her face. Setting her chin, she positioned her arms ever so gracefully at her sides and awaited the arrival of the man she now knew she was very much in love with.

SCANDAL TWELVE

'Tis fascinating that something as undesirable as the gritty soil beneath our feet is the only thing that enables a flower to sprout, flourish and bloom. And so it is that a lady must learn from this miracle and never disregard the worth of anything she considers beneath her. For one never knows where an opportunity may bloom. Unfortunately, one must also accept that there will also always be weeds festering in that very same soil. ~~*I suppose that is the way of life. With every glorious bloom, there will always be a damn weed trying to piss on its roots.*~~

—*How To Avoid A Scandal,*
Moreland's Original Manuscript

TRISTAN LEANED AGAINST the wall at the far end of the corridor, tapping his right pocket and rattling his razor case. Though he could hear the exchange of quiet, female voices drifting toward him, he had long given up straining to hear what he knew the conversation was about: him and his cutting.

It was degrading. He felt as if he was being passed on from one set of panicked hands to another. It wasn't as if he did it anymore. He only hoped his grandmother hadn't driven Zosia to feel pity for him now. Because he didn't want Zosia's affections to be reduced to pity. He wanted to be a man in her eyes. Not a pathetic pup.

The clicking of slippers against the marble tile made him glance up and over toward his grandmother. He pushed himself away from the wall and straightened, walking toward her until they finally paused before one another.

After a long moment, he offered coolly, "I take it I will now have to crawl in an effort to redeem myself in her eyes."

His grandmother's dark eyes met his and a tremulous smile overtook her lips. She reached up her aged, pale hands, placing their warmth upon his cheeks, and whispered up at him, "You will never crawl again. Not in her presence. You have done well for yourself, Moreland. Very well indeed."

He stared wordlessly down at her.

Raising herself on her toes, she lowered his head toward her and kissed his forehead gently. "I will inform His Majesty of the match I have made. He will think I and I alone arranged your disappearance. It is the least I can do. May God bless you both. Now I am asking you to leave. Go." She released him and stepped back.

He grabbed her and yanked her back against himself, burying her head against his chest and kissing the top of her soft, white curls. It had been some time since he had held her and acknowledged how much he truly loved her. The fact that she approved of Zosia meant everything to him. More than she would ever know. "I will write the first of every month after we arrive in New York. The moment she is with child, you will be the first to know of it."

She pushed herself out of his arms and stepped back, tears streaming down her cheeks. She choked back a sob. Covering her mouth with a shaky hand, she rounded him and hurried down the corridor.

He jerked toward her direction as she bustled farther away. *"Grandmother!"* he called out, his own voice choked, unable to let her leave without ensuring she would survive on her own. "Assure me I have no cause or need to worry."

She curved toward the wall and paused, leaning a hand against it, but kept her back and the long row of ivory buttons on her gown to him. "I am much stronger than I appear."

He swallowed and stepped toward her. "Come with us. I will carry you beyond that doorstep."

She shook her head. "I have lived my life. It is time you live yours."

"At least look at me," he insisted. "I need assurance you will do well on your own."

She pushed herself away from the wall, stubbornly keeping her rigid, slim back to him. "Do not make our parting any more difficult than it needs to be. I have my books and you have your happiness. That is all I could ever hope for. I look forward to your letters, Moreland. Be sure to send a family portrait once a year, and I expect the first girl to be named after me." Setting her chin, she walked down the corridor and disappeared into her favorite room: the library.

Tristan momentarily closed his eyes, drawing in a steadying breath. She would have no one once he was gone. No one who would understand her, that is. But she was right. It was time for him to live out his life. He had waited long enough to live it. If he hesitated now, everything could unravel.

Reopening his eyes, he turned and strode down the corridor, back toward the sitting room where he knew Zosia was waiting. He dreaded the look of pity he was going to see her in her eyes.

Veering into the sitting room, he jerked to a halt and drew in a savage breath at seeing an incredibly beautiful woman serenely and gracefully standing before him, her nightdress draped to the floor and her long black hair tousled about her slim shoulders. For a moment he actually did not recognize that this was his Zosia *standing* before him.

She smiled playfully, her gray-blue eyes brightening. "I grew a leg while you were gone."

He choked on a laugh, almost believing it, and dared not approach or breathe lest this beautiful vision of her disappear. "By God. You look…stunning. Taller."

She shrugged, her body still poised and elegant, not betraying a single sway or that she was standing on one leg. "I thought it was time I share my little secret. I can stand quite well on my own without any assistance whatsoever. I can even hop about an entire room without growing tired, though it is anything but graceful."

She observed him and confided softly, "I can stand on my own without crutches, Moreland. It is my hope you will one day be able to do the same for yourself. To go through life without a razor in your pocket. I know if I can survive on one leg, you can survive without your blade."

He swallowed, his chest tightening with a burning need to believe that he *could* survive without a blade, knowing she was at his side. Why was it she had far more faith in him than he had in himself? It was humbling.

He slowly approached. Closing the distance between them, he paused and lingered before her, realizing her true height without crutches was in fact at his shoulder. She was much taller than he thought.

Holding her gaze, he allowed his ungloved hand to drift toward her hair. He fingered the long, silken black strands she'd loosened from her braid, following their smooth length down past her shoulder until his knuckles grazed her full, uncorseted breast. He paused and met her gaze.

Cupping her face with both hands, he leaned toward her and gently kissed the warmth of her soft lips. There wasn't even time to appreciate how wondrous this moment was. Here, he had expected pity and coddling, but instead found a bursting pride and strength that fed into his own. He had finally found someone who truly and completely understood him.

He drew his mouth away from hers and dropped his hands, knowing they had to start making their journey to the coast. "We should have you dress more respectably for the journey ahead. Come."

Grabbing her waist, he yanked her up into his arms, ensuring she was comfortable. She wrapped her arms around him as he quickly strode toward the sitting couch where she had left his greatcoat.

He met her gaze and leaned slightly forward, tilting her hand toward the greatcoat. He silently willed her to sweep it up for him. *Show me you understand me without even needing me to say a single word.*

She smiled and snatched up the greatcoat, dragging it onto herself and over his shoulder. "We do not even need to speak anymore to have an understanding of each other. Do we?"

He smiled and murmured, "Bless me enough to never speak again."

SCANDAL THIRTEEN

To love and be loved is everyone's right.
~~*Though I may be wrong, depending on who*~~
~~*"everyone" is.*~~

—*How To Avoid A Scandal,*
Moreland's Original Manuscript

THE VIOLENT JERK OF HIS BODY made Tristan snap wide awake from a dreamless slumber he didn't even remember falling into. As the carriage jerked back and forward again, he tightened his hold on Zosia and dug both of his booted feet against the floor in an effort to keep them from spilling forward. He leaned back against the seat, trying to balance them against the motion.

Muffled shouts from the driver and the footman made him freeze as the carriage jolted again, lurching the entire coach from side to side. It was slowing drastically from the fast pace he had demanded the driver keep. The tugging of the horses reducing their gallop slanted them forward and backward.

"Moreland?" Zosia sat up sleepily against him, swaying within his arms. "What is it?"

"I don't know." Yet something whispered that his time with her was coming to a quick end. Dearest God, why did fate hate him so? Was he that unworthy?

Releasing his hold on Zosia, he slid across the seat, shoved aside the curtains and unlatched the carriage window. "Clayton!" Tristan shouted out into the night toward the driver seated high above. "Why are we slowing?"

"Benson needed an opportunity to better prime our pistols, my lord!" Clayton shouted back. "I'll be returning the horses to a faster pace the moment he's done."

"Why is Benson priming pistols?" he demanded.

"A group of riders have been following us! Since Greenwich. They've kept their distance, for the most part, but appear to be moving in and we thought it best to take precautions."

The carriage jerked steadily forward at a faster speed, sending the misty night wind whistling around him. Tristan leaned farther out the window, searching for the riders, and glanced around the fast-moving landscape, barely illuminated by the moon breaking through the clouds. The violent swinging of the lighted lanterns outside the carriage cast just enough light to extend beyond the gravel road crunching beneath the wheels as they whizzed by.

He froze.

The faceless shadows of two men in large military hats galloped into view several feet behind the carriage. One shouted something to the other in another language.

Russian.

One of the riders pushed his horse forward and closer, his hand jerking up from beneath his cloak. The outline of a pistol hovered, aiming straight at Tristan's own head.

"Shit!" Tristan lunged back into the carriage as a thundering shot rang out amidst the storming clatter of hooves and wheels. He gasped for breath, steadying himself against the door. One horseman he could easily overtake. Benson and his pistols could oversee the others.

Hissing out a breath, Tristan gathered Zosia and yanked her off the seat, setting her gently on the floor of the carriage. "Remain on the floor." He tried to keep his voice calm. "Whatever happens, I want you to remain right where you are."

She scrambled to push herself up. "Tell me what to do. Tell me and I will—"

"No!" he shouted, grabbing hold of her shoulders and shaking her hard, until every muscle in his body felt like fire. "They won't hurt you, Zosia. They are

not here to hurt you. But if you accidentally get in the way of a stray bullet, I cannot very well protect you from it, can I? Now, remain where you are. Promise me you will." He held her intent, shadowed gaze, willing her to submit.

She hesitated, but eventually half nodded.

Although he could see fear etched within her pale face as the carriage bobbed them from side to side, her eyes were steadily fixed on him. It was as if she had no doubt he could protect them and was simply waiting for him to do something.

And do something he would.

He scrambled up and slid back to the open window. He could make out the shadow of a cloaked man galloping steadily closer.

At least he had one reliable weapon.

Tristan yanked out his razor case, flicked open the hinged lid and grabbed the razor out of the box. Snapping it closed, he tossed it onto the seat and unfolded the blade, angling the handle in his right hand. Gripping the looped leather handle hanging from the ceiling of the carriage, he propped himself on the ledge of the open window.

He leaned out as far as he could, the wind trying to push him back against the carriage. Shadows of the night whirled fast around him, but his eyes instantly focused on the closest faceless man.

Lifting his left hand, he drew the steel of the razor

level to the side of his jaw, fighting against the wind that whipped around him and vibrated his entire arm.

He suddenly paused, swaying against the lashing wind. There, just beyond the glow cast by the lanterns and the moonlight that appeared and disappeared behind clouds, a total of six shadowed riders—not two—now visibly trailed the carriage, all of them wearing similar military hats and cloaks.

His eyes widened as he sucked in a ravaged breath. He couldn't fight them all. Not even if he was armed to the teeth. Which he wasn't.

One rider shouted out in a heavy accent above the thrashing and whistling wind, *"By order of the Emperor and Autocrat of All the Russias, halt! Halt or blood will soon pour!"*

His throat burned. This had all warped into something far beyond his control. He wasn't about to put Zosia, his driver and his footman at risk. Even if it cost him everything. Which he knew it would.

He released his blade, letting it clatter against the side of the carriage and disappear beneath the fast-spinning wheels, and shouted up at the driver, *"Stop the coach! Now!"*

"My lord?" the footman shouted. "Is it wise that we—"

"Stop the goddamn coach!" he roared against the thundering noise around him. "Benson, put away

your pistols and don't *ever* question my authority again!"

"Yes, my lord!"

His body weakening, Tristan leaned in through the window and slid back inside the carriage. He stumbled as the carriage kept jerking against progressive sharp halts. He yanked the carriage window shut and sagged onto the floor beside Zosia.

Dragging in deep, ragged breaths, he looked over at her, knowing nothing would ever be the same. It was over before it had even begun. Before he ever had the chance to know what it would be like to truly be loved by her.

He met her solemn gaze within the jumping shadows the small lantern made above their heads and wondered if she would ever forgive him.

Christ. This was all a nightmare. "We have to stop. They are not here to harm you. If I cooperate, they may spare my life."

Zosia scooted close to him, burying her dark head and soft shoulder against his chest.

"Hold me," she whispered softly, her hands fisting his coat. "Please hold me."

"Shh. All will be well. I promise."

"Why are we being chased? What do they want?"

"Forgive me, Zosia. Forgive me for putting you through this. I should have never..." Shifting against her on the floor, he wrapped his arms tightly around her and pulled her close to him, setting his chin on her soft hair. It didn't matter what happened to him. It was time to stop being so viciously selfish and let her go. It was time to give her the dream she had always wanted. A dream that included her hero and the opportunity to be a much bigger voice for her nation. Dreams that had never included him.

The carriage slowed, tugging and pulling until it soon clattered to an abrupt halt, rocking them from side to side. An eerie silence now pulsed around them, interrupted by the approaching thudding hooves and shouts of men in the distance. Shouts in a flurry of Russian.

Her soft warmth dug into his. "Russian?"

He swallowed. "Do you understand what they're saying?"

She shook her head against him. "No. I never learned Russian. My mother thought it unpatriotic."

If the situation weren't so dire, he would have actually laughed. Her mother had been one determined devil of a woman to have placed *this* many divides between Zosia and Russia. It was time to bury those intentions by honoring Zosia in the only manner he knew how. "Zosia, your mother *was* Russian. She was Russian royalty, in fact. Which is what you are."

She stilled in his arms. "What?"

He tightened his hold on her, trying to pour whatever strength he had within his own body into hers.

"Empress Catherine—*your grandmother*—shared a liaison with your grandfather, Poniatowski. It resulted in the birth of your mother. That is the only true connection you share with the Polish crown. The Empress sought to bury her association with him by staging your mother's death and giving her a new identity in Warsaw. Though the Empress eventually sought to reinstate your mother to the Russian Court, she died before she could. Before her death, however, she issued a letter to your mother that was delivered to her by a young Russian, who fell in love with her, but did not disclose who he was until after your birth."

"My father?" she rasped against him.

"Yes. Your father. The former Emperor of Russia, Alexander the First. Upon discovering his identity, your mother denied him of you and refused any association with Russia, turning to the Poniatowski family. To the end, your mother, as well as your cousin, sought to keep you out of the Russian Court. That is why the Russians are here, Zosia. They want to take you home. They seek to make you Grand Duchess."

"My father…he was…he was…the Emperor?" She choked and shook her head against him. *"Nie. Boże, nie rozumie jak moja własna matka—"*

"Dearest," he whispered, fighting the burn in his

own throat. He didn't need to understand her words to understand her anguish. "I am so sorry. I—"

"What am I to do now?" her voice pitched in panic. She choked back a sob. "If they seek to make me Grand Duchess, they will expect me to support Russia. And I...I cannot. I cannot! Not after what I have seen done to innocent people under their power. What am I to do, Moreland? *What am I to do?*"

"Shhh. Listen and listen well. His Majesty insisted that this duplicity would dismantle you, but he doesn't know you the way I do. You are *meant* for a role like this and will guide the Russian Court in better understanding your people. A true leader, which I know you are, understands both sides and seeks to bring them together as one. Regardless of who your father was, you were raised a Pole and will do right by those who raised you, without turning against your heritage. This is your dream, Zosia. Embrace it as one."

"Embrace being Russian? But Moreland, I—"

The carriage door banged open, making them both tilt toward its direction.

A tall, well-muscled gentleman garbed in black military ensemble, with golden-tasseled epaulets and rows of medals pinned on his upper left chest, stepped forward and pointed the muzzle of a large pistol into the carriage. At Tristan's head.

It was none other than her damn gallant. How

fitting. The man had said that the next time they met Tristan would find himself at the end of the man's pistol.

"Do not hurt him!" Zosia cried, her warm hands jumping up to Tristan's own face, as she used her own body to try to shield him.

A glowing pride filled Tristan as he yanked her down and away from the pistol. "Zosia. Please. Don't."

The man's sharp features softened. *"Velikaya Knyazha."* His shadowed gaze drifted appreciatively down her gown before drifting back up to her face.

Tristan's throat tightened as he jerked Zosia down against himself, trying to shield her from far more than just the man's pistol. "Lower your pistol, sir, lest you misfire with all that damn amorous intent."

"Moreland. Is this not the same man who…" Zosia pushed at his arms and leaned far forward, ignoring Tristan's attempt to shield her from the pistol. "Why, I know you," she whispered at the man, her voice soft and full of wonder. "Heavens above, 'tis you. *You.* I barely recognized you. Your hair is so much longer and you shaved your mustache."

Tristan's breath hitched as his hands slipped down to Zosia's waist. He swept the length of the interloper's large, muscled frame boasting a well-fitted military uniform. He supposed it was something a woman would appreciate.

The officer lowered his pistol and grinned, a visible dimple—the man had to have a dimple—indenting his shaven right cheek. He shrugged as his other hand adjusted the red ribbon holding his dark mane at the base of his high collar. Russian words flew rapidly from his lips, his commanding voice dipping and rising, conveying God knew what.

Zosia glanced up at Tristan, her cheeks flushing to a deep crimson that was noticeable despite the shadows and dim lantern lighting the carriage. "He seems to think I speak Russian."

Why was she blushing? She never blushed like that around him. Why was she—

The Russian leaned in, his dark, arched brows coming together. "Do you not also speak…?"

Tristan tightened his hold on her. "No. She does not speak Russian."

The man leaned back, glancing toward the small group of soldiers who had gathered behind him, and cleared his throat. He shifted back toward them, as if debating which language he should be using.

"English," Zosia insisted. "So that we might all understand."

The man leveled an intimate gaze at Zosia, a smile flitting across his lips. "English it is, Grand Duchess. 'Tis an honor to behold you in such health, and to be remembered, given the number of years it has been. Allow me to formally introduce myself. I am Count

Maksim Nikolaevich, and by royal decree, as was ordained by your father, I am here to return you to Saint Petersburg and reinstate you as Grand Duchess by making you my wife."

She gasped. *"Your wife?"*

Tristan cringed. This just kept getting worse.

Maksim grinned, genuine pride warming that heavy accent. "I have waited years for the honor. *Years.*"

The dimple-toting Russian popinjay had only met her once! "'Tis a strong sentiment to hold for a woman you don't even know."

Maksim set his knee-high black-leather boot on the unfolded steps of the carriage. "You have no right to mock me after all that you have done." Maksim stared him down. "We will take this matter before your King and allow the Grand Duchess to decide how this will end."

Tristan clenched his jaw tighter and dug his fingers into Zosia's softness. How was he ever going to let her go? He couldn't. He wouldn't.

"So I am not expected to go?" Zosia asked softly. "I am not expected to become your wife? Or Grand Duchess?"

Maksim leaned toward her and lowered his voice as if wanting to keep Tristan out of their conversation. "Though I have the right to seize you and hold you to what has been decreed, I am a gentleman and will submit to whatever decision you make." He hesitated. "Might we speak in Polish? I prefer it over English."

Zosia let out an impish laugh against Tristan's shoulder, nudging herself into it. "He wishes to speak in Polish. How charming."

Tristan refrained from punching the man in the face, knowing Zosia was tripping over her own blushes. Even worse, he knew how this was going to end if it went before His Majesty. His Majesty held no patience for those who went against his name. Tristan would be fortunate if he wasn't stripped of everything he had, including his title. It was a mess. One that he and he alone had created, and one he doubted Zosia would ever forgive him for once she knew the truth.

Tristan lifted her off the floor, rising with her, and set her on the upholstered seat, removing himself completely from her arms. He couldn't hold her anymore. Not knowing—

"Moreland." Her hands grabbed hold of his arms once again, ferociously holding on to them and yanking him back toward her.

He stared down at her, trying to conceal the torment of wondering if this would be the last night he'd ever see her. "We ride to Windsor. You have a decision to make."

She shook his arms. "There is no decision to be

made in this. Count Nikolaevich may be ordained to be my fiancé, but I could never..." She shook her head. "No. I am not prepared to play a role of this magnitude, Moreland. I do not speak the language, I know nothing of the customs or the people or what will be expected of me." She feigned a laugh. "Can you imagine me and my one leg hobbling into the Russian Court and commanding the Emperor to free all of Poland or die? The very notion is laughable. Nothing would ever come of it."

It wasn't laughable at all, and he sensed she was only saying that it was because of whatever attachment she might have formed to him. Somehow, and he knew not how, he had allowed his passion to not only destroy the last of his own values, but hers, as well. Because the Zosia he had come to passionately know and love would have never turned away an incredible opportunity like this. Not when it came to helping her people.

He was going to lose her. He was going to forever lose her to a politically important marriage, that he knew, but if didn't let her go, if he didn't let her do this, he would hate himself for the rest of his life. Because this was so much bigger than him and his stupid happiness. A nation's fate was at stake. Christ, he *had* to let her go.

Swallowing against the tightness of his throat, he

glanced toward the Count, who was intently watching them. "Allow me to speak to her alone, sir."

Maksim angled a tasseled shoulder toward him and leveled his pistol at Tristan's chest. "Speak to her at the point of my pistol or not at all. You have taken enough liberties with her good name. She will be returned to His Majesty at once."

"I only wish to speak to her." Tristan tried to remain calm.

Maksim kept the pistol pointed at Tristan. "Then speak."

Knowing he had no choice, Tristan turned to Zosia. He leaned toward her and cupped the sides of her soft face with both of his hands. Her face was still moist and streaked from earlier tears, which reflected his own agony. "Zosia," he whispered. "This is an opportunity you cannot turn away. Not for me, not for anyone. Leading others is not only your duty, but your birthright. It is in your blood, in your words, in your mind. It is who you are and what you will always be. Imagine what you could do for Poland if you became part of the Russian Court. *Imagine*. No battle is ever won without a fight from within. You must go. You must do this."

She hesitated, crinkling her brows. "I suppose I could try to guide and influence the Emperor, but—" Her gray-blue eyes lifted and searched his face, her grip tightening on his arms. "What about us, Moreland?"

He vowed not to break beneath those words and that sentiment. Now was not the time to break. He needed to love her in a way no one else had. In a way not even her own mother had. It was time to let her go and allow her to pursue not only who she really was, but the dream he had never been a part of to begin with.

He met her gaze and held it intently, willing her to understand that her happiness was all that mattered to him. "There is no us, Zosia. There never was. You were always meant for far greater things than I. I knew that from the moment we met."

Her eyes widened. "You mean to let me go? Completely?"

"Yes. There is no other way. You must marry Count Nikolaevich."

She gasped. "After everything we have shared?"

"Zosia, please. Do not—"

"What if I told you that I love you, Moreland? Would that change anything? Would that change how you feel about this or me? Because I love you. I do. And you love me. You do love me, do you not?"

His jaw tightened as he fought against claiming those lips and thanking her for honoring him with the words he longed to hear. He traced his thumbs against the smooth, soft contours of her face, hoping to sear this moment in his mind always. A moment in which she believed she was in love with him even after everything he had done. Of course, she had yet to understand what he had done. "Your hero whom you have loved long before me is no longer nameless and stands here beside us. As was ordained by your father, *he* is your rightful husband. Not I. I knew who he was, Zosia. I knew it all along."

She searched his face. "Whatever do you mean?"

He swallowed and focused on the words he knew he needed to say. "It was my plan to never tell you about Count Nikolaevich or the opportunity Russia was giving you as Grand Duchess."

Her fingers dug into his arms. "What? Why?"

"Because my happiness meant more to me than yours." Tristan squeezed her face hard with his palms, willing her to feel the twisting pain he was feeling inside. He needed to ensure she took the right path. The only path that was left to take. And it was up to him to lead her in this. "You asked me if I loved you, Zosia, and I must answer in earnest. No. I never loved you." *I never loved you enough...*

Her eyes widened as she drew in a sharp breath. Her hands slipped away from his arms. "Did I mean nothing to you? At all?"

He couldn't breathe. Though he tried. "You and I are done. There is nothing more to say. Accept it. I have."

She choked. "Why are you saying this? Why are you doing this?"

Because I will never *put myself before you again. Never. And as much as it rips my soul apart, I cannot have you abandoning everything you are for a man who does not deserve you.*

"In time, Zosia, you will forget. As you should." Tristan released her, feeling as if one massive weight had been lifted only to be replaced by another, much heavier one. "I will ensure you are returned to His Majesty so this can be resolved appropriately." He quickly turned away from her before his resolve fissured.

Maksim had long lowered his pistol and taken several steps back and away from the door of the carriage. The man had no doubt been expecting more resistance.

What Maksim didn't realize was that Zosia's aspirations and happiness meant far more to Tristan than his own. Stepping toward the ledge of the carriage, Tristan jumped down, his riding boots thudding against the gravel. He squared his shoulders and met Maksim's gaze.

Prominent green eyes dimly displayed by the surrounding lanterns and the flitting moonlight above continued to warily observe him. Everything about the man was annoyingly perfect. His stance, his attire, his noble, sharp features, the color of his eyes, his square shaven jaw. He even had a dimple. It was as if he'd stepped forth from a painting on the wall of a gallery.

Fisting his hands, Tristan strode toward him, wanting to swing at his skull out of rage and jealousy but unable to do so out of pride and respect for Zosia. "Honor her at every turn or, by God, I will kill you."

"Fine words coming from a man who has no respect for his own King and has no doubt defiled what is rightfully mine." The man's pistol jumped up, pointing at his head. "You blackguard! On your knees. *Now!*"

"Maksim!" Zosia's commanding voice echoed around them. "Makim, *nie. Przestań!*"

A thud against the gravel behind him made Tristan snap around. His pulse thundered as he realized Zosia had fallen from the carriage, her traveling gown scattered around her sprawled body. She gasped, trying to push herself up, her lone shapely, stockinged leg exposed to the knee as Russian soldiers hurried to her side.

"Zosia!" Tristan sprinted toward her. He slid to her side, shoving men away from her, and stumbled onto the gravel. Hoisting her up off the ground and into his arms, he quickly covered her exposed limb from the eyes of those around them, smoothing her dress against her leg. His hands trembled

as he cradled her in his lap and rocked her against himself.

She shoved him and hit his shoulder with his own razor case, which she clutched in her hand. "Though I cannot walk when it matters most, I still have my pride!" she shouted. "I have my pride, damn you, and I will not allow you to take away the last of it. Release me. *Release me!*"

He swallowed and grabbed her wrist, yanking the brass case out of her hand. He didn't want her touching his own shame in their last moment together. Shoving it into his pocket, he seized her again and held her even tighter against himself. "I am so sorry," he whispered. "I am so sorry I violated you and your trust. Forgive me. You and I simply were not meant to be."

She let out a choked sob, still punching at his arms.

He wanted to die knowing he was breaking her and making her cry in an effort to ensure her happiness. It seemed so wrong.

Maksim kneeled beside them. "Release her!" He forcefully pried Tristan's hands and arms from Zosia, dragging her over and gathering her into his own.

Tristan didn't resist or stand. His body was too numb to do either.

Maksim tucked Zosia protectively against himself as if she had always belonged there. He rose with her, as she continued to sob, and towered above Tristan. He stared down at him beneath the large rim of his feathered hat. "Why is she like this?" he demanded. "Have you defiled her? Is that it? You defiled her!"

He was *not* about to let him smear the last of Zosia's name in front of a group of soldiers. Her good name was going to be her greatest weapon in the Russian Court. "Mind your bloody tongue and her honor. I never touched her. Not once." His voice was cold and to the point.

"You lie. And I will defend her honor in the only manner I know how." Maksim stepped back, readjusting Zosia in his arms, and shouted a curt command in Russian.

Death was a universal language. Tristan knew he was a dead man.

The crunching of gravel beneath boots thudded closer. Two large cavalry men swept out their swords from their sides, the clang of metal sweeping through the night air.

He closed his eyes and waited, one knee still on the ground. How ironic that a blade was going to end it all.

"Maksim!" Zosia choked out. "You would be a savage to do this. This is not how a man defends a woman's honor. Leave him be. Leave him be and take me to His Majesty at once. It is my duty to set him

aside and oversee my father's wish and the rights of my people. Now, please…leave him be."

There was a moment of silence.

"As you wish." Maksim issued another command and, except for the horses shifting their hooves and huffing through their nostrils, nothing more happened.

Tristan reopened his eyes and snapped his gaze toward Zosia, who had wrapped her arms around the broad shoulders of her Russian. Though Tristan tried to hold her gaze to silently thank her for her mercy, she averted her tear-ridden face, burying it against Maksim. Her shoulders sagged. It was as if she were no longer that strong born-leader he knew and loved, but a rag doll unable to even hold up its own head.

"Leave," Maksim announced.

Tristan slowly got to his feet, a pulsing knot rising from his stomach to his chest. Zosia was not happy. His Zosia was not happy despite the fact that he had let her go without resistance and she now had everything she had ever wanted, including her hero.

Which meant…

She loved him. She really did.

His jaw tightened so hard his teeth ached. He couldn't leave her to suffer like this. He couldn't walk away and leave her to think he had never cared or loved her in turn. It would be violating her trust all over again and that he swore he would never do.

Tristan drew in a steadying breath and stepped forward. "I need to approach the Grand Duchess."

"Leave," Maksim warned as he stepped back, bringing Zosia up higher against his chest. "I will not spare your life twice."

The cavalry surrounding him inched in, as if sensing something was about to detonate.

Tristan narrowed his gaze. "I will not leave unless *she* wishes it. Grand Duchess. Might I approach and amend my earlier words? That is all I ask. Allow me to amend my words." *Zosia. Show me you will not turn me away in senseless anger, but that you will fight for me, and in turn, I vow to make you proud.*

She jerked her head back toward Tristan, her tear-streaked, shadowed face softening under the moonlight. "Let Moreland approach."

Tristan sucked in a breath and fought from growling, *God, do I love you. How I love you for always extending more faith in me than I have ever had in myself.*

Maksim glared down at her. "He seeks to sway you."

"No man sways me. I sway myself."

Maksim huffed out a breath and grudgingly toted Zosia toward him. Maksim paused within an arm's length of where Tristan stood and coolly stared him down.

Odd though it was, Tristan couldn't help but

respect this Russian. After all, he was proving to be a far greater gentleman toward Zosia than he himself had ever been.

"Moreland?" Zosia expectantly met his gaze. "What is it? What do you wish to say? Now is the time before our paths divert and nothing can be changed."

Mere words were going to be meaningless. He needed far more than words to prove to her what he felt. Which is why he was going to openly offer her that one piece of his heart he'd kept hidden from everyone, including his own grandmother, for thirteen years.

He dug into his coat pocket, his fingers pressing against the razor case, and pulled it out. Opening it, he dug out the aged, folded parchment and tossed aside the empty case. He swallowed and held out the page, hoping to God she knew what it was. Hoping to God his grandmother had told her about it during her little pity fest so he wouldn't have to explain things. Because he didn't have the strength to explain.

Zosia's eyes widened. "Why are you giving that to me?"

Though he had never once spoken of it or removed the folded parchment from his razor case in her presence, it was obvious by the dread in her face she knew exactly what it was. His grandmother *had* told her. And he, for one, was thankful she had, for he was able to silently convey how important this moment was for him—for them—without shattering the last of his resolve.

He stepped closer, still holding it out. "I hope one day you will be able to forgive me for all that I have said and done. By giving you this, I vow to become a better man in your honor. You must understand that I could never agree to you giving up an opportunity to help your own people. Not when so much is at stake. It has nothing to do with what we share and what I feel for you. Do you understand?"

Her eyes jumped to his and searched his face. She hesitated, reached out and slipped the faded parchment from his fingers. Edging it back toward herself, she pressed it against her chest with both hands and leaned back against Maksim, who was already stepping back. "What will become of us?" she whispered, clearly wanting to understand what he was saying.

He leveled her with a firm gaze and offered, in a soft tone that he hoped conveyed all the love he held for her, "Perhaps our paths will cross again when I am more deserving." He bowed and stepped back, trying to control the trembling in his body.

Tristan gestured toward the carriage, his hand quaking visibly. "Take my carriage, sir," he announced to Maksim. "Her condition will not allow her to ride upon a horse." He turned and yelled over to Benson and Clayton, "Escort her to Windsor and ensure her safe arrival! Is that understood?"

Benson and Clayton, who solemnly stood in the driving box, offered compliant nods.

Tristan swiveled back toward Maksim. "I will ride on any horse you generously offer, though I have no qualms about walking, either. After all, my life was spared and for that I am grateful." *Although I do need a damn horse. Give me a horse, man.*

Maksim eyed him, blew out a breath and offered matter-of-factly, "Allow me." He issued a few curt words over his shoulder to the surrounding men.

A saddled stallion was brought over.

Tristan silently offered an appreciative nod toward Maksim, ensuring his gaze didn't meet Zosia's. Or he'd never leave. He yanked himself up and swung his leg over and onto the horse, shoving his booted feet into both stirrups. Tightening his hold on the reins, he veered the horse away from the carriage and toward the direction of what he knew was Windsor.

He dug his heels into the sides of the horse and galloped into the night, which was beginning to fade and give way to the soft pinkish-blue hue of day that illuminated the long road ahead. The cool wind whipped at him, flapping and lifting and pushing his coat all around him. As dirt kicked up from the hooves of the horse, stinging his eyes, he welcomed the discomfort and pushed the beast faster and harder, praying he got to Windsor long before Zosia and Maksim.

SCANDAL FOURTEEN

A lady ought to wait a respectable amount of time before announcing her engagement to society. This will prevent any breach of prom-ise that may occur and whatever vile compli-cations come with it. There is no guarantee that a breach of promise will not occur, but it will eliminate those offers that were not of any worth to begin with. ~~Sadly, we men can be such stupid creatures, holding no regard as to what we say or do in the name of riled emotions that even we do not understand. I will admit, however, that there are times that stupidity can lead to happiness.~~

—How To Avoid A Scandal,
Moreland's Original Manuscript

Late morning, on the outskirts of Windsor Castle

"*Velikaya Knyazha.*"

Zosia opened her eyes and blinked, realizing she was still tucked against the upholstered seat of

Moreland's carriage. Only it wasn't Moreland sitting across from her. It was Maksim.

She swallowed and glanced down at the yellowing, folded parchment still pressed between her fingers. She hadn't been able to bring herself to open it. Eerily, she felt that if she opened it, Tristan would cease to exist. That *they* would cease to exist.

Maksim slid his dark, wide, feathered hat onto his lap. He cleared his throat, squaring his broad shoulders against the seat. "We arrive soon."

She tried not to dwell on how terrified she was, anticipating stepping into the Russian Court without knowing the language or the faces or the politics or the expectations or the customs. How was she to fight for her people's cause when she couldn't even do it in their own language? She had always wanted to be a voice, that she knew, but with each step she took that brought her closer and closer to her dream, she was beginning to realize that becoming a voice for a nation meant giving up one's *own* voice and, in turn, sacrificing everything. Including one's own heart.

Maksim lowered his gaze, his gloved fingers rounding the rim of his hat. "You will find the Emperor to be most welcoming. He is your uncle. He believes you will create a symbolic union between Poland and Russia. One that Russia needs. He will listen to your views and apply them as he sees fit, but expects you to convert and become part of our

Greek church. By becoming part of our church, we will then be allowed to marry."

It appeared that majestic manipulation—better known as male politics—had already commenced without her having even stepped into Russia. She knew that by submitting to being Grand Duchess she would never be anything more than a symbol to be emblazoned upon whatever flag the Emperor wanted to hold up. But if the Emperor thought he would ever be able to control her or her thoughts or her religion, he didn't know anything about Polish women. Which she still was, despite the Russian blood she now knew warmed her veins.

Her fingers tightened on the parchment Moreland had given her. She drew strength from it. "I have no objection to any church outside of my own, but I do object when others think my church is worth less than theirs. I was born a Catholic and will die a Catholic, like my mother before me. And though I may become Grand Duchess, I will not become anyone's pawn. Which is why, despite the decree, you and I will not wed."

He glanced up, his green eyes sharpening. "You have a duty to Russia and to me."

She slowly shook her head. "No. I have a duty to Poland and its people first. Russia comes second, though only out of respect for the father I never knew.

And as for you, Maksim, though I do owe you my life, regrettably, there is no place for you at all."

He rose, swaying against the movement of the carriage, and settled beside her. Leaning toward her, he gently pushed her braided hair over her shoulder. "I have not forgotten that day. I have not forgotten what we shared. It haunts me. *You* still haunt me."

She glanced toward him and swallowed, leaning away. "You lost whatever claim you might have had, Maksim, when you abandoned me and left me to never even know your name."

"Do you not remember anything?" he insisted. "Do you not remember when I…" He searched her face.

She shook her head, wishing he would stop. She didn't want him digging into her head or the past. Not when her heart belonged to Moreland. "I only remember you being kind. That is all I remember."

"I did not abandon you willingly." He leaned closer, his hand curving down her shoulder, his fingers grazing the sleeve of her gown in a lingering manner. "I inquired many, many times, but your mother demanded I cease. And so I did. Out of respect for the love a mother has for her child. She knew what was best for you. Not I." He reached into her lap and grasped her hand. The one holding Moreland's parchment.

Zosia's heart pounded as she tried to yank her

hand away, feeling he was violating whatever was left of her and Moreland.

He tightened his hold and threaded his fingers between hers, crinkling the parchment between their hands. "As I was leaving for my military duties abroad, several months later, the Emperor requested to see me and hailed me for my heroism in assisting you. He apparently followed all the events of your life as well as your mother's through various informants. I learned everything I wanted to know about you from your father, including who you were and how, despite my efforts, your limb had been amputated. He boasted of your strength in having survived what usually killed his own soldiers, and went on to insist you had formed an attachment to me—a Russian— and that you had forced your own mother to post monetary awards throughout Warszawa to find me. I was touched, as was the Emperor. He thought we would be a good match. I agreed." He squeezed her hand, crinkling the paper even more.

Zosia yanked her hand out of his. "Please do not impose yourself upon me like this. That part of my life no longer exists. I still hope to wed Lord Moreland and ask that you respect that." She tucked Moreland's letter into her bosom and scooted toward the other side of the carriage, even though there was nowhere to go.

He was quiet for a moment. "Your title of Grand

Duchess will only be extended to you through our union. It was ordained by your father that if by your twenty-third birthday you had remained unwed due to the tragic circumstance of your amputation, you would be married to me and brought back into the Russian Court."

Zosia jerked toward him, her throat tightening. Oh, God. Now she understood why Karol had made use of that old private agreement her grandfather had made with England offering protection during any revolt. Karol's fear had been far greater than that of revolt when she had arrived in London barely before her twenty-third birthday. Karol had feared she would become part of the Russian Court.

Much like her mother, her cousin's patriotism had caused him to overreact. "I must marry you if I am to be reinstated as Grand Duchess?"

"Yes."

"And did Karol know about this decree?"

"Yes. Several months prior, he was contacted and informed of the upcoming decree and its expectations. He agreed to submit, as was expected of him, and gave us an appointed time and place for you to be passed into the Emperor's hands. A spy informed the Emperor that you had been removed from the country and placed into England's hands. The Emperor was anything but pleased."

She swallowed. "Karol has not been harmed or reprimanded in any way for his intervention, has he?"

"No. Out of respect for you, I requested that the Emperor offer your cousin leniency."

She drew in a shaky breath. "I thank you."

He hesitated and added in a low tone, "Thank me by allowing me to reinstate you to what is rightfully yours."

A pounding fear crept into her heart, paralyzing her as the carriage pulled in beneath the arching stone portico of Windsor. If she became Grand Duchess, she would have to marry Maksim and give up Moreland forever. And she was not ready to give him up. Not yet. It was time to take on her *own* voice. One she refused to silence.

She gathered her locket with trembling hands, a locket that had not been removed from around her throat since it had left her mother's four years earlier, and slipped it up and off. She kissed it, turned to Maksim and draped it over his head. She lovingly adjusted it around his neck. "My father, your former Emperor, gave this to my mother. I am now giving it to you, Maksim. By doing so, I announce that we are friends and only friends, and with it, I end whatever duty my father sought for me to uphold. I will do right by Poland in another way."

The carriage door opened. Royal footmen

unfolded the steps, formally announcing their arrival at Windsor.

Maksim's gloved hand fisted the locket, the leather around his knuckles creaking softly in protest. He hesitated before finally saying in Polish, "You will give up your heritage, your honor, your right and your duty for a man who did not respect you enough to tell you the truth?"

She nodded. Staring out before her, she replied in English, "Moreland is still learning how to love himself. He is bound to make mistakes. And for that, I cannot fault him."

Maksim leaned in very close, causing the hilt of his dagger attached at the sash of his uniform to graze against her thigh. "Come with me to Saint Petersburg. Meet your people. Meet your Emperor." His warm lips traced her cheek. "Offer me the same chance you offered him, *Velikaya Knyazha*. Do I not deserve it?"

"Cease," she choked out, leaning away. "Cease this. Cease touching me."

He leaned closer. "No. I will not. Not until—"

She shoved his solid body away from her. Grasping the thick silver hilt at his side, she yanked the heavy blade out of its scabbard and pointed the tip of its steel blade toward his chest. "*Never* touch me or think you can sway me, or I will carve off whatever makes you a man and serve it to your own horse after I grind it into a barrel of oats."

Maksim let out a gruff laugh and held up both hands, rising to his booted feet and away from the blade. "I genuinely fear for myself and all of Russia."

"As well you should."

SITTING IN THE SILENCE OF the oversized gray, red and gold receiving room, whose sweeping walls were covered with gilded paintings of former royalty, Zosia fingered Moreland's parchment.

She had waited long enough. She needed to read it.

Shakily, she unfolded the yellowing, frayed paper, dreading the words she was about to read. She blinked and stared at what she had unfolded. Aside from faded ink unevenly spattering the parchment, there was not a single word written upon it.

She turned it over and then back again, confused. As she stared at the splatter of ink, trying to understand, her eyes widened and her breath caught.

It wasn't ink.

It was dried blood.

Blood from thirteen years past.

Her fingers slid to the edges of the parchment. There had never been a letter. He had been cruelly left to never know why. "Oh, Moreland," she whispered brokenly, tears blinding her as she tightened her hold on the edges of the parchment. "I am so sorry. You deserved more."

She sniffed, carefully refolding the paper so she didn't have to look at it. She swiped away the tears with the back of her hand. She couldn't abandon him. Not after he had entrusted her with his greatest secret. He deserved an opportunity to redeem himself.

"Damn my cousin for all eternity!" a booming male voice echoed in the huge room, making her jump. "This is all her doing, you realize. That is all women are ever good for. Gossip."

Zosia tucked Morcland's parchment into her bosom, and glanced up as His Majesty's stocky frame stalked across the room toward her. Patting her face dry with her hands, she slowly rose from her gilded chair. She regally balanced on her one leg, arranging her traveling skirts about herself, and offered the King a deep bow of her head. "Your Majesty. Please forgive the intrusion and the hour."

"Sit, sit." He waved her back into the chair, the rubies and emeralds on his gold rings glinting against thick, white fingers. "I have had more intrusions this morning than I have had in my entire years as King. Damn annoying is what it is."

She sat, wobbling for a moment, and took a deeply needed breath. She was thankful Maksim had been forced to wait in the adjoining room.

His Majesty swiped at wizened gray hair, shoving it away from his prominent brow, and then dragged a chair closer to hers, wafting the subtle scent of almond powder toward her. With a hefty breath, he sat, adjusting his long morning robe. Smoothing the lace neck cloth against his throat, he eyed her. "Be forewarned. The Russians will use leeches the size of my scepter to bleed out whatever love you think you have for your country."

She smiled. "You will be pleased to know that I am relinquishing my right and claim to the title of Grand Duchess."

His gray, bushy brows rose. "Relinquishing, you say? Rubbish. Whatever for? I thought you would dash at it."

She drew in a shaky breath and let it out, setting the tips of her fingers against Moreland's parchment hidden within her stay. "Since coming to England, Your Majesty, I have learned something invaluable from a remarkable man who has yet to recognize how remarkable he truly is. I have learned that I must fight one battle at a time, not a dozen. For the more battles I dedicate myself to, the less effective I will be. Which is why I must learn to conquer what matters first and foremost first: my heart. I come to thank you for the protection you have so gener-ously bestowed upon me, and humbly ask to remain in England so that Moreland and I may wed. I intend to convert to the Protestant church."

He pulled in his chin and gawked at her for a long moment. "You jest."

She laughed. "No. I know my God will forgive me, for I submit to love."

The King chortled and shifted in his chair, smacking a hand against his thigh. "In my opinion, you may be better off drinking arsenic, my dear, than becoming a Protestant and marrying that boy. A scandalmonger is what he is. A damn scandalmonger. To have reduced you to this!"

"I confess I have always been fond of scandalmongers."

"Is that so? I happen to be an even greater scandalmonger than he. So why the devil do you continue to deny me? Eh? Too old? Or is it—" he slapped his protruding belly "—*this?* The belly isn't quite as large as what lies beneath it."

She pinched her lips together, her cheeks unexpectedly burning like fire. She lowered her gaze, unwilling to entertain the man with so much as a reprimand, for she knew it would only rile him and his naughty nature.

His Majesty chuckled and leaned forward, his full face brightening. "I take great pride in knowing that I can still make a woman blush." He cleared his throat and searched her face. "Let us be done with this.

Seeing you are renouncing your title in the hopes of wedding Moreland, we regret to inform you of a quandary. A quandary involving Moreland."

She glanced up, her heart pounding. "What is it?"

"He swept through here not even an hour ago, personally informing me of all that has come to pass." He heaved out a breath, shook his head and leaned back against the chair. "I was so outraged. I almost seized everything associated to his name. I would have done it, too, but I know my cousin would have never forgiven me for it, and in truth, Camille means far more to me than that boy ever will."

Zosia shifted forward in the chair, her pulse heightening. "Is Moreland still here? Might I see him?"

"No. The man has already left for London."

Her heart sank. "With your permission, Your Majesty, I request an opportunity to make my way to London and see him."

"I am afraid, my dear, he has requested there be no further contact between you and him. And I, for one, think it very wise. Let the passion settle."

She gasped, snapping her spine straight. "He does not want to see me? Not ever again?"

"Oh, he does. He most certainly does. The boy is merely being honorable and leaving it up to you as to whether you wish to see *him* again."

A breath rushed out of her. "Oh. Well. Of course I want to see him. He and I have quite a bit to discuss."

"If that sentiment upholds, you will be allowed to see him in a year. Though not sooner."

Her eyes widened. "What?"

"He is asking for a year on his own and will not have it any other way." He rubbed at his round, shaven chin with thick fingers. "Aside from wanting to campaign extensively in England and Europe over the next year, he intends to also sail to New York, Boston, Washington, Philadelphia and heaven knows where else as a means of garnering support for Poles. He told me to assure you of his devotion, but that you need time to pursue what is most important to you and he needs time to develop his self-worth. Whatever the devil that means. So as not to send you into a complete panic, if after a whole year you still wish to pursue him and matrimony, Moreland wishes it and will ensure it. Though not prior to a year. He hopes you will understand."

Zosia pinched her lips together, tears trembling against her eyelids. She pressed a hand against the parchment hidden within her bosom. Moreland was doing this for her. For himself. For them. All while going out into the world and supporting *her* dream. She had never felt so honored. She would willingly wait ten whole years for his return, if he wished it. "Will I at least be able to write to him?"

"No. If there is any news of importance you believe he must be privy to, you are to relate it to me, and I, in turn, will relate it to him. He is of the mind that you deserve complete freedom apart from him, which continued communication would only warp."

Moreland was trying to prove his worth and she couldn't help but be in awe of him. And though it would be a nauseating form of despair to live a whole year without seeing him or touching him or talking to him, it was something she was going to have to respect.

His Majesty raised a bushy brow. "'Tis obvious what needs to be done. I think we respect both sides and wait for a year to pass. But we cannot have Moreland doing all of *your* work, can we? That would be boorish. Which is why, despite you relinquishing your title, you will go to Saint Petersburg and make use of the year you are being given. A year alongside the Emperor should progress your cause considerably."

Her lips thinned as she flattened her moist palms against her lap. "You expect a hen to cluck its way into a kitchen and rip off its own feathers for the chef?"

Throwing back his gray head, he let out a long peel of laughter. "You exaggerate. I know Emperor Nicholas quite well and you needn't worry about getting your feathers plucked. He and I overturned many a good card together in our younger years. Why, he used to live in London, right on Stradford Place for a time when your father was still on the throne. A more animated and intelligent soul you'll never meet. You think the man is all blood, war and politics? You should have seen him at Almack's whisking our women about the floor. The man has charm."

Zosia stared at His Majesty, her throat tightening. "Forgive my words, Your Majesty, but life is *very* different for those trying to breathe beneath his tyrannical rule. Poles are wilting very, very fast beneath the cold shadow he casts. While he dances, my people and their way of life are being obliterated. We Poles have no rights. *And it is our country!* How is that just?"

His Majesty's amused grin faded, revealing the harsh, wrinkled features of a very old and very tired man. He sighed and nodded. "Yes. I *deplore* his politics and his irrational dread of intellectual improvement. His hostility toward the Ottoman Porte in and of itself is vile and unacceptable. And that is why you must go. Use the year Moreland is giving you to guide the Emperor into better understanding your people. You have a duty to uphold, Moreland has his duties to uphold and I have my duty to uphold. Therefore it is done. You and our Russian guests will depart in three weeks. You will stay here at Windsor for a small while so that I may offer you fortitude and rest, while better acquainting you with what you can expect. Russian Court etiquette alone will take us a damn week to discuss." He rose with a groan and winced as he straightened his hefty frame. "I am getting far too old for this. I need to die."

Zosia choked back a laugh and rose, bowing her head to hide her smile. "'Tis my hope you live indefinitely, Your Majesty. Thank you for your wisdom and assistance."

He gestured toward her chair. "Yes, yes. Sit. 'Tis exhausting watching you stand on one leg. However do you do it?"

She grinned and set her chin but did not sit. "With practice."

"I am infinitely impressed. Why, I can barely stand on *two* legs." He snorted and regally trudged across the room toward the footmen set against the wall. He paused and clapped his hands at them. "Prepare several rooms for the Countess and all our Russian guests. See to it their needs are well provided for and have some damn port and a plate of sausages delivered into the reading room."

The men bowed and breezed off to oversee the request.

His Majesty paused and glanced back at her. "Be at ease with your decision, dear girl. I will write a letter to the Emperor and have it sent straightaway, so he can properly greet you and be prepared. I will also remind him that George will have his head if you are not treated with the same hospitality my family showed him whilst he was here in England."

"Thank you, Your Majesty. I am honored by your endless generosity."

"As well you should be, you Catholic wench. I confess I am rather annoyed Moreland gets *my* trinket, after I do all the work! God carry you." He turned and disappeared out through the oversized double doors.

"Long live the King!" she called out after him. *"For no greater man has ever lived!"* She paused and added playfully, *"Except for Moreland, that is!"*

"There is no need for blasphemy!" he called back without reappearing. "I will see you at supper. And you had best wear a pretty gown or I will not have you at my table."

She smiled and repeated softly, "Long live the King, long live Poland and long live my Moreland. Amen."

SCANDAL FIFTEEN

In London, the excellence of one's soul mat-
ters very little compared to the excellence of
the clothing one wears and the barouche one
rides. ~~Ah, yes. Society favors all those super-~~
~~ficial bastards who ought to be disemboweled~~
~~for even breathing.~~ *Try to achieve excellence*
in all. Not only will London be pleased, but so
will you and the Lord above.
                              —*How To Avoid A Scandal,*
                        Moreland's Original Manuscript

TRISTAN HAD BEEN TOSSING OUT so many orders to
his servants every hour, he was beginning to forget
what orders he had already issued and why.

Shortly after meeting with his secretary, his book-
keeper and solicitor, he reorganized and restructured
his entire schedule to reflect the new life he was
taking on for the next eight weeks while he prepared
for his upcoming debate before Parliament concerning Russia's growing power, not only over the Ottoman but, of course, Poland. By keeping the focus

solely on Russia, as opposed to what England could do to salvage Poland, he hoped everything would fall into place without creating full opposition.

His newly arranged schedule included meetings with titled peers, merchants and gentry who were either Catholic or bore Catholic sentiment. His schedule also included attending any and all sessions and debates at the House of Lords, while designating two days to his grandmother, instead of one. He also terminated his membership to Angelo's Fencing Academy and commenced a new sport that required more grit, valor and far less clothing: boxing at Jackson's.

Fridays and Saturdays he'd completely allotted to the British Museum so he could delve into its extensive library and archives pertaining to history, politics and economics of the Ottoman Porte, Poland and Russia over the past hundred years. His debate depended on it. His Majesty had generously offered him access to the crown's own personal library, which included pamphlets, maps and documents unavailable to the public.

As the daily routine of his new schedule fell into place, so did his way of thinking. He slowly gathered all of the dirks, stilettos, razors, blades, dagger pistols, whips and riding crops that he'd collected throughout the years. It was an extensive collection that astounded even him, comprising a hundred and twenty-eight different pieces. He only kept one blade. A rare silver-and-gold piece from Nepal he hoped to one day display in a glass case in the library. After he had carefully bundled the blade in velvet, he stashed it in a locked drawer at the bottom of his writing desk and gave the key to his butler.

He then hefted the remaining collection of weapons, whips and riding crops into several wool sacks and had everything delivered to a pawn shop, donating whatever money was acquired to a local orphanage. The only razor he kept in the house was his shaving razor, and that he assigned to his new valet, Winslow, with strict instructions to only deliver it for the twenty minutes he required each morning to shave.

Tristan also opted to altogether remove every object connected to his mother and father. Furniture, vases, books, paintings, stationery, letters, even inkwells and stubs of old wax in tins. He felt the need to purge and commence anew. Not as a means of forgetting—for his parents did not deserve such disrespect—but as a means of decluttering his life and his thoughts. As days went on, and more and more objects were removed from each room, he realized he was going to have to purchase countless items for the entire house.

After donating his entire wardrobe to a workhouse, he invested over a thousand pounds in new coats, cravats, boots, trousers, gloves, cloaks, hats, waistcoats and linen shirts. He opted for less gray and far more color. It pleased his grandmother no end and made him feel more attractive.

Though he felt awkward the first few dozen times he did it, he still joined all of the men at Jackson's in the routine of removing his coat, cravat, waistcoat and linen shirt and leaving his chest bare whenever he stepped into the roped arena. Men stared like prim misses gauging his scars, but he became surprisingly popular. Men eagerly sought to go up against him in the arena, thinking his scars reflected he was a tougher challenge. And *that* motivated him to remove his shirt every single time.

Sadly, tragedy momentarily touched his world when he received word that his father's good friend, Lord Linford, had succumbed to syphilis and had, in fact, passed. Tristan sent condolences and baskets of flowers to Lady Victoria and her husband, Lord Remington, but avoided them and the funeral. Silent prayers in church extended over several Sundays were about all he could afford to give without teetering off his designated path.

With each visit to his grandmother, he encouraged her to join him on his journey toward a new way of thinking and a new way of life by stepping outside the house. She wasn't quite as enthused as he'd hoped she'd be.

Eventually, he was able to get the woman to extend her arm past the open doorway of the entrance. He had to stand on the doorstep and extend her arm for her, but even that was far more than she'd been capable of in nineteen years.

She protested and panicked, but soon grudgingly opened the door herself and extended her arm beyond the entrance and held it out so that he would cease nagging. He wagered antique books for minutes spent holding out that hand, which motivated her, and eventually he was able to get her to stand in the doorway for over twenty minutes. Of course, whenever a gentleman passed and nodded his pleasantries, she would scramble back in and slam the door, bolting all eight locks. She usually wouldn't let him back inside the house when she fell into one of her panics, and he had to wait until his next scheduled visit to see her.

It was his hope that after his speech, which he'd aligned to occur two sessions before the closing of Parliament for the Season, he could get his grandmother to sail with him to America to campaign from city to city and from state to state. And from there, campaign and tour all of Europe.

Despite there being no guarantee that Zosia would even be waiting for him at the end of the set year, he had promised himself to enthusiastically count down each and every day, hoping it edged him closer to seeing and holding and kissing and loving and marrying the incredible woman who had inspired him to put *more* into Moreland.

THE LONG JOURNEY FROM ENGLAND to Saint Petersburg had commenced aboard the overly crowded and overly rustic *W. Jolliffe Steamer.* A more luxurious steamship could have been chartered, but would have delayed the trip by another week, and Zosia had no intention on putting off the inevitable.

The boasting terrain and coast of Kent and Essex eventually shrank to the size of a hand, fading against the sea's vast horizon until it disappeared, and it was as if England and her Moreland had never been.

The chugging vessel trailed constant veils of sooty smoke from its stacks, sweeping them out toward cloud-ridden skies, strong winds and massive waves that relentlessly rocked far more than the ship. It rocked her very gut to the core, threatening to slap her own innards up and out through her nostrils.

There was very little comfort to be had, although her newly acquired lady's maid did everything to make her journey comfortable. Their cabin, though sizable, was musty and at night was lit by several lanterns that all flickered incessantly as if chatting away amongst themselves.

Limited accommodations had forced her to set aside pretense and offer sections of her large cabin to Maksim, his five cavalry men and all four guards

His Majesty had graced her with. She insisted on sharing quarters, despite panicked protests from her lady's maid, after discovering all ten men had been sleeping on a rain-drenched deck, using their cloaks for blankets and bundling ropes for pillows.

What was far worse than sharing sleeping quarters with ten grown men—four of whom snored with the strength of the north winds snapping off branches—was having to endure the *stench* of grouping said ten men in one cabin.

Most of the meals served in the designated dining hall were tasteless, pasty and cold by the time they found their way into her mouth. Oddly, the less she ate, the better she felt.

Whenever weather permitted, she spent most of her hours on deck, reading the wonderful, extensive array of books His Majesty had gifted her with. Her favorite, by far, was the 1787 French eighteen-volume edition of *Correspondance Secrète, Politique et Littéraire*. It was a witty and salacious journalistic chronicle that wove truths, half truths and lies into intriguing tales about the reign, politics and personal affairs of Louis XVI. She kept her place marked with Moreland's folded, old parchment, hoping that on the day of their reunion, they'd burn it together in symbolic celebration.

Maksim watched over her and her lady's maid at every turn, always keeping them in sight and constantly reprimanding any man who wished to be familiar. After she had threatened what was most dear to Maksim that day in the carriage, he himself maintained a very respectable distance she was grateful for.

Her own guards spent most of their bored hours playing cards with Maksim's cavalry. No one ever liked when she played. Between her luck, her competitive nature and her tendency to count cards, she almost always won. So she refrained from spoiling their fun and kept to reading instead.

Despite the notable language barrier between the two groups of men, the moment drink, food and cards were involved, they seemed to understand each other *very* well. They even knew to wordlessly nudge each other whenever a pretty face breezed past on deck. There were some things that were simply universal to all men.

When the ship finally arrived in Hamburg, Germany, almost two weeks later, and all of their papers had been inspected, three four-horse carriages were hired for the remaining distance to Russia. They took their time, stopping to refresh the horses and themselves often and visiting many cities along the way.

Upon entering the borders leading into the Kingdom of Poland, where their papers were inspected by young Polish sentinels who offered amiable conversation in her own language, a sense of peace and pride propelled her onward, reminding her of her purpose. She didn't feel like a one-legged woman anymore. She felt like a dignitary.

During the very last week of their journey, after six long weeks Zosia realized something. The lacings on her corset were a tad uncomfortable, both of her breasts were unusually sore and she hadn't had her menses since London. Well before she and Moreland had...

And yes. She knew. She was pregnant with Moreland's babe. Though there was no visible belly, she still kept her hands protectively on it, secretly cherishing what she'd been gifted with in all but one moment of intimacy. She was thrilled to know that the year apart which Moreland had set was going to be shortened considerably, as she intended to send word about their babe upon her arrival in Saint Petersburg. She only hoped he would be able to rush to her side and marry her before her belly exposed them both to scandal.

When at long last she had arrived at the territory of Polangen, which admitted them into the expanse of Russia, their carriages were greeted by several blockades and countless Russian sentinels asking them to step out.

Far more than their papers were inspected. They were. She worried the sentinels were going to insist she remove her gown and dismantle both of her crutches. Fortunately, it never came to that.

The inspection also included unstrapping and hefting off all of their trunks from the back of each carriage and sifting through each one. To her astonishment, the only trunk to have created a panic was the one holding her books. Stern, bearded faces paged through all fifty-eight of them, as if they were cannons. She considered whipping a book at each of their heads to demonstrate that a book against their skull would in fact hurt far more than propaganda.

After many shared mutterings and curt Russian words tossed over their shoulders to fellow sentinels, each book was returned to her trunk one by one. They returned everything except for her precious eighteen volumes of *Correspondance Secrète, Politique et Littéraire*. The Russian blighters shoved all eighteen volumes into several satchels, explaining books containing political subjects were not allowed.

Astounded, she protested by explaining that they had been gifts from His Majesty of England, and that the political content was more satire than truth. But the men only repeatedly waved her and her crutches off. When she demanded Maksim seize her rare 1787 editions, he only shrugged and confided there was nothing to be done.

So she showed him what could be done.

She commanded all four of her own British guards

to ambush the sentinels and seize her French volumes by force. Only…she found herself ambushed. Maksim hoisted her up and threatened to use her own crutches against her backside if she didn't get into the carriage. And such was her first impression of the great Russian Empire under Emperor Nicholas's ludicrous rule.

SCANDAL SIXTEEN

There are nuances that reveal more about a person than their own words ever will. They are revealed in their mannerisms, their gestures, the expressions that flit across their face and, above all, seen in the depths of their eyes. It is referred to as soul recognition or soul revelation. It is when one quietly recognizes who a person is and in turn must decide if it is time to bask in that presence or dash from it. ~~*Most of the men and women I meet fall into the dash category. Even the way these people breathe annoys me, because I know with each breath they take, they are using those breaths to purposefully limit the intake of air for others.*~~

—*How To Avoid A Scandal,*
Moreland's Original Manuscript

ARRIVING IN SAINT PETERSBURG was like drifting into a massive, mythic city that had been hidden within the mist from the rest of the world for ages. Enormous cobbled streets as wide as any river were surrounded by looming, magnificent buildings that boasted Grecian arcades, giant columns of granite, white stucco, brick and polished and carved marble that could have only been built by deities, not humans.

By far the most haunting aspect of Saint Petersburg was beholding such magnificence against a soft, grayish glow of light that lit the sky and whispered to all that it was neither day or night. As Maksim went on to explain, during spring and summer, night disappeared and only light pervaded all of morning, noon and night.

It was a city of opal nights.

As her four-horse carriage approached the riverbanks of Neva, the Winter Palace that adjoined the Hermitage stretched and stretched in sweeping architectural splendor, making Zosia feel as if she had arrived upon the doorstep of God himself. It was as eerie as it was breathtaking.

After passing through large iron gates emblazoned with eagle emblems of Imperial Russia, her carriage disappeared into the hidden realm of the Winter Palace. The coach lulled to a halt, aligning her window with a grand entrance guarded by soldiers whose military sashes all held sheathed swords.

Her throat tightened, depleting her of whatever courage she thought she had. The carriage door opened and the steps were unfolded. The soft, warm air of the gray, illuminated summer night drifted in, bringing with it the scent of damp leaves.

Maksim stepped out of the carriage and wordlessly extended his black-gloved hand to her. She stood, swaying for balance, and grabbed hold of his hand, leaning toward the opening of the carriage.

Maksim reached up and grabbed hold of her corseted waist and swept her out onto the paved ground. Though he momentarily allowed her slippered foot to touch the ground, he retained his hold and, without warning, scooped her up and into his arms, ensuring her traveling gown was well in place.

She stiffened, glancing up at him.

"Do not resist my good intentions," he provided in Polish. "There are countless stairs and we do not have all night."

She sighed and allowed him to carry her up the wide set of stone stairs lit by burning torches and lanterns. Several red tarps draped the vast entryway, restlessly flapping against the wind.

The double doors before them were instantly swept open by dark-skinned men dressed in flowing, dark green Turkish garbs bound by red, thick sashes around their waists.

Maksim's arms tightened more noticeably against her body as they entered, as if he were silently demanding her full cooperation. His riding boots echoed against the gleaming, Siberian marble floor as he proceeded up another set of wide stairs with carved, gray wood railings. Countless gold-and-silver sconces lit with tapers softly lighted the white ornate hall.

They veered down a cathedral-like corridor. Her eyes scanned the walls, which gleamed like honey-colored china against the expanse of high, soaring ceilings. Large, gilded paintings of life-size men and women floated past, their frozen eyes and proud expressions seemingly following her.

Maksim eventually paused before a wigged footman draped in laced livery, issuing several curt commands in Russian. The young footman responded in a suave flow of Russian, bowed and guided them toward an incised, gray wood door on the right, which was dutifully opened.

"The Emperor has already been informed of your arrival and will be here to greet you shortly," Maksim announced as he carried her through what appeared to be a small study. Lowering her into a large, wing-back leather chair, he swept up each hand and, to her astonishment, stripped her kid glove from each.

His jade-green eyes momentarily met hers as he held out her gloves. "I will wait out in the corridor should you need me."

She smiled tightly and slipped her gloves from his hand. "Thank you."

He offered a curt bow, turned and strode across the room. He paused in the doorway, glancing back at her one last time, as if concerned for her well-being, and then disappeared. The footman closed the door behind him with a soft click.

Zosia drew in a quivering breath and exhaled, the silence of the small study unnerving her. She glanced around the oak-paneled room, noting chairs, a French writing desk, maps, countless models of ships displayed on wooden shelves and leather-bound books in gleaming glass cases. It was a simple room meant for thought, not grandeur.

The echoing of heavy steps made her freeze. The footfalls faded past and she was left in silence yet again. She waited and waited, and felt as if she were sucking in the last of whatever air was left in the room. The echoing of another set of steps made her freeze again. This time, the door breezed open.

"The Emperor and Autocrat of All the Russias," a wigged footman announced in English.

Zosia rose and bowed her head in expected recognition.

A stout but very tall mustached gentleman dressed in a simple, gray military uniform with high black boots strode into the room. A large hound scampered in alongside him, veering toward her with a wagging tail.

The Emperor gestured for Zosia to sit with a quick sweep of his hand.

So she did.

A large, furry head found its way into her lap, nudging her bare hands for affection. She smiled, rubbing the soft gray-and-white fur, and peered into those large brown eyes, which quietly observed her with great appreciation for the affection she was offering.

"He likes you," the Emperor announced in a low and casual tone as he settled into the chair across from her. "That is good. It means you and I will get along despite your arriving on a Monday."

She glanced up, still affectionately rubbing the hound's head. "Monday?"

"Yes."

"I do not understand."

He smirked. "Today is Monday. Is it not?"

She blinked, her hands momentarily stilling against the dog's head. "I still do not understand. What does Monday have to do with whether we get along or not?"

He chuckled. "Forgive me. Some Russians believe Mondays to be unlucky and therefore anything occurring on that day will carry itself as being unlucky."

"Oh." This did not bode well.

"Ah. But I took the Russian crown on a Monday." He winked. "So such superstitious raff cannot be of any merit, can it?" He snapped his fingers toward the dog. "Hussar. Enough. You will exhaust her."

The hound turned and darted back over to its master, settling across the length of the man's booted feet with timed obedience. The Emperor observed her pensively, long fingers stroking the tip of his waxed mustache as his brown eyes intimately met hers. A small smile lingered on his lips as he nodded. "I see the resemblance," he murmured more to himself than to her.

Those soft words and soft brown eyes laced with warmth were not at all what she had expected to find gracing a man of such lethal power. She clasped her moist hands together, reminding herself that it took more than a mere brushstroke to create a true likeness and understanding of a man. "I am grateful for your willingness to host me despite my refusal of the decree."

"And why would I not host you?" His hand fell away from his mustache, his brows coming together. "I wish to become better acquainted with my niece. Despite your vile Catholic upbringing, you and I are family."

She stared at him, astonished at how flippantly and openly he dashed her religion. Was nothing sacred?

He hesitated, as if sensing her unease. "I am disappointed you are turning away your title. Do you not realize Maksim has passed on several good matches in the hopes that my brother's decree would sweep him into the Russian Court?"

She lowered her gaze. "No. I did not."

He sighed. "You do him and all of Russia great injustice, *Velikaya Knyazha*. Great injustice. I have already briefly spoken to him about enforcing the decree, but he does not wish to insist upon it. I fear he likes you too much to impose."

Zosia felt as if the Emperor were sticking a fork of guilt into her side, trying to get her to submit. "Maksim has proven to be quite the gentleman."

"Yes. A flaw of his, I believe." He laughed. "The man can aim a pistol at anything but a woman's heart."

She couldn't help but smile. "If that is a flaw, Uncle, may everyone be cursed with it."

He leaned forward, reached down and rubbed Hussar's outstretched belly, the large gold-and-onyx ring on his finger appearing and disappearing. He glanced up. "We will be hosting a gathering in your honor in a few weeks. I would have hosted it sooner, but Madame Nicholas and I only arrived a short week ago from Antichkoff and have had little time for anything."

Her brows came together. "Is Madame Nicholas your…?"

He grinned, his eyes and face brightening. "Yes. My wife. Your aunt." He lowered his chin and his voice playfully. "Though I would refrain from calling her Madame Nicholas. It will only rile her, and that, you do not want. She may appear regal and dutiful and quiet, but she is anything but."

He leaned back against his chair, setting his head of brown-and-gray side-swept hair against its wingback leather cushion. "I wish to settle whatever unease you may have. I have heard much of your sentiment. I understand it quite well, but the Poles are not your people. We here in Russia are your people. Do not ever forget that."

Lucifer's oversized hoof was already tapping.

She met his gaze and retorted in a flat tone, "Poles are not your people, either, Uncle. So why is it you seek to hold their way of life and their entire country hostage? 'Tis no different than an elephant ordering a herd of sheep to grow tusks. Improbable. Ludicrous. Pointless. You may wish to consider taking care of your own people first before taking on other nations. I hear the Russians are as unhappy as the Poles. Why do you suppose that is?"

The Emperor's brows rose as he leveled his head. "You appear to have inherited your grandmother's tongue." He shifted toward her. "Allow me to explain something, *Velikaya Knyazha*. In a position such as mine, it is necessary to rule with a thumb pressing against the pulse of everyone's throat. Otherwise it is *my* throat that is pressed, squeezed and slit. Do you understand?"

She feigned a laugh. "Perhaps people would not be so eager to press, squeeze and slit if you were not so busy pressing, squeezing and slitting *their* throats. Have you ever given thought to that?"

He *tsk*ed and wagged a forefinger. "You have no understanding of me or my politics."

"I am here to entertain an understanding of you, Uncle. But only if you are willing to entertain an understanding of me."

"Good. That is good. I will share." He cleared his throat. "On that very first day I took the throne as Emperor of Russia, without even being given an opportunity to demonstrate my worth to my own people, revolts echoed throughout the streets and swept out into the world. It was my duty to demonstrate from that very moment that defiance will only earn blood. My words of assurance meant nothing to them, you see. They only mocked assurance. But fear? Ah. No one ever dares mock fear or death. For they know it is permanent. You obviously seek to educate me, *Velikaya Knyazha,* and I respect that. I do. I hope you will educate me on all that is important to you and your people. When you are ready, I will graciously grant you an hour to convey all of those concerns and then you and I will never speak of this again. That is how we will settle our differences."

Which meant it wasn't going to be settled and that her time in his presence would bring nothing but angst and frustration. He expected her to educate him in *an hour* about a crisis that affected millions of people? Ludicrous!

"I beseech you for more than a mere hour, Uncle," she insisted. "Aside from Russian noblemen controlling far too many political seats, thus choking out the vote of *any* Pole, there is a very long list of basic constitutional rights that need to be addressed. I am asking for six months of continuous discussions. Six months will enable me to fully explain the hardships that extend from basic education to land to military training, all of which is completely controlled by the Russians and benefits no one but the Russians. There needs to be a balance of power."

He observed her pensively for a very long moment, running the tips of his fingers across his lips. "You understand the politics."

She shook her head. "No. My mother understood the politics, Uncle. Not I. I only ever understood the people. I spent my entire life listening to their discontent. The discontent of a university student whose education is being censored and limited, preventing him from becoming more. The discontent of a professor who is not allowed to improve the minds of those around him without being punished or intimidated. The discontent of a soldier who is forced to salute a flag that is not his own. The discontent of a priest who cannot pray within his own church without meeting God Himself first. *Those* are the politics I understand."

His eyes brightened. He pointed at her. "I need someone like you. I do. I need someone who will be able to speak to the restlessness the Poles feel. As you just did! Your passion, Niece, is brilliant. Absolutely brilliant." He shifted in his seat. "How about this. I am willing to negotiate certain rights for your people over whatever period of time you desire if you give me what I want. What do you say to that, eh?"

She stared at him. "And what is it that you want?"

He eyed her, slowly rolling his palms together as if about to toss a pair of dice he hid within his hands. "I want you to take your place in this court as was decreed by my brother. Your presence is one of great importance to me and Russia. As Grand Duchess, I would expect you to use your understanding of the people and your position to eliminate every last whisper concerning revolt. I wish to instill a form of stability without money and bloodshed. In return, I will negotiate certain rights to appease you and them."

Zosia felt as if the man were holding up her beating heart and slowly squeezing it. How could she gamble away her own happiness and Moreland's for something that held no guarantee? "What sort of rights would you be willing to negotiate? And how would they be guaranteed?"

The Emperor shrugged. "You and I will discuss that after you become Grand Duchess. Prior to that, there is nothing to discuss."

Oh, God. Oh, dear God. How could she—

She leaned forward, attempting to soften her tone. "I would be more than willing to become Grand Duchess and take my place in this court. But only if I am permitted to marry a man of my choosing. Otherwise, Uncle, I would be sacrificing what matters most to me. My heart."

He leveled her with a cool stare. "I care nothing about the sacrifices you must make. As Emperor, I make sacrifices all the time. That is what a leader must do. And that is what you must do."

Her breath burned against her own throat.

He set his elbows on the armrests and folded his hands together, holding them below his chin. "Are we done, Niece? It is late and I wish to retire."

Trying to keep her voice steady and calm, she confided, "If there is one thing you can do, which I know will appease the people and keep them from revolt, it would be to cease the tyranny you impose upon civilians. No one understands the extent of that tyranny more than I. I lost my leg after Russian soldiers burned down a home they had no right to burn."

He grunted. "You are fortunate it was only a leg."

Zosia kept herself from jumping forward and smacking him. Instead, she drew in a calming breath, allowing her features to soften, and offered in a tone that was neither condemning or loving, "I beseech you, Uncle, upon whatever goodness you have, to consider giving Poles, who are *Catholic,* an opportunity to exist on their own land apart from your *Greek* empire. There are too many differences between your people and mine and it creates nothing but perpetual discontent. If you do not wish to offer them freedom, at the very least allow them to retain their dignity and their basic rights. Allow them to live by the constitution that was set by the Congress of Vienna. It is a worthy constitution every Pole will uphold, yet it is being violated at every turn."

"I would sooner reduce Poland to a province than enforce a constitution that should have never been created to begin with." He rose to his imposing height of well over six feet. "I know a revolt is coming, *Velikaya Knyazha.* You are but a petal upon its impending bloom. That is why I need you. If you care for your people at all, you will lead them by taking your place as Grand Duchess and warn them that their thorns will be crushed by the gauntlet covering my hand if they choose to revolt. You will become my voice, and in turn, we will both earn respect."

She gasped. "If I were to become Grand Duchess, I would never submit to being *your* voice. I would only submit to being a voice for my people."

"Enough!" He stared her down, his mouth tight and grim. "For however long you are here, and as long as you choose to deny your duty, you will show your uncle respect by speaking no more of what you will and will not submit to. If you decide to unroll that tongue of yours in defiance even once in my presence or to anyone in this court, you will disappear into Siberia *permanently*. And no one, not even the mighty good George of England, will know of it until you are dead. Do we understand each other?"

Zosia rose upon her one foot, unwilling to sit this one out. Though her sole limb quaked, she kept herself balanced and steady and strong and whispered hatefully up at him, "If you can terrorize, intimidate and condemn your own niece to death to better serve your own vile purpose, there is no hope for any Pole beneath your rule. Is there?"

He pointed down at her. "Exactly. *Now* we understand each other." He smiled, enthusiastically patting her cheek, and turned, sweeping toward the door.

Hussar glanced toward her with wary eyes, as if announcing in dog language that Zosia had best respect the master, before scampering out after him.

The Emperor paused. He turned, gesturing toward her. "I will have Maksim personally escort you to your suite. Maybe you and he can reach an amorous understanding that will benefit us all. Yes? It was a pleasure, Niece. Good night." He disappeared, his steps echoing down the corridor.

Zosia collapsed onto the chair behind her, squeezing her eyes shut, and pressed the tips of her quivering fingers to her temples, which were beginning to pinch, ache and throb. She should have never come. She should have never thought it was possible to forge an alliance with a man who took great pride in ruthlessly crushing anyone who opposed his way of thinking.

For an opportunity to lead her people, without a guarantee anything would come of it, she would have to give up everything. Including Moreland. She would have to give up the father of her babe before it even made her belly large. What if she sacrificed him and their happiness only to find herself left with nothing, not even the respect of her own people? It was not something she was prepared to do.

She choked on a sob, tears pushing their way through her closed lids. It was horrid knowing that she, Zosia Urszula Kwiatkowska, was a coward and a failure. She had never thought of herself as a coward and a failure. Until now. Until faced with the reality

that she was never meant to be a leader or a voice.
Another choked sob escaped her.

"Velikaya Knyazha?" a low, male voice softly
inquired.

Startled, she dropped her hands from her temples
and glanced up at Maksim, who lingered before her.
She sniffed and swiped away tears, trying to calm
herself. "Forgive me."

Maksim leaned toward her, his brow pinching in
concern. "It did not go as well as you had hoped. Did
it?"

She lowered her gaze and shook her head. "No."

He sighed. "We are all but pawns until we are
made King. That is the way of this world. Come."
He leaned closer and slid a bare hand beneath her
thighs and curved his other hand around her waist.
"You have endured enough. It is time you retire."

She slid her arms around his shoulders, latching
on to his warmth and allowed herself to be carried
out of the study and through endless, vast corridors
that turned and turned and turned.

Eventually, they arrived at a suite of chambers.

How she prayed Maksim held no expectations.

He veered through an open doorway leading into
an ornate, enormous bedchamber. The embellished
ceilings were upheld not by columns but massive,
Greek caryatids. Each female figure was positioned

differently, all frozen and forever cursed to never move or speak.

Zosia blinked up at the stoic gazes and large stone faces, her hold on Maksim instinctively tightening, wondering how she was ever going to sleep surrounded by such imposing monstrosities. Was it not unnerving enough being sentenced to sleep for months on end beneath the same roof as her uncle?

Maksim casually carried her past the bed, taking her into what appeared to be an adjoining library. She glanced up at him. "Where are we going?"

"You will see." He paused before a large bookcase. He lowered her onto her slippered foot, ensuring she was well balanced, and then removed a book from the shelf, setting it aside. Reaching into the space, he took hold of a hidden doorknob and drew back the entire bookcase, revealing a narrow staircase lit by a single gold lantern.

Her eyes widened as she hopped forward and peered down the carpeted stairs descended into what appeared to be a room that disappeared into heaven knew where.

Maksim smiled and held out his hand. "The Emperor insisted I show you. It belonged to your grandmother. It is where she escaped from the pressure of her duties and reveled in being human. It is timely and yours to revel in for however long you remain here with us."

Zosia eyed that large, outstretched hand and the candles that lit the hidden realm. She shook her head. Though Maksim had proven to be a gentleman throughout their entire journey, she was now in his realm and the Emperor's, and refused to trust either of them. "I will see it at another time. I wish to retire."

He gestured toward the opening. "This is where your quarters will be, *Velikaya Knyazha*."

She gasped. "Behind a bookshelf? I think not." She waved toward the adjoining bedchamber beyond the library, teetering for a moment. "I would rather sleep in that bed with all those women."

Maksim laughed, his smooth cheek dimpling. "That sounded far more exciting than I am certain you intended." He shook his dark head and leaned toward her. Meeting her gaze, he pointed toward his eyes. "Trust." His low, accented voice held a challenge. "You will be rewarded for setting aside your prejudice, which you are only basing upon what you *see* and not upon what you *know*. Yes?"

Her heart pounded at receiving such an endearing fleck of wisdom. With a trust she hoped she would not come to regret, she grasped his large, warm hand and allowed him to guide her both by hand and waist, hop by hop, down all thirty steps. The scent of oiled jasmine lingered in the cool air.

Zosia drew in a breath at finding a massive suite

encased in expansive mirrors, both on the walls and ceiling alike, reflecting prisms of candlelight in lush, soft brilliance. A wide burgundy-colored, embroidered couch that stretched and rounded like a bed was laden with plush pillows and coverlets, allowing for both lounging and sleeping. With an exotic flare, colorful paper lanterns, pagodas, sculpted griffins and dragons adorned the room, which appeared to connect to two other sweeping apartments beyond. It was...incredible.

Her grandmother, Empress *la Grande,* had once breezed through these same rooms. Given the woman's notorious reputation, she had no doubt her grandmother had more than just breezed through them. She'd probably entertained countless lovers in this domain, watching them writhe within those reflections beneath her rule.

Maksim rounded her and lingered, drawing close. He eyed her intently, as if wanting to do or say something.

She swallowed, uncomfortable with the way he continued to observe her. "Do not look upon me so intimately."

"You misunderstand."

"Do I?"

"I seek to be your friend."

"I certainly hope those are your intentions, Maksim, because my situation is already complicated enough without you insisting upon *your* needs now being met."

He sighed, as if he were already exhausted listening to her reasons of resistance. "Please. Allow me to advise you."

"Advise me? Advise me on what? That I should convert and marry you? That I should become Grand Duchess because millions of people are depending on me? Including you, who have given up opportunities for a chance that I am denying you?" Her voice rose steadily louder and louder and angrier and angrier. "Or perhaps you wish to advise me on how I should toss aside my happiness and my entire life without any guarantee any good will come of it at all? All for an Emperor as deranged as the devil himself? Is that what you should advise me on?"

He *tsk*ed. Then *tsk*ed again. Shaking his head, he leaned in and lowered his voice. "I am not like the Emperor. Do not treat me as such. The Emperor has great expectations, yes, and he will use those expectations to create opportunities for himself. I advise you not to give him opportunities. That is my advice."

She swallowed. "What should I do?"

"You must write and inform your British boy to come and protect your honor. You must do it before your belly betrays you and the Emperor thinks it is my doing. Even if the Emperor were to believe otherwise, he will force you and I to wed as a means of ensuring you become Grand Duchess. I know him. He will use your scandal against you."

She gawked up at him, her cheeks burning, and placed a protective hand against her stomach. "How did you...know? My belly has yet to show."

A flirtatious smile ruffled his lips. "I have eight sisters, two of whom strayed. It was obvious what had already occurred between you and Lord Moreland, despite him valiantly protecting your honor before my soldiers. I became concerned about your constant illness and demanded your lady's maid confirm whether you had had your menses throughout our journey. She informed me that you had not."

She winced, wanting to altogether faint from embarrassment.

He smiled and tapped her cheek with a finger. "Worry not. I will protect you and your secret, *Velikaya Knyazha*. Until he arrives and can oversee your honor himself."

She lowered her gaze. "Thank you."

"He will come if you write. Yes?"

"Yes. I know he will." Oh, how she prayed Moreland would come. Before she was forced onto a path she wouldn't be able to escape.

"Come." Maksim scooped her up into his arms and carried her over to the round, oversized couch. Setting her on the plush cushions, he slid his length beside her and propped himself up on an elbow, extending his long, booted legs. "Ah. What would you like to do with Maksim tonight? I am yours to do with as you please."

She scrambled up and scooted away from him to the edge of the couch. "I would like to retire. *Without* Maksim."

He chuckled. "Did you know that Russians are far better lovers than the British will ever be? I am willing to prove it if you let me."

Her eyes widened as she whipped a finger toward the stairwell. "I do not find you amusing! Leave."

Merriment flickered in his green eyes as he playfully clicked his tongue. "While you wait for your British boy to arrive, I can entertain you. He does not need to know and we will not have to worry about a mishap that is already his."

She gasped, grabbed up a pillow and bounced it off his head, wishing the pillow were made of concrete. "You vile—"

He laughed in a boisterous, jovial manner, grabbing the pillow out of her hand. "Have you no humor?" He whipped the pillow aside with a laugh, grabbed hold of her and gently tugged her down onto the couch, his hands skimming her face. He grinned. "We Russian officers have a savage fondness for Polish women. Why else do you think we keep invading your country?"

She gargled out an exasperated laugh, smacked his

hands away and pushed his body off to the side. "Off with you. Off my bed, you ungovernable Russian."

He jumped up to his feet and adjusted his uniform. He pointed down at her, his features stern. "Write your letter tonight. I will ensure your missive is sent by express military courier. It will arrive in London faster than any other courier available."

Zosia blinked up at him, and sat up, touched by his sentiment. "Maksim? Can I really trust you? Are we friends? True friends?"

"Someone has to keep you from being sent to Siberia. It might as well be me. So, yes. We are friends. All I ask is that you now name your first son in my honor. Maksim is a good name."

She grinned. "I highly doubt Moreland would allow me to name our first son after a Russian I used to fantasize about."

He lowered his chin, his brows rising. "You used to…?"

"*Used to,* Maksim. I have long since learned that the British are *far* more reliable than you Russians will ever be."

SCANDAL SEVENTEEN

A lady who wishes to be admired must, above all, know how to dance and dance well. Dancing is representative of life. It requires innate rhythm and an understanding of the steps needed to take to be successful. This inner rhythm can only be pulled forth from one's self and one's self only. Not even the greatest of dance masters can teach that rhythm to a heart and soul that does not carry it. That rhythm is further guided by music that propels one to glide forward and submit to the dance. That inner rhythm is what is most important. For when the outer music unexpectedly stops, for whatever reason, one can either fumble and make a disgrace of themselves ~~and their lives~~, or they can smile and keep dancing, while waiting for the music to return.

—How To Avoid A Scandal,
Moreland's Original Manuscript

The 18th of September
Early afternoon

A CURT KNOCK MADE TRISTAN open his eyes. He blinked, realizing the side of his face was plastered against the parchment of an open ledger he'd earlier set upon his desk. He sat up, swiping his face and blew out an exhausted breath.

Though his never-ending crusade to rally support for Poland had ended weeks earlier, his body and his mind were still recovering from the stress. His scheduled debate had been a good one, his best by far, but it had roused little sentiment from a Parliament that was still transitioning to accepting its new Catholic peers into the realm. He only hoped America would prove to be more supportive.

Another knock against the closed doors of his study reminded him how he'd been roused from a state of slumber.

He cleared his throat. "Is it urgent?"

"A letter arrived by express royal courier," the butler called back. "His Majesty ordered it delivered into your hands at once."

News. From His Majesty. Zosia. It had to be news pertaining to Zosia. It was the first he'd been privy to since he had last seen her over four months ago.

Tristan jumped up and onto his booted feet. Jogging around the desk and across the room, he threw open the doors, a renewed burst of energy overtaking him. "Where is it?"

The butler stepped toward him, stoically presenting him with the silver mailing tray.

Tristan reached out and was about to swipe up the correspondence, but paused. He edged back his hand. On the tray's reflective center was an old faded parchment with spattered discoloration and sloppy creases that had been strategically refolded into a letter and sealed with a large red wax embossed with a Russian eagle crest.

His breath hitched, recognizing the parchment. The lone piece of parchment he had slipped off his father's blood-smeared desk thirteen years ago, shortly after his body had been removed by the doctor and authorities. It was a parchment Tristan had folded away and kept, wishing it held his father's last thoughts. The parchment he'd given to Zosia. What did it mean? Was she done waiting? Had she already married her Russian and taken her place as Grand Duchess?

Tristan met the butler's gaze but did not reach for it. "What instructions came with it?"

"You are to read it, my lord," the butler confided, still holding out the tray.

He shifted toward the man in agitation. "Yes, I gathered as much. But am I to respond to it? Is there a request for a response?"

"No. There was no request for a response, my lord."

Tristan swung away and swiped a hand over his face. He didn't know if he was strong enough to even touch that parchment, let alone read whatever words Zosia had written upon it. Dearest God. She'd actually written words upon a parchment still bearing his father's own blood. She'd actually written words upon it. *Words!* Damn her. Damn her!

He swung back to the tray and snatched up the letter. "Leave. Now."

Bowing, the butler lowered the tray and departed.

Tristan slammed the doors into each other, turned and paced back and forth, tapping the parchment against the open palm of his hand. "It's only been a little over four months, Zosia," he growled aloud, tapping it against his palm harder and harder. "If you aren't capable of dedicating yourself to me this long, there is no hope for us. None."

He stalked over to the desk and slapped the letter onto it with a big downward sweep of his arm. He raked his hands through his hair and then turned, trudging over to the nearest sideboard to keep himself from even *thinking* about the blade.

Brandy. He needed brandy. He deserved to get soused after choking on Catholic politics for weeks and weeks on end. Hell, if it hadn't been for the boys at Jackson's, where he'd thrashed out every single one of his frustrations over the fact that no one gave a spit about Poland, he would have never survived.

Grabbing the crystal decanter of brandy, he toted it back to his desk, eyed the letter and slammed the decanter onto the gleaming surface beside it. His throat tightened and he suddenly felt his skin swell with heat.

He couldn't breathe.

Stepping back, he lifted his chin and unraveled his cravat as fast as his fingers would allow. Yanking it off, he whipped it aside. He then stripped his coat, his waistcoat and his linen shirt from his body, lashing them all one by one onto the floor of the study.

Though the pricking heat against his exposed skin was rapidly cooling, he felt restless as he rounded his writing desk. He grabbed up all of the ledgers, stacking them, and paused before the row of carved wooden drawers. He stared at that bottom drawer, knowing his blade from Nepal was buried within it. All he had to do was ask the butler for the key.

His chest tightened as he struggled to steady his breathing. He shook his head, knowing he was stronger than this. He was stronger than resorting to the blade. He'd proven that to himself when he opted to box every time he felt like slicing himself out of frustration.

He was going to have a drink. The way an ordinary

man would after a long day. Only he wasn't about to use a glass or limit his intake. God, no.

Leaning over, he tossed the glass stopper from the decanter onto the desk, causing it to chink, and grabbed the decanter, the amber liquid within sloshing. He brought the rim of the smooth crystal to his lips, tilting it and his head back, guzzling the burning liquid into his mouth. He swallowed and swallowed and swallowed, trying to finish as much as he could without coming up for air.

Only…it didn't feel right. He felt like he was drowning himself, instead of facing reality. It was but a different form of the blade.

Tristan broke away from the brandy, but couldn't level out the decanter in time. Cool, razor-stinging liquid exploded across the front of his chest and trousers. He winced and hissed out a breath.

"You clod," he muttered. "You can't even drink." He slammed the almost-empty decanter on the table and swiped at all the liquid covering the expanse of his bare chest. His brows creased, and he paused as his wet fingers slid against sections of his scarred skin that felt…smoother.

He glanced down, drawing away his hands, and stared down at himself. He didn't look the same, and had been too damn preoccupied to even notice it. Despite the discolored scars creating jagged angles that whispered of every incident that had ever upset him, his upper body looked...decent.

His chest was far more muscled, far more taut and far more defined from all the countless hours of boxing he'd thrown himself into. It was as if his skin had been pulled tight against whatever scarring there was. He'd never looked this fit in all his eight and twenty years. *He* did this. He had done it all on his own, without anyone, not Zosia and not even his own grandmother, holding him up by the collar.

He was finally his own man. He felt it. He knew it.

He leveled his gaze toward the desk where Zosia's letter waited for him, his nostrils flaring. Her face and her body echoed within his mind, and though he still desperately needed her and desperately wanted to be with her, a part of him dared her to defy him. He was his own man now and could damn well box his way through anything. No matter what that letter said, he would survive. He would.

Tristan set his jaw, rounded the desk and snatched up Zosia's letter. Drawing in a calming breath, he cracked the red wax seal and unfolded the parchment.

He stared at the perfectly scribed words that had filled the yellow, faded, blood-spattered page.

Mój Kochany,
    Though I have much to share, and most of it

does not bode well for my people, I intend to only share what matters most: my love for you. We never had a chance to truly come to terms with all that has happened to us, but please know that all is forgiven. I am humbled by all that you have already done. I am humbled by your attempt to prove your worth to yourself and to me. I apologize for writing upon what I know is sacred to you, but I thought it fitting I share my wondrous news upon a page that I hope will replace all of the sorrows you have ever known. You must come to the Winter Palace in Saint Petersburg at once. I am with child. Your child. We must be wed before this belly of mine becomes too noticeable and these Russians begin to think I am the Virgin Mary reincarnated. In truth, if you do not come, the Emperor will insist I wed Maksim as a means of ensuring I take my place in the Russian Court. You must come. I do not wish to be anyone's bride but yours. Please. Please come. All of my love and our child await you.

Twoja zawsze,

Zosia Urszula Kwiatkowska

Tristan staggered in disbelief. Zosia was…*damn*… he was…*damn*…a babe? After only one moment of intimacy?

Upon all that was holy.

The words on the parchment blurred as tears overwhelmed him. He was going to be a father. Him. A father. He was going to be a father.

He sniffed hard, and then let out an exasperated laugh, shaking his head, unable to suppress all of the emotions bursting and whirling through him. He was going to be a father! And here he'd thought—

He huffed out a breath and glanced around his study. So much for the rest of his campaign. He had to get to Saint Petersburg and protect her honor. Before the Emperor—

He fumbled to refold the parchment and dashed out of the room, his heart pounding. "Winslow!" he shouted at the top of his lungs to his valet. *"Winslow!"*

He sprinted up the staircase, skipping three full steps at a time. "Winslow! Where the blazes are you? Christ, we need to pack. Winslow? *Winslow!"*

"Yes, my lord?" his valet echoed from down the corridor.

Skidding to a halt at the top of the stairwell, Tristan whipped toward the direction of the young man he'd hired when his other valet had dashed off to Scotland.

Tristan pointed at Winslow repeatedly with the parchment. "See to it you pack all of my best clothes, boots, hats and gloves into every trunk I own. Some summer clothing, too, but overall, the warmer the better. Oh. And include my beaver hat. Have yourself ready, as well. You're going with me."

Winslow stared at him. "Wherever to, my lord?"

"Russia."

"Russia?" Winslow cleared his throat and set his chin. "I regret to inform you, my lord, that I will… require time to inform my wife and therefore cannot leave quite yet."

"Send a missive to your wife telling her if she lets you go, you will each receive an additional thousand pounds on top of all your regular wages."

Winslow slowly grinned, his full face brightening. "I will send a missive at once, my lord, and ready us both for the journey ahead."

"Good. Once you do that, and pack all of my clothes and yours, have all of our trunks delivered to Benson so they can be attached to the coach. Oh. And have the butler gather all of my traveling papers. I will oversee the rest. Now go. *Go!* We need to leave within the hour. No less than an hour."

Winslow blinked at him, his lips notably thinning.

"What?" Tristan demanded. "Too many instructions?"

Winslow cleared his throat. "No. Not at all, my lord. Will you require assistance into a set of traveling clothes before I commence my round of duties?"

"There is no time for bloody traveling clothes!" he

exclaimed in exasperation, waving toward the man. "I'll go as I am. Now go. *Go!* Get packing."

Windslow smirked. "As you wish, my lord." He bowed and departed with an amused swagger.

Tristan blinked, wondering what the devil that swagger and smirk was about. He then paused and glanced down at himself, realizing he was only wearing a pair of boots and brandy-covered trousers. He cringed. It appeared he was going to need a set of traveling clothes, after all.

"Milord?" Miss Henderson echoed, pulling open the entrance door he'd been pounding against. "What—"

Tristan darted past her and skidded into the foyer, swinging back toward her. "Where is my grandmother?" he demanded. "Where is she? I must speak to her. *Now.*"

Miss Henderson wordlessly gestured toward the staircase. He whipped around and glanced up toward the very top of the sweeping stairs.

His grandmother lingered, her pale hand already on the railing, her cream-and-lilac morning gown rustling with her movements. "Moreland?" she echoed, her silvery brows coming together. She slowly descended the stairs to greet him. "Whatever are you doing?" She *tsk*ed. "With all that rude pounding I thought my husband had risen from the dead."

He bit back a grin, waiting until she found the last step. The moment that slippered foot touched the marble floor, he sprinted toward her and yanked her up into his arms with a single sweep and whirled her around the foyer, unable to contain himself.

"Moreland!" She laughed down at him. "What—"

He plopped her down onto her slippered feet, re-adjusted his traveling coat and leaned in close and confided in a very low, cocky tone, "I'm going to be a father. I'm leaving for Russia on the next ship out to ensure our babe isn't born without me."

She covered her mouth with the tips of her fingers, her silver brows flickering. "Moreland—" She smothered an astonished giggle. "I'm going to be a..."

"Yes. A great-grandmother. Congratulations."

She paused. "But how is that even—" Her eyes widened as her hands came plopping down to her sides. She gawked up at him, her cheeks heightening in color. "Moreland. You didn't actually..."

He winced. "I did."

She gasped, leaned toward him and smacked the side of his arm. *"That* is for being a libertine and a lecher of the worst sort! Is this what I raised?"

He let out a mortified laugh and put up both gloved hands, stepping back. "I have no excuses except that I was and am still ardently in love with her."

She rolled her eyes and waved him toward the door,

where Miss Henderson lingered. "Off with you. Off with you to Russia, you rake! Go. The moment you get there, marry the girl at whatever church will do it, wait for the babe and then carry them all straight back. Russia is no place for my great-grandchild. No place at all. I cringe at the thought of exposing our dear babe to weather that I hear freezes everyone's noses off."

He hesitated, knowing his grandmother was about to officially panic. For he hadn't come merely to announce that he was going to be a father.

Tristan swung toward Miss Henderson. "Miss Henderson. Round up all of the servants and have Lady Moreland's papers and trunks packed within the hour. She and I are going to Russia."

Miss Henderson grinned and scurried past. "Yes, of course, milord."

A choked gasp escaped his grandmother's lips as she scrambled backward, shaking her head of white, bundled curls. She kept shaking and shaking and shaking her head. "I…no. Moreland. No. I am not…I cannot…no."

He stepped toward her and grabbed hold of her shoulders, forcing her to look up at him and into his eyes. "You only need to do this once. *Once*. Long enough to survive going to Russia and back. That is all I ask. If I can walk without a blade, after thirteen years, you can walk out that door. You have to do this. If not for yourself, do it for me, Zosia and our babe. I cannot imagine you not being part of this. Do you not want to be part of this? Do you not want to see me wed? Do you not want to be the first to hold your own great-grandchild?"

She pinched her trembling lips together, tears streaming down her cheeks.

He tightened his hold on her shoulders and whispered, "You can do this. I know you can. And I will remain at your side through every breathing moment of it. Now, please. I need you to do this. I need you at my side. I know nothing about babes or birthing. *Nothing.* Does that not frighten you or move you to pity?"

She let out an anguished laugh. She half nodded, closing her eyes. Drawing in a breath, she let it out and whispered, "I will. For you, Zosia and the babe. I can. I know I can. I have to."

"You have always gifted me with so much. Bless you." He cradled her face with both hands and softly kissed her forehead. "I promise I will never leave your side."

SCANDAL EIGHTEEN

The world is already well practiced in all things woeful, dismal and wretched. There is no need to add to it by shrinking the last of your soul. I recommend practicing the art of happiness and submitting to mastering it. It may take all of life, this author will agree, but oh! To master true happiness would be like mastering the very beat of one's heart. Do that and that is when life will truly start. ~~One day, true happiness will be mine to claim. I know not when and I know not how, but one day, it will be all mine to cradle, that I vow.~~

—*How To Avoid A Scandal,*
Moreland's Original Manuscript

The 29th of October, evening
The Winter Palace

ZOSIA HAD NO DOUBT that the Emperor was beginning to suspect something, despite her trying to conceal her pregnancy, which was beginning to balloon.

She expected him to storm into her room at any time, point at her and announce her betrothal to Maksim. It was exhausting constantly worrying about it.

The only tolerable part of her stay in the palace had been Maksim and all the good food she'd been eating. Though she hadn't been eating it at any table. Oh, no. She feared the Emperor would question her appetite.

Instead, she ate whilst lounging upon her grandmother's plush burgundy bed, surrounded by the flickering prisms of mirrored candlelight, draped in a French lace robe embroidered with pearls and reading books Maksim kept sneaking in from her uncle's covert library. It was an entire library of more than a hundred thousand books, consisting of every volume the Emperor had confiscated, and she was strictly forbidden from entering. She had no doubt her eighteen volumes of *Correspondance Secrète, Politique et Littéraire* was in that library somewhere, but Maksim had yet to find it.

Stretching out a hand toward the sideboard set next to her oval bed, she plucked up another marmalade tart stacked upon the gold porcelain plate and lowered her gaze back to Miss Porter's second volume of *Thaddeus of Warsaw,* which was actually quite good. She fully understood why it had been confiscated by her uncle.

He opened the drawer which contained his few valuables. With a trembling hand, he took them out one by one. There were several trinkets that had been given to him by his mother, and a pair of inlaid pistols which his grandfather put into his belt on the morning of that dreadful tenth of October.

Zosia shoved the entire large tart into her mouth, its divine sweetness coating her tongue, and sat up, bringing the book closer, wondering if Thaddeus was actually going to use said pistols from that dreadful tenth of October.

"By God," a deep British voice drawled in clear amusement. "And I thought you were missing me."

She jumped, her book cascading out of her hands, and almost choked on the tart pushing against her cheeks. Was it…Moreland? She froze, mid-chew, the mirrors around her reflecting eight images of a muscled frame garbed in black trousers, a matching evening coat, a moss-green waistcoat and a matching cravat. The man casually leaned against the ascending stairwell directly behind her, heatedly observing her in the reflection, longer, windswept auburn hair cascading into dark brown eyes.

Her eyes widened. Moreland!

She would have joyously shrieked out his name for all of Russia to hear, only the tart still filled her entire mouth. She jerked around, toward where he stood, trying to desperately finish chewing. She gestured toward her cheeks in exasperation.

He grinned and tapped a bare forefinger against his lips. His eyes intently held hers as he crossed the expanse of the mirrored chamber, his movements slow and commanding, with an intent to do far, far more than simply greet her.

She gawked at him, the tingling within the pit of her stomach having nothing to do with the babe at all. She suddenly felt like she was Catherine la Grande about to be reunited with the greatest lover known to all of humanity. All while trying to finish chewing on a stupid marmalade tart.

He paused, towering right beside where she was draped on the large oval couch.

She swallowed the last of the annoying pastry and eagerly pushed herself up toward him. "Moreland! *Kochanie!*"

His forefinger came to his lips again, demanding silence. He met her gaze and said in a soft, husky tone, "Words cannot describe this incredible moment we are sharing. Therefore let us refrain from saying anything for a small while."

He lowered himself onto the embroidered cushion surrounding her and took up her hand. His fingers tightened, conveying a pulsing restraint. He lowered his head to her hand, his warm lips trailing and grazing her knuckles, toward her wrist and up again. He closed his eyes and seemed to revel in what he was doing.

Her breath hitched as she watched those lips make love to her hand. Oh, how she had missed him. She swallowed and felt her hand trembling in a joy no words could ever describe, knowing he was at long last at her side. It was a moment she would remember for the rest of her days.

He reopened his eyes and released her hand, his gaze momentarily meeting hers. He smiled, then lowered himself to her uncorseted belly hidden beneath her robe. A rounding belly that was protruding.

He lowered his head, placing both hands on her belly, and kissed it repeatedly, giving her belly and their child within it as much attention as he had just bestowed upon her hand.

She smoothed the soft, silken strands of his hair, her fingers trailing through its thickness, savoring the feel of him and reveling in what was finally hers. All hers.

There were so many things she wanted to say and so many things she wanted to share. But for now, she would have to settle for the only words that came to mind. *"Kocham cię,"* she whispered down at him.

He paused and drew away from her belly, slowly rising up until their faces and their lips were mere inches away. "You just said you loved me in Polish. Didn't you?"

Her lips curved into a smile as she placed her hands against his smooth-shaven jaw. "I did."

"Good. Now say it in English so I can understand."

She nuzzled her nose against his, loose strands of her black hair grazing both her face and his. She trailed her hands down to his broad shoulders, rubbing their solid curves, and whispered, "I love you."

"And how I love you," he whispered back. "Please say you do in fact forgive me for what I did."

She smiled. "Undress me."

"Oh, I will." He hesitated. "Does this mean—"

"There is no need to linger on a matter that has long since resolved itself."

"I know, but—"

"Touch me, Moreland. That is the only form of apology I will accept."

He grinned. "I should sin against you more often."

"Cease procrastinating."

"Gladly." He tilted his head, his eyes trailing down to her lips. He edged in, the heat of his mouth feathering her own mouth. "What about our babe?"

"I know you will be gentle."

"I don't know if I can be," he growled back.

"You will have to be." She tilted her lips closer, until her bottom lip playfully grazed his. "Your babe depends upon it."

"And I depend upon you," he said against her mouth, crushing her lips against his own. His wet tongue slid against the lower lip she'd given him, the scent and flavor of sweet champagne coating her own lip.

Champagne? She bit back a laugh, her hands rubbing his shoulders. "You taste of champagne."

"Hmm." He slid his tongue across her cheek and back again. "I've been here almost an hour," he murmured, in between tongue strokes. "I had to settle in my grandmother and try to look decent for the mother of my child, all while being forced to a share a bottle of champagne with Maksim to celebrate my fatherhood. He wouldn't show me where you were until I did."

She blinked, his tongue causing her to fade in and out of reality. "Your grandmother? She—"

"Oh, yes. I not only got the woman out of the house but out of the damn country. She survived, too. Though barely." He nipped her cheek. "I don't want to talk right now. Not unless it's about what we are doing."

He grabbed her face and edged her head back, exposing her entire throat to him and forcing her to look up toward the ceiling of mirrors, where she saw her own face reflected in flushed ecstasy as his large frame hovered over her body and his head shifted against her throat.

He licked the entire curve of her neck, then buried his face against her, his mouth viciously sucking on her delicate skin. She gasped against the unexpected torrent of sensations rippling down the length of her neck and watched what was happening to her in a mesmerized daze.

He sucked harder and harder, making her gasp repeatedly against him, while his hands trailed down from her face and curved down around her breasts. A groan escaped him as he unraveled the silk sash holding her French robe together. Whipping aside the sash, he released her throat and shifted toward her, against the large cushion. He opened the entire length of the robe and swept it down her naked arms and away from her nude body. She was so grateful she had opted to wear only a robe that evening for comfort.

His eyes watched as his own large hands curved and traced her shoulders, her breasts, her waist, his fingers dragging and pressing against her skin with a rigid intensity that made her entire body feel as if it were being remolded by his hands. His jaw tightened as he slid a palm and his gaze down the sweeping length of her full limb and then back over to her amputated limb. "Heaven keep me from ever leaving your side again," he rasped.

She leaned toward him. Her fingers trailed toward his linen cravat, wondering if he would let her undress him. "Moreland?"

His hands stilled against her heated skin. His dark eyes met her gaze, his brows both rising. "Yes?"

She tugged at the cravat and eyed him. "You will not deny me from seeing you, will you?"

He grinned, leaned toward her and *tsk*ed. "Rather randy, aren't you? About as randy as the first time."

Her cheeks burned as she gestured toward herself in exasperation. "I have everything off."

His eyes traced the length of her, lingering on her breasts as he seethed out a slow breath. "So you do." He slid his frame from the cushion and rose, rounding the large oval couch she was draped on, his image and hers flitting around them. He paused at the base of her bare foot and stared her down, making her fully aware she was not only naked but pregnant with his babe.

She awkwardly reached for her robe to cover herself.

"Don't cover yourself." His voice was gruff as he continued to stare her down, removing his evening coat from his shoulders and the length of his arms. He held the coat out beside him, quirking a brow, and then let it drop to the floor with a rustle. With his coat now gone, the bulge of his erection pressed against his trousers *very* visibly. "If you want to see everything I have, you have to show me everything you have. Now spread yourself open. Wide."

Her entire body was ablaze with a prickling heat that was almost intolerable. A tremor and a sense of complete vulnerability she had never known overtook her as she slowly willed her thighs apart.

"Tell me what you want removed," he offered in a low, seductive tone. "Tell me and I will remove it upon your command."

She wet her lips and prayed she hadn't fallen asleep from overindulging in marmalade tarts. Moreland was here and doing this, wasn't he?

"I'm waiting," he taunted, lowering his chin.

"Waistcoat."

His fingers undid the row of silver buttons one by one, his eyes glancing from his hands to her face until he was done. He removed it and held out his waistcoat for her to see, emphasizing how accommodating he was being, and let it fall to the floor. "What else?"

She stared at his exposed linen shirt, noting that she could already see a sliver of his chest through the slit held closed by his cravat.

He lowered his chin again. "You are taking far too long deciding what I should remove. At this pace, our babe will be three years old."

She choked on a laugh, cleared her throat and quickly said, "Boots."

"*Boots?*" he echoed, glancing toward his feet and then back up again. "My feet aren't nearly as exciting as the rest of me, woman."

She burst into laughter and rolled her eyes. "Your cravat, then."

"You said boots first. I therefore must oblige my lady or I'm not being very considerate of her needs." He bent and yanked off each boot and sent them thudding and skidding to the floor, yanking off his stockings along with them. "I threw in the stockings for good measure or this will never end."

He straightened, his mouth quirking as he lifted his chin and unraveled his cravat, his eyes never once leaving hers. "*Now* the cravat." He slid the length of linen from around his throat and whipped it aside. He angled himself toward her, challenging her to continue.

She'd never been so physically aware of *needing* him. "Shirt. Then everything else. Only faster. Much faster. You are going much too slow."

He grinned, the edges of his eyes and mouth crinkling. "We have the rest of our lives. Therefore I am not going any faster than is absolutely necessary."

"*Moreland!*" She closed her thighs, pressing them together, and grabbed up her robe and covered herself. "There. I intend to punish you. Now what?"

"I'll be right there to punish you in turn, *after* I am done." He unclasped the two buttons at his throat that held his shirt closed. The collar fell away, exposing the upper portion of his chest. In a single sweep, without any hesitation, he yanked up the linen shirt and stripped it from his body, leaving his entire chest bare.

He set his hands on his trouser-clad hips and blew out a breath, eyeing her. "I've been boxing."

"Oh, that you have," she purred.

He cleared his throat. "So, what do you think? Tolerable?" He sounded like he needed an answer.

She drew in a breath and let it all out in vast, vast appreciation. The faded scars on his chest and arms rather delectably emphasized every well-defined, taut muscle on that broad chest and chiseled stomach. It was like beholding her own personal warrior. Even the bulk of his arms appeared more defined than the rest of him.

"Moreland," she breathed, her chest rising and falling unevenly out of her own desperate need to touch him. "You are torturing me with the perfection I see. Now remove your trousers and come here. I need to know that you are more than a fantasy."

He smoothed a hand against his chest as he angled toward her. "So you like it?"

She groaned in disbelief that he still could not see what she saw. "I am madly in love with it. Now let me touch it before I call in the Russian guards just so they can drag you over to where I am."

He chuckled and fumbled to unbutton the flap on his trousers. He stripped both his trousers and undergarment, his thick erection now on full display, and tossed both items away.

Kneeling on the cushion of the oval couch, he slowly crawled toward her as if he were no longer a man but an animal, the muscles on his arms shifting as he drew closer. "How I have missed you."

Her heart pounded as he whipped off her robe.

His arm circled her, dragging her toward the carved armrest of the couch. "After a good long kiss, we are going to turn you around so that there is no bumping against our babe. Are we in agreement in this?"

"Full agreement." She ran her hands over his smooth skin, fingering the scars scattered across his chest.

He wrapped a muscled arm around her neck, locking her nude length against his own velvet naked body, and grabbed her face with his other hand.

He brushed his lips softly against hers.

"There is no need to be *that* gentle, Moreland." She grabbed a handful of his hair and forced him to press his lips harder against hers, thrusting her tongue into his mouth.

A low growl escaped him, echoing within the quiet

chamber. His hot, wet mouth devoured hers as his hand slid down to her right breast. He rubbed and flicked her nipple, his tongue delving so deep into her mouth she could hardly breathe. He drew her even closer against his hard body until his erection dug into her side.

The urgency within his tense, muscled body grew as did her need to touch him. She slid her hand down the length of his hard chest. Down his stomach, down to—

Her fingers gripped the hard length of his erection.

He groaned. His hips jerked against her hand, shoving the head of his erection harder against her entire palm. She rubbed its length up and down, enjoying its smooth yet rigid feel.

He released her mouth, his chest heaving.

The rush of cool air drifted against her lips and for a few passing moments, she couldn't even bring herself to open her eyes, let alone move. All she could do was focus on their heavy breaths and how his erection, his body and warm hands felt against her.

"I will turn you," he said in a low tone, lifting her and turning her.

She opened her eyes and kneeled, setting her hands on the carved armrest. She watched their reflection in the massive gilded mirror set directly before her as his muscled body kneeled behind her.

He glanced down, his hands spreading her thighs apart. He leaned her forward just a bit more and slid his fingers in between her folds and slowly rubbed.

She moaned, her fingers digging into the carved wood as she closed her eyes to the sensations overtaking her.

"Watch everything I do," he challenged, rubbing faster and faster, until she felt as if she would collapse.

She gasped and reopened her eyes. She met his heated gaze in the reflection as he positioned himself and his erection dug into her backside.

"We will do this slow," he whispered.

"Slow," she repeated in a whisper.

She saw his hand position his length against her incredibly wet opening. Their gazes remained locked as he slowly pushed into her, sliding his entire hard length inside. They both moaned at the same time, their lips parting in unison.

His hands grabbed hold of her waist and he stilled against her, his chest heaving. His dark eyes held hers in the reflection. "How does it feel?"

Though it felt tight, she was so wet, it also felt so incredibly—

"Divine."

He pulled out and pushed in, slow out and slow in, repeating the easing motions against her tightness until they were both gasping. "Should I go faster?"

"Yes," she choked out.

He increased his pace and pumped until nothing but their ragged breaths, moans and flesh slapping against flesh echoed throughout the room.

She watched her breasts swaying with each gentle thrust as she pushed back against him, trying to remain balanced even as the mirrors around her seemed to spin and she could no longer see but only feel. She edged closer and closer to bliss. She gasped, feeling her core tightening, and lowered her head.

"Hold up your head," he growled from behind, jerking in and out of her tightness faster and faster. "I want to see your beautiful face. I want you to watch yourself and me as we cry out. Do it."

She lifted her head and watched him as he pushed her toward that perfect rapture she knew was going to overtake her at any moment. Her cheeks were so flushed, her hair was hanging over her shoulders and one side of her face. She hardly recognized herself as her body and her breath folded into one and she cried out against the onslaught of pleasure that was reflected all around her. She cried out again in disbelief as Moreland kept jerking in and out of her, causing the rapture to last longer than her body was capable of enduring.

Soon, it faded, and though weak and almost unable to keep holding herself up against the armrest, she remained in place, waiting for him to finish.

His fingers dug into her hips as he leveled a feral gaze at her and ground into her one last time. A guttural groan exploded from his lips, his body stiffening against hers. She felt his seed pulsing into her, and saw him seethe out fierce breaths through his teeth in a rigid resolve to keep holding not only her but her gaze in that reflection.

It was the most erotic thing she had ever seen. Him, in the ultimate moment of pleasure, desperately wanting *her* to see him in that ultimate moment of pleasure.

He stilled, his chest heaving, and lowered his head, as if he, too, were unable to keep himself upright.

She smiled as he pulled out and gently turned her, pulling her and himself flush against the large, soft cushion. She nestled herself against his chest as he wrapped his arms around her.

Her finger traced all the different jagged scars, following them around the curves of his muscled chest. "One day," she whispered, "you will never even know they exist."

His hold tightened on her. "That day is today, I assure you."

She kept tracing and tracing them. "Are you walking without your razor, Moreland?"

"I am. Why else do you think my body looks so damn good?"

She let out a soft laugh, poking him. "A bit conceited now, are we?"

"A bit." He chuckled, smoothing a hand against her hair. "I was going to ask if you were being treated well, but judging by the amount of tarts on the tray over there, I don't need to."

She sighed, nuzzling her cheek against him, and confided, "Those tarts made life bearable while I waited for you to come. The chef has been most kind. He makes them every week just for me."

He hesitated. "And how goes it with you and the Emperor? Any progress? At all?"

Her heart sank as she replied in a soft, sad tone, "I might have had an opportunity to make progress, but he is set in changing nothing and so the people will continue to be nothing. Revolt might very well be the only path if people seek change. Which is senseless. Why can words never be enough to settle the world's battles? Why can words never be enough to make that rainbow appear?"

He drew in a deep breath and let it out, kissing the top of her head ever so softly. After a long moment, he replied, "*Non sine sole iris,* my dear."

She blinked, translating the Latin aloud, "No rainbow without the sun." She sighed and half nodded, closing her eyes. "True. Right now, there is no sun. Only dark, dark clouds, thunder and rain."

"It can't rain forever." He tightened his hold on her.

"After we marry, we will wait for our babe to be born. Then you, I, the babe and our dear grandmother can board a ship and start dining every American willing to listen. What do you say?"

She smiled against his chest, taking comfort in knowing that perhaps all wasn't lost. "Yes and yes."

"Good." He rubbed her shoulders. "I regret to inform you that if we have a daughter, her name is already spoken for."

She adjusted her chin against him. "Oh? And what name is that?"

"Camille. After my grandmother. 'Twas all the woman ever talked about on the way over. Little Camille this and little Camille that. We had better have a girl or she may very well name our poor son after herself."

She giggled. "And what if we do have a son?"

"Then I will give you the honor of naming him yourself."

She shifted against him so she could better meet his gaze. "Maksim."

He lifted a brow. "Oh, I see. And is the man going to be godfather, too?"

"The man has earned both privileges. On that point, you cannot argue."

He shrugged against her. "Maksim it is."

She kissed his chest lovingly. "Might we leave Russia?"

He paused. "In your state? God, no. We stay until the babe arrives."

She sighed, knowing he was right. "Might we at least leave the Winter Palace? Before the Emperor takes it into his head that we name our child after him instead?"

Tristan rumbled out a laugh and kissed the top of her head. "We leave tomorrow morning. Will that be soon enough for you?"

She breathed out a huge sigh and closed her eyes, finally feeling at peace. "Yes. That will indeed be soon enough for me."

Author's Historical Note

WHILE THE MAIN CHARACTERS in this story (Maksim, Zosia, Tristan and Lady Moreland) are but figments of my overactive imagination, the historical facts underpinning this story are for the most part true. Before Count Poniatowski became the King of Poland in a formal coronation that took place in Warsaw in 1764, he was indeed Catherine the Great's lover. The Empress, despite already being married, bore Poniatowski's child, Anna Petrovna (not to be confused with Catherine the Great's daughter, Grand Duchess Anna Petrovna, who died at age twenty).

As mentioned in the story, the child's birth was recorded to have taken place in Saint Petersburg in 1757. Anna Petrovna mysteriously died fifteen months after her birth and, oddly, there is very little to no information about this child. This sparked a "what if" Anastasia-like story. What if that mysterious death had, in fact, been staged? There certainly would have been reasons for it and it whispered of possibilities. Possibilities I tweaked in order to create Zosia's story.

Not even a decade after the Empress had assisted Poniatowski in seizing the throne, everything rapidly fell apart under his rule and the whole of Poland was partitioned into three sections by Prussia, Austria and Russia. The first partition occurred in 1772, the second in 1793 and the third and final partition that eliminated Poland as an independent nation was in 1795.

King Poniatowski was promptly dethroned. Interestingly enough, Poniatowski was kept under close surveillance in Saint Petersburg and was given a pension by the Empress until his death in 1798, even though the Empress herself unexpectedly died two years before he did.

With that last partition of Poland in 1795, the liberties offered to what little remained of Poland and its people were set under a new constitution, established by the Congress of Vienna and regulated by the Russian Empire. Those liberties quickly eroded. Freedom of speech and press ceased to exist under the Emperor's dread of intellectual improvement. Any Polish noblemen who didn't succumb to the wish of the Emperor soon found themselves replaced by Russian noblemen who were far more cooperative.

By 1825, to be a patriotic Pole was to be a rebel that Russians sought to crush through secret organizations similar to the KGB. Relentless oppression kept stacking until it created a revolt. What riled the first Poles into revolting was the recovery of Russia's plans to use Polish officers and its military to suppress other countries.

On November 29, 1830, a young Polish cadet by the name of Piotr Wysocki from the Imperial Russian Army's Military Academy, seized arms from that Academy with fellow Poles in Warsaw. They stormed Belweder Palace, which held Russia's governing seat, thus sending a clear message to the entire Russian Empire that freedom was what they sought.

The city's main arsenal in Warsaw was seized as Poles took back their city, and soon they sought to take back their entire country. More and more Poles jumped onto the revolt and, in December of 1830, the entire Polish Sejm (their administrative council) joined in and announced the National Uprising against Russia.

Emperor Nicholas I sent approximately one hundred eighty thousand troops to crush Poland's approximate seventy thousand. Of those seventy thousand Poles, about a fourth had no formal military training, but simply the will to fight for freedom. Poland surrendered to Russia on October 5, 1831, with approximately twenty thousand men remaining of the original seventy thousand. After their surrender, Poles were stripped of all rights, many fleeing into other countries. Polish women were known to wear tokens of black in mourning for their men and their lost homeland.

During that revolt and bloodshed, the British paid little to no attention to the Poles. It wasn't until after Poland was crushed that the sentiment arose in Britain, and an idea to preserve an understanding of Poland bloomed in 1832, creating a society known as the London Literary Association of the Friends of Poland.

Due to the sad outcome that I knew could not be reflected within this story, as there was no happily-ever-after for Poland, I commenced the action in THE PERFECT SCANDAL a year before the uprising, to pay homage to the bubbling patriotism that was about to explode.

After another attempted uprising against the Russians in 1864, which also failed, Poland didn't regain its independence as a country until one hundred and twenty-three years later, during World War One. Sadly, Poland only remained independent for a brief twenty-one years (1918-1939).

The Nazis brought a quick end to its short-lived independence when they marched in, assisted by Russia, which was now led by Stalin. Together, they seized the still-frail Poland, eliminating the country from the map again, as England and the entire world stepped back, allowing Hitler and Stalin to effortlessly crush Poland without offering assistance until it was too late.

Stalin assisted Hitler in overtaking Poland by conducting mass murders separate from Hitler's own agenda of exterminating Jews. Stalin personally arranged the Katyn massacre, rounding up and executing approximately twenty-two thousand Polish officers, doctors, police, professors and public servants, all as a means of eliminating intellectual resistance within the country itself and, in turn, achieving complete control. Stalin also supplied Hitler with every possible resource he needed so Germany could continue to fight against the rest of the world.

Despite being Hitler's accomplice throughout most of World War Two, when Hitler fell, Stalin strategically aligned himself with the British (Churchill) and the Americans (Franklin D. Roosevelt) and found himself well rewarded. World War Two ended, and despite Poland pleading to the world for its freedom apart from Stalin's regime, Poland was handed off to Russia. Yet again.

It wasn't until the Solidarity movement and the fall of the Communist Wall in 1989 that Poland *finally* achieved its freedom after a total of one hundred and seventy-three years of oppression under the Great Russian Empire.

* * * * *

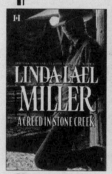
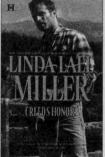
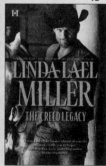

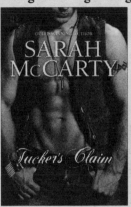

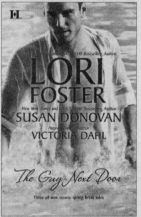

REQUEST YOUR FREE BOOKS!

2 FREE NOVELS
FROM THE ROMANCE COLLECTION
PLUS 2 FREE GIFTS!

YES! Please send me 2 FREE novels from the Romance Collection and my 2 FREE gifts (gifts are worth about $10). After receiving them, if I don't wish to receive any more books, I can return the shipping statement marked "cancel." If I don't cancel, I will receive 4 brand-new novels every month and be billed just $5.74 per book in the U.S. or $6.24 per book in Canada. That's a saving of at least 28% off the cover price. It's quite a bargain! Shipping and handling is just 50¢ per book in the U.S. and 75¢ per book in Canada.* I understand that accepting the 2 free books and gifts places me under no obligation to buy anything. I can always return a shipment and cancel at any time. Even if I never buy another book, the two free books and gifts are mine to keep forever.

194/394 MDN FDC5

Name	(PLEASE PRINT)	

Address		Apt. #

City	State/Prov.	Zip/Postal Code

Signature (if under 18, a parent or guardian must sign)

Mail to the **Reader Service:**
IN U.S.A.: P.O. Box 1867, Buffalo, NY 14240-1867
IN CANADA: P.O. Box 609, Fort Erie, Ontario L2A 5X3

Not valid for current subscribers to the Romance Collection
or the Romance/Suspense Collection.

Want to try two free books from another line?
Call 1-800-873-8635 or visit www.ReaderService.com.

* Terms and prices subject to change without notice. Prices do not include applicable taxes. Sales tax applicable in N.Y. Canadian residents will be charged applicable taxes. Offer not valid in Quebec. This offer is limited to one order per household. All orders subject to credit approval. Credit or debit balances in a customer's account(s) may be offset by any other outstanding balance owed by or to the customer. Please allow 4 to 6 weeks for delivery. Offer available while quantities last.

Your Privacy—The Reader Service is committed to protecting your privacy. Our Privacy Policy is available online at www.ReaderService.com or upon request from the Reader Service.

We make a portion of our mailing list available to reputable third parties that offer products we believe may interest you. If you prefer that we not exchange your name with third parties, or if you wish to clarify or modify your communication preferences, please visit us at www.ReaderService.com/consumerschoice or write to us at Reader Service Preference Service, P.O. Box 9062, Buffalo, NY 14269. Include your complete name and address.

MNOM11

DELILAH MARVELLE